Praise for Lois Greiman

"Dangerously funny stuff."
—JANET EVANOVICH

"Lois Greiman is a modern-day Dorothy Sayers. Witty as hell, yet talented enough to write like an angel with a broken wing."
—KINKY FRIEDMAN, author of *Ten Little New Yorkers*

"Simple sexy sport may well be just what the doctor ordered."
—*Publishers Weekly*

"Fast and fun, with twists and turns that will keep you guessing. Enjoy the ride!"
—SUZANNE ENOCH, *USA Today* bestselling author of *Flirting with Danger*

"Sexy, sassy, suspenseful, sensational!! Lois Greiman delivers with incomparable style."
—CINDY GERARD, *USA Today* bestselling author of *To the Edge*

"Lucy Ricardo meets Dr. Frasier Crane in Lois Greiman's humorous, suspenseful [series]. The result is a highly successful, tongue-in-cheek, comical suspense guaranteed to entice and entertain."
—BookLoons

"Move over Stephanie Plum and Bubbles Yablonsky to make way for Christina McMullen, the newest blue collar sexy professional woman who finds herself in hair raising predicaments that almost get her murdered. The chemistry between the psychologist and the police lieutenant is so hot that readers will see sparks fly off the pages."
—thebestreviews.com

"A fun mystery that will keep you interested and rooting for the characters until the last page is turned."
—Fresh Fiction

"Greiman makes you feel for all of her characters. Whether you hate, love or fear for them, she brings forth every emotion."
—*Romantic Times* (Top Pick!)

"L.A. psychologist Chrissy McMullen is back to prove that boobs, brass and brains make for one heck of a good time . . . laugh-out-loud-funny . . . sassy . . . clever."
—*Mystery Scene*

Not One Clue

Not One Clue

A Mystery

Lois Greiman

A DELL BOOK

NEW YORK

A Dell Mass Market Original

Copyright © 2010 by Lois Greiman

Published in the United States by Dell,
an imprint of The Random House Publishing Group,
a division of Random House, Inc., New York.

DELL is a registered trademark of Random House, Inc., and
the colophon is a trademark of Random House, Inc.

ISBN 978-0-440-24478-3

Cover design and illustration: Jae Song

Printed in the United States of America

www.bantamdell.com

2 4 6 8 9 7 5 3 1

To my sister, Gail, who inspires me daily
with her love and devotion.
You're my hero.

1

Give me ice cream or give me death.

—*Chrissy McMullen, during*
an ongoing bout of teenage
angst

I had just drifted into the feathery nest of Sleepdom when the phone rang. Cracking one aggravated eye, I glared at my bedside clock. Eleven-seventeen. Okay, eleven-seventeen may not exactly be the wee hours of the morning, but I have a deep and abiding affection for sleep and tend to get somewhat miffed when I and my beloved are separated. I happen to consider REM to be the next best thing to chocolate, which is the next best thing to . . . damnit. I couldn't remember anything that beat the cocoa bean for sheer unadulterated bliss, and that wasn't a good sign. I was pretty sure there had once been something rather titillating.

The phone blasted my eardrums a second time. I gave

it a jaundiced glare, but it remained unrepressed and rang again. Cheeky bastard. Snaking an arm across Harlequin, a dog who disguises himself as a hundred-pound door-stop, I hauled the receiver from its cradle, dragged it into my lair, and rumbled an impolite salutation.

There was a moment of silence followed by, "Jesus, McMullen." Rivera's smoky voice sizzled through my system like cheap wine. "Did your larynx have a run-in with a sander or are you just on a bender?"

Meet Lieutenant Jack Rivera, LAPD down to his cotton boxers. He and I go back a ways. When Bomber Bomstad, client and ex–football star, dropped deader than kibble on my overpriced berber, Rivera was the first on the scene. Irritating, smart-mouthed, and preposterously hot, he's as tempting as truffles. He is also equally restricted, because although a little dark chocolate may boost your serotonin levels, a steady diet is likely to be fatal. And I had no intention of suffering death by Rivera. On the other hand, I had no qualms about a little Latin appetizer. I turned on my side, letting the cord drape over Harley's bicolored ear. He ignored it as if it were the "sit" command.

"Maybe this is how I sound when I'm satisfied, Lieutenant." My voice was sexy-low and husky.

"Like you need a defibrillator?"

I grinned a little. After all, he couldn't see me, so it was okay to admit that sometimes I kind of appreciate his smart-ass wit. "You a doctor now, Rivera?"

"If that's what floats your boat." I could hear the sigh in his voice as he started to unwind. A cop's day can be as stressful as a shrink's, which just happens to be my calling.

"In your dreams," I said, but the dreams were more

likely to be mine. I'd had enough fantasies about Rivera to fill an erotic miniseries.

"You're usually Catwoman in my dreams."

"Catwoman." My stomach tightened a little at the thought that I might occupy his late-night imaginings.

"Crime fighter with a tail."

"You're one sick bastard," I said, and he laughed.

There was something about the sound of it that did naughty things to my otherwise saintly equilibrium.

"Maybe *you* could play the doctor this time." His voice rumbled through me, but I fought off the effects. After all, I was no longer a pubescent tuba-player. In fact, I had worked like the proverbial dog to become a card-carrying psychologist. Even harder to become immune to the kind of low-level charm Rivera exudes like rush hour exhaust fumes.

"Did you have a reason for calling?" I asked.

"This is it," he said.

"Sexual harassment?"

I could hear the shrug in his tone. "I won't call the cops if you don't."

I snorted. Sometimes when I'm really tired I tend to sound like an overwrought Guernsey and it was now . . . holy cow . . . 11:22.

"So what do you think?" he asked.

"About what?"

"Sex."

The buzz that had begun in my overzealous endocrine system geared up to an insistent hum. "In general or—"

"Now."

My breath caught in my throat. "You're not under my bed or something, are you?"

"Freaky," he said. "But if that's what trips your trigger, I'll try to squeeze in."

"Big of you," I said, and refrained from dropping my head over the edge of the mattress to take a peek.

"You've no idea," he said.

I resisted rolling my eyes, mostly because, in actuality, I *did* have something of an idea. There had been a rather memorable episode involving an overdose of Nyquil and Rivera . . . in the shower.

"Listen, Rivera, as much fun as this is, I have to work tomorrow."

"I didn't think it would take *that* long, but I'm willing to call in sick if you think it's necessary."

"Are you drunk?" I asked.

"That's not the adjective I'd use."

"*Adjective* . . ." I rolled onto my back, warming to the conversation. "I'm impressed."

"They've been teaching us to read down at the station."

"Our taxes," I said, "hard at work."

"I'm willing to share what I've learned."

"Maybe you can send me a syllabus."

"I could deliver it in person."

"I said 'syllabus,' not 'syphilis.' "

He chuckled. I could hear his chair squeak as he leaned back, and imagined him stretching, body arched, cuffs rolled away from well-muscled forearms, black hair teasing his button-down collar. "You always this mean when you're sleeping alone?"

"Who said I'm alone?"

"Me."

"Maybe you're wrong."

"I'm willing to put money on it."

I considered swearing at him, but that was the old Chrissy. The new Chrissy was saving the "f" word for major emergencies. And L.A. drivers. Low-fat muffins. And Mondays.

"Unless Elaine's sleeping with you," he said.

"I'm not that desperate."

"Yes you are. But if she's not doing her fiancé I think I can trust her with you."

I scowled. He had inadvertently touched on a raw nerve. Brainy Laney Butterfield, beauty personified, and my best friend since the fifth grade, was betrothed to a man I referred to in nothing but four-letter words. The kindest of them was "nerd."

"So how you doing with that?" he asked, and I wondered in my sleep-deprived brain if that was why he had called in the first place. It didn't take a genius—or a Homo sapien—to know that I was patently unhappy about the impending nuptials. It wasn't just because Elaine would forever belong to someone else. It was because she would belong to the geekiest guy on the planet. And that made my skin crawl.

"Fine."

"Yeah?"

"Of course." Reaching out, I fiddled with the pad on Harlequin's left hind paw. I'd learned early on that Great Danes did not necessarily make stupendous watchdogs. He was a gift from Rivera. As was my Mace, the cactus that guarded my yard, and the baseball bat I'd stuck in my hall closet. Rivera had a penchant for things that could inflict pain. "I'm a grown woman."

I waited for his comeback but he was silent for a moment, then, "He'll be good to her."

For a moment I couldn't say anything. Elaine had been my pillar through every major catastrophe in my life: my first period, zits, and the devastating realization that most guys *are* like my brothers. That truth can still bring me to tears. But the thought of her wedding looming over me like a gawking gargoyle was almost more than I could bear. The only positive thing to come out of the impending ceremony was the fact that this would be the first time my bridesmaid gown wouldn't look like a pink train wreck.

"You know that, don't you?" Rivera asked. "That he'll be good to her?"

"Sure." My voice sounded a little strange. I glanced up. The iron knob on the antique bed Laney had given me as a bridesmaid gift gleamed dully. She'd found it at a Hollywood estate sale. Upon examination, I had discovered the initials "A.A.L." scratched in the metal. With my luck, it probably stood for the forerunner of Alcoholics Anonymous.

"Besides, you can always kick his ass if he isn't," Rivera said.

I refrained from sniffling. "It wasn't his *ass* I was thinking of."

He was silent for a moment, then, "Jesus, McMullen, if you're considering *any* part of Solberg's anatomy, it might be too late for me to save you."

I scowled at the ceiling.

"But I'm willing to make the effort."

Despite myself, I laughed. "You're a giver."

"Like a saint."

"God, I hope not," I said, and he chuckled.

"Last chance," he said.

"Promise?"

There was a momentary pause, then, "Not on your life," he said, and hung up.

I did the same, shuffled the receiver into its cradle, and smiled even though there was less than a month left until my best friend's wedding. A month during which she was staying with me since she'd given up her apartment long ago and didn't relish the idea of hotel life. I had hoped we would have some time to spend alone together, but her schedule was pretty hairy. Not only was there the wedding from Elm Street to contend with, there was also a considerable amount of hoopla involving the upcoming spin-off of her popular television series, *Amazon Queen. Jungle Heat* featured several of Laney's coactors and would premiere soon. Wesley Donovan, a relative newcomer to female fantasies, played the male lead and was creating most of the hoped-for heat.

All this meant that the Geekster would not only be nearby, he could damned well be *in my house*. The idea made my skin crawl, but the phone rang again, pulling me from my morbid musings.

I grinned through the darkness at it. There's nothing like a trash-talking stalker to make a girl feel special.

I picked up the receiver on the third ring. "Okay. But bring a condom," I whispered, then squirmed a little and wondered how I was going to sneak Rivera past Laney. "Hell," I corrected, "bring a box of 'em. Do they still come in boxes? It's been—"

"He's dead," a voice hissed.

I jerked upright in bed, heart crammed tight in my throat. "What? Who is this?" I rasped.

But the dial tone was already buzzing in my ear.

2

I been a pretty good mama. Too bad I'll have to wait for
my funeral to hear it said out loud.

—Shirley Templeton—mother
of seven, and a vocal
proponent of birth control

*M*y muscles were frozen, my lungs petrified. I jerked
my gaze toward the hall, sure someone was watching me,
but the doorway was empty, so I yanked my imagination
under control and jabbed Rivera's number into the key-
pad.

His line was busy. I hung up and tried again. Same results. Settling the receiver into the cradle, I stepped off the
bed, stiff as a pool cue, but just then the phone rang. I
squawked as I swung toward it.

Atop the bed, Harlequin stared at me, sleepy-eyed,
head half lifted from the mattress, one ear cocked up.
Slowly I reached once again for the receiver.

"Who is this?" My voice quivered like a falsetto's.

"I think I killed him," the voice hissed again. It was juxtaposed eerily against a keening noise in the background.

"I'm calling the police."

"They're already coming."

I moved to hang up, but in that instant a sliver of recognition pierced my foggy brain. Squinting, I tightened my grip on the phone. "Who—"

"I came to see the boy. Just wanted to see him. You know? Never had much family. Not really. Didn't intend to . . . Didn't think . . ."

"Micky?" The name came out on a rasp of surprise. Micky Goldenstone was one of my clients, but even I'm not stupid enough to hand out my home phone number like a suicidal real estate agent. "How did you get this—"

"Listen . . ." He drew a heavy breath as if searching for calm, and when he next spoke, his voice was steady, cool even, carefully enunciated. "I don't have much time before the cops show up."

"The cops . . ." I shook my head. Sometimes it's the most intelligent thing I can think to do. "What—"

"I need you to drive over."

"Over where?" Or whom? "What are you talking about?"

"Glendale. I don't want the boy to spend the night here. Or with the county."

"Jamel?" I was guessing wildly, mind spinning.

"Yeah."

"I thought he was living in Lynwood with his aunt."

"I guess Lavonn's boyfriend's loaded. Bought himself this big-ass house in Glendale. But that don't . . ." His voice, calm just moments before, broke. "There's a shit-load of blood, Doc."

My stomach pinched up tight, but sometimes in a crisis the professional me manages to squeeze past the real me and see the light of day. This was one of those auspicious moments. "I need you to take a deep breath, Micky, and start at the beginning."

"I didn't mean to—"

The keening in the background changed pitch, setting my teeth on edge and my nerves on stun.

"At the beginning," I said again.

I heard him inhale. It sounded shaky, but when next he spoke, his tone had settled into default mode. "Like I says, I just wanted to see 'im." Under duress, Micky's lexicon tends to slip toward ghetto. Apparently, a "shitload of blood," tended to cause duress.

"Yes. You told me."

"But when I come to the door they was—"

"Whose?" I asked, voice firm and strong. "Whose door?"

"Lavonn's. When I come to the door, her and Jackson was stoned out of their minds. Higher than—"

"We wasn't stoned!" The voice in the background was pitched high with hysteria. "We wasn't. We don't do that no more. We was just relaxin'. That's all. Jesus Christ! You didn't have to shoot 'im," she said and sobbed brokenly. In my mind I imagined her rocking back and forth, arms hugging her chest, head dropped.

"I don't know what the fuck—" Micky began, but I interrupted.

"Did you shoot him?"

There was a pause, during which I could hear him swallow. "Bastard had a gun."

"Jackson?"

Maybe he nodded. It was damned hard to tell. "He had a piece and he was high. I'll swear to that."

"Where's the gun now?"

He drew a shuddering breath. "In my hand."

I closed my eyes and swallowed bile. "You think the police are on the way?"

"I called 'em."

I could imagine him doing that. "Okay. You have to put the gun down, Micky."

There was a pause, long and wearing and filled with the residue of someone sobbing.

"I ain't going to the pen," he said finally. "They're like caged animals there."

And he would know. He'd been a guard at Folsom before becoming a third-grade schoolteacher. "So what's your plan?"

I could imagine him glancing at the body. At Lavonn, crouching beside it. Maybe at the boy. "Could be, this is when I buy it."

My mind went into a kind of slow spin, picking up a hundred crystal-sharp memories of my sessions with him. Micky had a past that would have doomed a lesser man. He had a history and he had a conscience. Sometimes that's too much for anybody. "You think now's the time to kill yourself?" I asked.

Another pause, long and painful. "Good a time as any."

I kept my voice steady. "In front of your son."

"I sent him to his room. Right after I called you the first time. Didn't want him seein' . . ." His voice broke again. "Didn't want . . ." Words failed.

"I thought you said he was a smart kid."

"Yeah." He sniffled. "He ain't got no one to help him

with his studies, but he's bright." His voice had gone very quiet. "You can tell sometimes. You can just tell when they're—"

"But you don't think he'll figure out that you killed yourself." I cut off his blooming paternal pride. Cut off the meandering musings, and that changed the tone of his voice.

"I won't be goin' to the pen, Doc. I seen what it's—"

"Yeah, he's probably not worth your trouble. Just a skinny black kid with ears that stick out." We'd discussed the boy's ears at some length in our sessions. But Micky wasn't talking now. The phone had gone quiet except for the sobbing in the background. "His mother was a druggie, wasn't she?" I asked.

"I know what you're doing," he said. His tone had gone tight and edgy.

"That's because you're smart, too, Micky," I said. "But it didn't save *you*, did it?"

I could almost hear him wince. "You owe me," he said.

I gripped the receiver tighter, because it was true. He'd done me a favor when my own life had been in danger, but I wasn't about to pay up without gaining something. "Promise me you won't use the gun and I'll come get him."

"I can't—"

"So you're going to screw him, too? Like you did his mother?"

"Fuck you," he said, but his voice had gone scratchy and he didn't hang up. A niggle of hope nudged me.

"Promise me and I'll make sure he's safe until you can take care of him yourself."

"I can't take care of no one." His voice cracked.

"Not if you're dead."

He swore, then the line went quiet, almost silent, except for the humming keen in the background.

"Promise," I said.

"Okay."

"Say it."

"Damn you!" His breath hissed into the receiver for a moment, then he said, "I promise," and after rattling off the address, hung up.

3

Maybe skinny's okay for them runway models and little girls who ain't yet got their monthlies. But *real* women oughtta have them some heft.

—Ella Brady, Chrissy's
favorite grandmother

My hands were shaking like castanets as I hung up the phone. Harlequin canted his head at me. "Micky Goldenstone," I said.

He blinked. I turned in a haze, searching for something. What was it? Shoes. I would need shoes. A pair of sneakers caught my eye. At least I thought they were a pair, but it hardly mattered. Crime scene victims rarely put a lot of stock in couture. I slipped into the tennies and remembered a half-dozen other victims I had seen in the past few years. Gooseflesh skittered across my arms. Scooping a denim jacket from the chair beside my bed, I dragged it on and searched for my purse. There. My keys. Beside it.

Checking for my cell, I said good-bye to Harley and

stepped into the night. It seemed unreasonably dark on Opus Street. Popping down the Saturn's noisy locks, I started the engine, flipped open my phone, and dialed Rivera. Still busy.

I called 911 next and was promptly put on hold, but I had already punched the address into my GPS and was turning onto Foothill Boulevard. Too late to turn back now.

The song with those lyrics popped erratically into my head. I tried to pop it back out, but it had a foothold. I mouthed a few words, feeling sick to my stomach. Traffic was light. Murphy's Law. The only time I didn't really want to go anywhere . . .

"It's too late . . ." My voice sounded hollow in the dark interior of the car. The lights from the dash made my knuckles look as sharp and fragile as bare bones.

". . . to turn back now."

"Nine-one-one. What's your emergency?"

"Yes!" My voice sounded spastic. I'd forgotten I had been put on hold. "I'd like to report a . . ." What? "Crime."

"What's your name?"

I gave it, then marched out all the information I could. It wasn't much. "I think someone may have already re- ported it," I said.

"Very well. Are you in a safe location?"

"Yes." The song was still humming through my mind when I hung up and wheeled onto Greenbriar. Something streaked across the road in the darkness ahead of me. I gasped. My foot jerked over the brake, but whatever it was had already disappeared.

By the time I pulled up to Jackson's curb my heart was pounding like Judge Judy's gavel. Lights were blazing in the two-story house. It was Spanish Colonial in design, old-world elegant with a railed second-floor balcony and tall, narrow windows. No ambulance loomed in the broad street out front. There wasn't a police car in sight.

"I believe, I believe, I believe . . ." I held my Mace in one wobbly hand and stepped from the dubious safety of the Saturn. My knees felt unsteady, but managed to carry me up the curving, red-tiled walkway. The world felt surreal and oddly skewed.

It was then that the screen door squeaked open. I jerked at the sound.

"That you, Doc?"

Micky stood in the doorway, dark skin shiny from the ambient light. A muscular Don Cheadle.

"Yes." Hallelujah and praise the Lord, my voice sounded as if I were not about to pee in my pants. "Are you okay?" I asked, and ascended the tiled steps. The interior of the house smelled odd. Like college with something added. Blood maybe. The idea made my guts twist.

A black man in his forties was propped upright against the wall in the foyer, his legs splayed and stretched out in front of him. A dark pool had seeped from the bullet hole and accumulated on the rosewood flooring.

His eyes were open, his teeth gritted. Even in pain, he was Hollywood handsome. A woman with a smooth, Michelle Obama hairstyle was kneeling beside him, holding a bloody towel to his side. She turned toward me. Her movements were jerky, her eyes very dark. "Who's that?" Her brow puckered.

Micky ignored her. "I'll get Jamel."

"What you talking about?" The woman rose to her feet.

She was approximately my height, but lacked some of my admirable "heft." Barefoot, she wore blue sweatpants and a white tank top. Still, her ensemble beat the hell out of mine. My bare legs felt cold and stubbly under the shabby shorts, my arms scratchy beneath the denim jacket.

"I'm Christina McMullen . . . Ph.D.," I said. Maybe I was trying to defuse the situation. Maybe I was nuts. She, on the other hand, looked higher than a Pasadena mortgage. "I'm a friend of . . ." For one fractured second I considered telling the truth, but I'd made that mistake before. "Jamel's," I said.

She cocked her head. "You're a liar is what you are."

Ahh, hostility. I kept my tone level. "Is he all right?"

" 'Course he's all right." Her tone was offended and a little slurred. "You think I'd hurt my own sister's kid?"

"There will be retribution," Jackson said, and smiled. They were the first words he'd spoken since my arrival. His voice was singsong smooth, like one in a trance.

"You should keep pressure on the wound," Micky told Lavonn. The ghetto had died from his voice.

"You're the asshole that shot him." Lavonn sounded near hysterics. I could feel myself slipping in that direction. "Made him bleed . . ." She paused to breathe. "Bleed all over my pretty rosewood."

"The girl loves her rosewood," Jackson said. His voice sounded dreamy. "Floor matches the hearth. You see that?"

"An ambulance should be here soon," Micky said. There was worry in his tone, but Lavonn snorted a laugh.

"You ain't lived in the hood for a while, have you, Michael?"

"This isn't the hood," he said.

She scowled, seeming to remember where she was, but Micky was already speaking.

"I have to get Jamel out of here."

"Just like that." She pursed her lips, eyes angry.

"I'm his father, Lavonn. Blood tests proved that."

It was a long story. But Micky had just discovered a few months ago that the boy was, in fact, his son.

"I don't care about no blood tests," Lavonn said.

"Your sister would have wanted—"

"I don't care about no blood tests!" she yelled, and jerked up her hands. There was a gun in them. It was pointed at Micky.

"No!" I rasped the word, and she swung the weapon toward me like a laser.

Terror squeezed my throat shut. I stumbled back a step.

"How'd you say you know Jamel?" she asked.

For a moment my voice failed me entirely. "I just . . ." It squeaked. "I'm his teacher."

"You're a liar!" She spat the words and took a step toward me, arms shaking as she snapped her head toward Micky. "You his ho, ain't you?"

I didn't dare glance away.

"Ain't you!"

"Listen . . ." The situation was spinning out of control. And I had been using my shrink voice. I was keeping my "dear God, don't let me die" voice in reserve.

"No!" She shook her head. "I ain't gonna listen. I been listening to him." She turned the gun toward Micky. "Says he's Jamel's poppa. Says Kaneasha woulda wanted him to have 'im. But why didn't she never tell me about the two of 'em?"

Micky was shaking his head.

" 'Cuz he's a liar, too. That's why," she said, and squeezed the trigger.

The bullet whined through the house like a banshee seeking souls. I screamed. Micky swore. Then someone spoke, her voice as firm and solid as the floor beneath our feet.

"Lavonn Amelia Blount!"

We jerked in unison toward the woman standing in the doorway. She was a hundred years old if she was a day. Her skin was black and wrinkled, her eyes as sharp as switchblades, her voice gravelly. "What in the good Lord's name do you think you're doing?"

"Grams!" Micky rasped.

Lavonn's face twitched. "What are you doing here?"

"I keep tabs on folks from the old neighborhood," she said. "What's going on?"

Lavonn's hands were wobbling, placing her aim somewhere between Micky's knee and his clavicle. "Your boy shot Jackson."

The old woman stared at her for a long eternity, then turned creakily toward Micky, completely ignoring the figure propped limp and motionless against the pristine wall. "Is that the gospel truth, Michael?"

"He—"

She stomped her cane against the rosewood flooring. "I asked if that was so!"

"Yes, ma'am."

All oxygen seemed to have left the building.

"How come?"

No one spoke. The old woman's brows lowered, and in

that moment she looked far more dangerous than the crazy gal with the gun.

"I thought he'd hurt Jamel," Micky said.

My eyes darted from one to the other.

"Who?" Grams asked, but in that moment a boy stepped into view. He was half-shadowed by the hallway but still you could make out his wide eyes, his protruding ears.

The room fell into silence as Grams turned to the child. A muscle jerked in her pemmican face, but then she straightened painfully to her full garden gnome stature. Her expression became flinty as the facts clicked together in her head. "Least my girl had sense enough to tape down your daddy's ears before he was old as you," she said.

The boy scowled. She watched him, eyes as bright as flares before she pulled in a hard breath and pursed her lips. "You'll be coming home with me, boy."

He shook his head. "I don't wanna—"

The cane slammed to the floor again. "You want more of this?" She skimmed her eyes disdainfully about the elegant room: Jackson, Lavonn, the bloodstained floor, the tattered lives.

The boy looked, too, then shook his head, slowly, as if he wasn't sure, or at least wasn't sure he should admit it.

Grams nodded once, sharp and succinct. "Come," she said, and he did, following her slow movements out the door and into the night with barely a backward glance.

The rest of us remained as we were, like marionettes without direction. Micky and I were frozen. Lavonn's arms were still trembling, but she didn't lower the gun.

"Put it down, Lavonn," Micky said.

"How come my sister didn't never tell me about you and her?" she asked again.

Micky's mouth was tense, his body stiff. "She was young." He winced and I prayed to God he would lie. There may be a time for absolute honesty, but so far I hadn't found it. "Maybe she was embarrassed."

"Embarrassed." She snorted. The pistol jumped. "She was always talkin' about how cute you was. How hot you was. How she was gonna rock your world. Then she does and she don't tell me?"

He glanced out the window. Self-loathing shone in his eyes. I was breathlessly grateful he wasn't the one holding the gun because he was unlikely to miss if he aimed for himself. "Where are those fuckin' paramedics?" he asked.

"Why didn't she tell me?" Lavonn asked again. Her voice was becoming strident and Micky was weakening. I could see the truth trembling on the tip of his conscience.

"Because I r—" he began, and in that moment I launched myself at her. I may have yelled at the same time. I may have raved like a lunatic. Or I may still have been singing "It's Too Late." My shoulder hit her square in the chest. We went down together. Me on top. The gun exploded in my ear. I jerked, but if I was hurt I was too revved up to feel it, and in a moment Micky was there. He wrestled the pistol from her fingers. Still, she didn't give up. She squirmed beneath me like a wild animal, knees, elbows, hands, fingernails. Hitting, scraping, kicking.

But finally she went limp. She was crying by the time I wedged myself to my feet.

Micky was standing there, pistol hanging loose by his thigh. "I don't think I pay you enough," he said, but I was beyond humor. In fact, I was a little pissed. Go figure.

"That Jackson's gun?" I asked.

He raised it the slightest degree. "Yeah."

"Maybe I should have been more specific about where to put it when I told you to put it down."

"I didn't want Jamel to get his hands on it."

"So you gave it to *her*?"

"Not exactly," he said, and almost smiled. It's funny how some people think it's funny when I'm pissed as hell.

I took a deep breath and tried to see the humor in the situation. Nothing yet.

"Where are Lavonn's kids?" I asked.

"With their dad." The amusement was already gone from his face, evaporated from his tone.

Our gazes met.

"They *have* a dad," he said.

"Don't start," I warned.

"What the hell have I—"

"Micky!" I stepped up to him. Maybe I was *past* pissed at this point. "Give me the gun."

A muscle bunched mutinously in his lean jaw, but I had seen him bow to his grandmother, and although I would never be the intimidating little gremlin she was, I was willing to do my dominatrix best.

"Give me the gun or I'll bitch slap you from here to . . . Easter," I said.

"Easter?" One eyebrow cocked up and for a moment a spark of laughter returned to his eyes.

We heard the sirens almost instantaneously.

Our gazes were sucked toward the window. I shifted my attention back to Micky. There was anger in his eyes now. Anger and angst and terror swirling in one toxic blend.

"Please," I said and after a lifetime of hell, he handed me the gun.

Everything seemed to happen at once then. Someone pounded on the door. Someone announced the arrival of the police. I was the one who answered, saying one man was injured but no one was hostile.

They came in guns drawn, nevertheless. Fast and low. All dressed in black, flak jackets in place. I had my hands above my head, pistol drooping from my fingers.

"Put the gun down." The officer who gave the order had his face half hidden behind his uplifted arms.

"I . . ." I began, but he barked at me.

"Put it down!"

I did so, already sullen. Chrissy McMullen, sleep deprived.

Another officer snatched up the gun and jerked his head toward Jackson. "He been shot?"

"Yes," I said.

"You shoot him?" asked the first cop. I could see his face now. It was a good one, like a young Errol Flynn.

"I did." Micky didn't step forward when he spoke. I noticed that he had his hands up, too, but his expression was haughty, his eyes hard. I prayed for the longevity of martyrs and fools.

"That right?" asked Hot Cop.

I gave Micky a look. "Mr. Goldenstone would prefer to save his comments for later."

"Would he?"

"Yes." Chrissy McMullen. Haughty. And maybe a little protective. Micky had already been through purgatory and come out looking pretty good. Why risk hell?

"You his counsel?"

Counsel? "In a manner of speaking," I said.

"Yeah?"

Behind Cop Two, paramedics were rushing into the room. One felt for a pulse. He nodded. Three others hurried over, carrying equipment I couldn't readily identify. They squatted by Jackson, pushing Lavonn aside. She moved away, teary-eyed and sullen.

"What manner of counsel?" asked Hot Cop.

I dragged my attention back to him.

I raised my chin. "I'm Mr. Goldenstone's psychologist."

Hot Cop's brows had risen. "His psychologist."

If he smirked I was pretty sure I could take him down. I didn't care if he did look like Captain Blood.

"Yes."

"What's your name?"

"Christina McMullen . . . Ph.D."

Cop Two, shorter and stouter, glanced my way. His gaze swept my bare legs for a nanosecond, but he kept his pistol trained on Micky. "McMullen?"

I pursed my lips and gave him my best scowl. "*Christina* McMullen."

The corner of his mouth jacked up the slightest degree. "Rivera's squeeze?" he asked, and I believe I cursed.

4

Dogs, they may drink from your toilet and pee on your carpet, but they will not cheat on you with your friends. Unless they are from Saltillo, Mexico. Then who can be sure.

—*Rosita, the mother of Jack
Rivera and the ex-wife of
Senator Rivera, who was
from Saltillo, Mexico*

The phone rang again. In all honesty, I didn't think it would have the nerve. In even more honesty, I thought I had taken it off the hook. I hadn't gotten to sleep until nearly two a.m. and every fiber ached where Lavonn had hit me with her knees and fists. I opened one eye to stare at the clock and refrained from swearing even though it was officially morning and I knew who was on the phone. The police station grapevine was a thousand miles long and news traveled at the speed of light. I answered on the fourth ring.

"Listen, I didn't do anything wrong," I said, and covered my eyes with my hand.

"Chrissy." The voice on the other end of the line was a mix between a jackhammer and a road-grader.

"Mom?" I snapped my eyes open and sat up straight. Harlequin trotted in, tags jingling, lips wet from slurping water from the toilet bowl. He was a big believer in hydrating. "How are you?"

"Why didn't you tell me Elaine's getting married?"

My throat felt as if it had been corked up tight. The previous night had been scary as hell: The sight of Jackson's bleeding body tilted against the foyer wall, Lavonn's oddly dilated eyes, the gun, the angst, the anger. But there are few things that can compete with my mother's righteous rage. Harley plopped his head on my foot and swore undying devotion with his eyes.

"What?" I said. It was the best I could do at seven o'clock in the morning. Maybe with a couple more hours of sleep I could have come up with "Whatever do you mean," in a dynamite antebellum lisp, but I wasn't up to that sort of clever wordplay just then. And besides, it would probably have been nothing short of verbal suicide. My parents love Laney. Well, maybe not my father. As far as I know, Dad only loves two things. One of them is his easy chair, the other is produced in Milwaukee. Neither of those things would be available at Laney's wedding. I hoped to say the same of my parents.

"Elaine's getting married and you didn't think I should know?" Mom asked.

"Know? No. I mean, yes. Didn't I tell you?" Harley was drooling on the coverlet. "I was sure I told you."

"Where's the ceremony?"

"Where?"

"Yes. Where?"

Oh God, oh God, oh God, maybe I could convince Laney to perform her ungodly act of matrimonial stupidity in Las Vegas. Or Disneyland. Or Timbuktu. Anywhere that wouldn't lead my sordid kindred to L.A. "I'm not sure."

"What do you mean you're not sure? You two haven't had an argument or something, have you?"

Silence hung in the air like smog. For a moment I thought I saw a glimpse of an out and almost made a mad dash for it, but mothers can be sneaky and I thought I smelled a trap. "Why do you ask?" I asked.

Silence stretched on again, then, "Because I spoke to Pastor Butterfield."

So I'd been right about the trap. It had been yawning right in front of my feet, but I'd managed to escape it. Still, I winced. "Laney's dad?"

"He said you're Elaine's maid of honor."

"Oh." I nodded, sure she was watching me. Some people can see through a thousand miles of telephone wire. It's called mother-vision.

"Is that true?" Her tone was slick, as if she didn't care.

There it was. That sneakiness. I mean, of course it was true. Would a pastor lie about his own daughter's wedding? And more important, could I pull off a lie involving a pastor's daughter?

No. Even I wasn't that good.

"Well . . ." I yawned. It was entirely fake. I hadn't been this wide-awake since my brothers put red ants in my underwear drawer. "It's just a little ceremony." A couple hundred of her closest friends and most of the Hollywood community. "I didn't think you'd be interested."

"Not interested? Elaine is like a daughter to me!"

The daughter she had never had. The daughter every mother longed for. I had never wished more that I could hate the little bride-to-be. But Brainy Laney's like spaghetti, long and slim and impossible to dislike.

"Give me her address. I'll send her a gift . . ." She paused. It was a lengthy pause, and about twelve months pregnant. ". . . since she doesn't care enough to invite me."

That's when the war began inside me. Because although I wanted with stark desperation for Mom to send a gift instead of delivering it in person, I couldn't bear to allow anyone to believe that Laney was callous enough to neglect to send an invitation to her maid of honor's mother.

"Chrissy?"

"Yes?"

"She didn't invite us, right?"

And suddenly I couldn't come up with a single lie. Me, a tuba-player, a woman, a psychologist. Nothing.

"Chrissy!"

"I—"

And then my cell rang. I couldn't believe it. It was like a trumpet call from the heavens. Like Gabriel's ethereal fanfare.

Sliding past Harley, I reached for the purse I had dropped on the floor. "Listen, Mom, I'd like to chat, but I have another call."

"I don't care if it's Saint Peter, himself. I want to know—"

"Oh, look. It's Rivera."

She was just inhaling for another blast, when she paused. "Gerald?"

I closed my eyes and covered them with my palm.

There was some sort of proverb about a frying pan and a fire. Which was preferable?

"So you two are still dating?" she asked.

"I've really got to go. This could be important."

"Important?" Her tone had sharpened to a needle point jabbing my eye. "Important how? Is it serious between you two?"

Yes, it was serious. As serious as a body tipped against the wall and bleeding onto the rosewood floor, but I had a feeling that wasn't exactly what she meant, and I didn't share the specifics. "I think it is," I said, and for that one statement I knew I could burn in hell. Or worse yet, be cornered by an irate mother insisting that I had misled her into believing there might be wedding bells in her only daughter's future.

Maybe it was that thought that made me stammer an apologetic good-bye. Maybe it was some long-dormant sense of masochism that made me snap open my cell phone.

"What the hell were you thinking?" Rivera snarled.

I closed my eyes and rubbed my gritty lids. "Whatever happened to early morning pleasantries such as 'good day' or 'top of the—' "

"You knew he had shot someone before you went skipping over to Glendale, didn't you?"

"Actually, I drove. I've never been good at skipping. Something about the rhythm of hopping and—"

"Why the fuck would you get involved with him?"

"Who? Micky?" I asked.

For a moment there was a silence. "Was there another shooter?"

"Well, there was Lavonn," I said, and froze. To this day,

I still don't know why I would say such a thing. In the past there has been some evidence to suggest that I'm not completely brain-dead. Not a lot, but—

"She shot at you?"

"Not at me exactly."

"Who exactly did she shoot at?" His voice had taken on that patient-father tone I had come to detest.

Laney appeared in my doorway wearing an oversized T-shirt and baggy sweatpants. Her hair was mussed, her face bare of makeup. She was beauty personified. It almost made me wish I had kept the gun, just in case I caught a glimpse of my own face before applying my usual half a gallon of foundation. But cops are funny about letting could-be psychopaths walk away bearing arms.

"Rivera?" She mouthed the name.

I nodded.

"How's it going?" Mouthed again.

"Excellent." My answer was silent, accompanied by a confident nod.

She grinned at my lie. "I'll wait to hear the story," she said, and headed for the bathroom.

It was impossible for me to guess how she knew there was a story. Laney hadn't returned home yet when I'd left for Glendale. I had privately hoped she was still honing wedding plans at midnight or maybe out knocking over 7-Elevens . . . anything besides sharing a bed with Solberg. But it's impossible to say for sure. Brainy Laney's spooky in a lot of ways.

"McMullen." Rivera's patience sounded a little strained now, which, oddly enough, made me feel better.

"Yeah?"

"Who did she shoot at?"

"I'm not sure she had decided exactly."

He mumbled something then. It might have been a swearword. Hell, it might have been several.

I waited, staring at my legs. They were pasty white and kind of jiggly. I gave the right one a poke.

". . . fallen for someone with a couple of brain cells?"

My attention snapped up. "What?"

"I suppose you didn't even consider letting me know where you were going."

"Actually I tried . . ." I began, then remembered his words. "What were you saying? Something about falling?"

"What did you try?" he asked. Impatience had slipped into pissed. It wasn't a long slide.

"I called you," I said, and scowled, remembering the night before. The panic I had felt at the sound of the voice on the phone. *"He's dead,"* Micky had said and the first person that had popped into my mind had been Rivera. What did that mean? "Your line was busy."

"When?"

"About two minutes after I turned you down."

"What the hell are you talking about?"

I stood up. "Why are you so pissy? Did the next woman reject you, too?"

For a moment there was silence, then, "Oh, for God's sake, you don't seriously think I was propositioning someone, do you?"

"You propositioned *me*." I could feel anger and doubt accumulate like tartar inside me.

"I'd just put in a ten-hour day. You seriously think I was trying to get you in the sack?"

"Me and probably a half-dozen others."

He snorted. "Jesus, McMullen, if I put my mind to it

you'd be flat on your back before you could even *remember* the word 'no.' "

I curled up a lip. "I prefer being on top."

"I'll keep that in . . ." He stopped himself, drew a deep breath. I swear I could hear him grind his teeth. "Are you okay or what?"

I narrowed my eyes. Mothers weren't the only ones who could be sneaky. Men were right up there with the champs. "Who were you talking to, Rivera?"

"What?"

"Last night, after we hung up. Who'd you call?"

"Are you seriously asking this?"

"Are you seriously evading the subject?"

There was a pause. I opened my mouth to blast him, but he spoke first. "Mamá."

I closed my mouth, scowled. Harlequin had trotted after Laney. She had that effect on males. "You were talking to your mother?"

"*Sí.*"

"At that hour?"

His laugh was more of a heavy exhalation. "I know that wildcats like you have to get to bed before nine, but Latina women are known to stay up well past dusk."

My hackles rose. There had been more than a few Latina women in his past. Hell, there had probably been *Chihuahuas* in his past.

"What did she say?"

"Mamá?"

"Yeah."

"She said you're a nut job."

"It wasn't her, was it?" I don't know what's wrong with me. Really, I don't. I'm not usually the jealous type. The nutty type, yes. The horny type, absolutely. The weird, "I want to sleep with you but I won't" type. But not the jealous type.

He cursed again. He was getting more inventive. Which, in my own warped brain, made me think he probably was hiding something. Still, maybe it's not my fault that I'm warped. Maybe it's the fact that I've dated approximately seventy-eight guys, most of whom were certified whackos.

"Listen, Rivera. It's not as if we swore to be exclusive or—"

"She said you told her all you wanted was a man who wouldn't wear your underwear."

I closed my mouth, closed my eyes, momentarily wished I had been born mute. Because, actually, I had told Rosita Rivera just that. In fact, I had said a whole lot of embarrassing things. A long time had passed since then, but some evenings are more memorable than others.

I rubbed my eyes but didn't entirely give up on my line of questioning. Better to sound jealous than nuts. "She told you that last night?"

"You think I wouldn't have mentioned it sooner if I had heard it before?"

Good point. Valid point. "Listen, I'm sorry. I'm just—"

"An idiot?"

I nodded a little. It was entirely possible, but I wasn't about to admit as much out loud. He already knew I had been discussing underwear with his mother. How much ammo did the man need?

"Do you *want* to be dead? Is that it?" he asked.

"A client called," I said. "He was—"

"Michael Goldenstone."

"Micky. Yes. He asked me to meet him in Glendale."

"Why?"

"I'm afraid I'm not at liberty to divulge that sort of information about my client."

"Are you fucking serious?"

Kind of. "Suffice it to say, the situation was defused and—"

"By tackling a woman with a gun!"

Oh. So he had heard that. Kind of heroic, really. He should be proud. He didn't sound proud. He sounded pissed enough to pee tacks.

"No one got hurt."

"Besides the guy in the ER."

"Which happened before I arrived," I reminded him. It was something of a feather in my hat, I thought. Generally, when people get shot, I'm Johnny-on-the-spot. Things were looking up.

"So you thought it a grand idea to trot on over so you could get in on the action."

I refrained from telling him that I didn't really *trot*, either. Maturity, thy name is Christina. "How is Jackson doing?"

"He'll live."

"That's good."

"Is it?" His voice was kind of growly.

"What?"

"He's a rich fucking drug dealer who holds a grudge. There's no reason to believe he won't blame you."

"He's rich?"

"Funny, I thought you'd focus on the part about blaming you."

"I was getting around to that."

I heard him sigh. It sounded like the conversation was kind of making him old. I decided to change the subject before he needed an oxygen tank.

"How about Micky?" I asked. "How's he?"

"I heard he's a pain in the ass."

"Sometimes he becomes fractious when he's feeling guilty about his past," I said.

"Are you being televised or is there another reason you're talking like a damned robot?"

I made a face. "Sometimes he gets nasty when he's scared."

"Why should he be scared? He said the gun was the other guy's. He said he acted in self-defense."

"And I suppose the legal system is just going to take his word for it."

"What do you know about this, McMullen?"

"I have no reason to believe he had a gun or would have chosen to use it on Jackson even if he did."

"So you believe his story."

"Doesn't it seem unlikely that he would have intentionally shot him, then called the paramedics, if he meant to kill him?"

"I believe you were the one who mentioned guilt. Maybe he makes a habit of doing shit, then feeling bad about it later."

I held my breath. Moms were sneaky. Men could be even sneakier. But men who were cops . . . they were the true experts. "What do you mean?"

"He's been accused of rape. Did you know that?"

I hoped to hell he didn't know about Jamel's mother. If Kaneasha's family knew the truth about the circumstances, Micky wouldn't have a chance of obtaining custody. "A woman named Sheila Branigan, I believe."

"But you hopped on over to Glendale to save him anyway."

"What is it with you and weird verbs today?"

"Did you ever consider your own life might be in danger?"

"Did you know that Sheila Branigan also accused three other black men of rape? All of whom had solid alibis?"

"Maybe you're not aware that most women don't cry rape just for the fun of it."

"I'm a licensed psychologist, Rivera. I'm well aware of the lasting effects of rape, but Sheila's accusations were entirely fabricated."

"You got something for this Micky guy?"

I raised my brows at the tangy sound of jealousy in his voice. Don't get me wrong, I'm not a masochist or anything, but jealousy is not necessarily frowned upon in Chrissyland. "He's a client, Rivera. We have a professional relationship. You've heard of that, haven't you? It's a situation where two people treat each other with mutual—"

"Lavonn says he raped her sister."

The air escaped my lungs like helium from an overfilled balloon. "What?"

"She's not denying that the kid's his, but she says he's a product of rape."

I kept my voice calm. "Does she have any proof?"

"The boy's eight years old. Unlikely to be proof after this much time."

I felt myself relax a little.

"Unless his shrink would step forward with evidence."

"Micky's made some mistakes," I admitted. "But he has nothing but good intentions where his son is concerned."

"Lompoc is full of men with good intentions."

"I guess it's a good thing he found me, then. To help him nurture those intentions."

"Is that your job, McMullen? To save the fallen angels of the world?" Rivera had made his share of mistakes. For better or worse, his father, an ex-senator with more charm than morals, had been able to sweep most of them under the rug.

"Some are too far gone," I said.

"Good to know you're aware of that."

"Micky's not one of them."

"Did he rape Lavonn's sister?"

"Did you see Lavonn's eyes?" I asked.

"You're avoiding the issue."

"That's my job. Did you see her?"

"I heard reports."

"Did they say she was stoned?"

"Tox hasn't gotten back to us yet."

It was my turn to snort. "I'm willing to bet Jackson was just as far gone."

"That give your boy the right to shoot him?"

"My *client* has the right to defend himself . . . and his son . . . even in L.A."

"Spoken like a gun-toting Midwesterner."

"You don't have to be an ass, Rivera, just because you're jealous."

There was a momentary pause. Maybe it was even thoughtful. "Is that what I am?"

"Sounds like it."

"And what would you say if I told you I was really talking to Rachel last night after I hung up with you?"

Anger zipped through me. Immediately hot. "Is that skank circus back in town?"

There was a moment of silence, then he chuckled, soft and low, sending the sound skimming over my nerve endings like fingers on sensitized skin.

"Mamá says you should come over for margaritas," he said, and hung up.

5

In my family, being an overachiever means drinking
your weight in the alcoholic beverage of your choice.

—Chrissy McMullen, whose
brothers had actually
achieved that feat on more
than one occasion

"Hey, girl." Shirley glanced up as I walked into the reception area of L.A. Counseling, then did a double take and
popped to her feet. She was freaky graceful for a woman
her size. Shirley Templeton is a big woman. Big hands, big
shoulders, big belly. *Huge* heart. "I didn't think there was
no trains in your part of town."

"I wasn't hit by a train," I said, carefully removing my
sunglasses as I lowered myself into a chair near her desk. It
had been hotter than jambalaya on Interstate 2 that morning and the Saturn's air-conditioning hadn't quite been up
to the task of keeping my brain from shriveling like over-
cooked bacon. I closed my eyes and rested my head
against the wall behind me.

"Well, what in God's good name happened to you, then?"

"Oh . . ." I may have limped a little as I made my way toward my office. Maybe I had even added a pathetic little mew of pain as I'd entered the building. Let it never be said that Christina McMullen is above soliciting sympathy. Shirley's usually comes in the form of sugar. Need I say more? "There was a little altercation." Lavonn might have been a scrawny little crackhead, but she could pack a wallop when cornered.

"Who was she?"

I opened my eyes and turned to look at my receptionist. There are times when she can be almost as spooky as Laney. Maybe that's why she had slipped so seamlessly into Elaine's position behind the front desk.

"What makes you think it was a woman?"

" 'Cuz I ain't heard 'bout no fatalities in your part of town and if there was a man involved, I got a feeling there woulda been a funeral."

"Actually, there *was* a man involved. Two, in fact." I frowned, remembering Jackson.

"They gonna be all right?"

"Who?"

"Whoever you're worried about."

I considered that for a moment. "Have you ever thought about becoming one of those psychic readers?"

She shook her head. "They make a lot of money?"

"Has to be more than what I pay you."

She thought about that for a second, then shrugged. "Money ain't all it's cracked up to be. My kids would just take it anyhow," she said, and turned back toward her desk. "You need any ice for those ribs?"

"No. I'll be fine." I'm extremely comfortable in the role

of martyr. More than once I had considered investing in a nice camel-hair tunic, but at that precise moment I was wearing a pair of black capris with a short-sleeved turquoise blouse. It may not be much in the way of fever-inducing itching, but the top was fairly new and I didn't want to get it wet from melting ice.

"How about a long john?" Shirley asked, and opening a drawer, drew out a little white paper bag.

The glorious smell of refined sugar permeated the air. Thompson's Bakery, I thought, then sniffed again, olfactory nerves twittering. No. Donuts Go Round, I decided judiciously. Two rolls. Fresh-baked that morning. Maple frosting. No filling. "I shouldn't," I said.

"You been in a scuffle," she argued, and came back around the desk, delectable bag held in her right hand like a balm from the gods. "You need healin' food."

"Long johns *have* been proven to have medicinal benefits."

"Nothing better."

"And you *are* wiser than I," I said.

"It's God's truth." Handing over the bag, she lumbered back to her post. "Got a new client coming in at nine," she said, but I was still staring at the bag and feeling a little mushy.

"Shirley . . ."

"I love you, too," she said, and not bothering to look up, waved me off. "Now go eat that before the new gal shows up and finds you got frosting in your hair."

Rising a little unsteadily, I turned away, knowing true wisdom when I heard it. I *do* tend to frost my hair when donuts become involved. Sometimes, in fact, my shoes get a little glaze on them.

It didn't occur to me till later that I was unwilling to dampen my turquoise blouse with melting ice but willing to risk a frosting encounter.

I had just finished up the second john when my first client arrived. She was tall and slim and as serious as a Hemingway novel.

I stood up and turned toward the door as she entered. According to her chart, she was seventeen years old, but she looked like a leggy fourteen who was trying hard for forty.

"Emily Christianson?" I asked.

"Yes." Her handshake was firm and quick, her complexion pale. There were purple crescents under her eyes.

I smiled. She didn't.

"I'm Christina McMullen. Have a seat." I motioned her toward the couch. She went, turned, and sat slowly, sitting very erect on the ivory cushions. She was wearing a pale pink button-up blouse tucked into black slacks that were cuffed at the bottom and neatly pressed. Her hair was dark, straight, and pulled into a high ponytail. Her lips were pursed in a somber expression that looked as if it had settled in for the long haul. "So, why are you here?"

She blinked at me. "I filled out the chart."

I didn't glance at it. It only stated the most rudimentary information . . . just a little less than nothing. "So you came at your parents' request?"

"They thought I seemed stressed."

Ah, perception, thy name is parent. "Can you tell me why you're stressed?"

She shrugged. Economical and stiff, as if she were afraid the motion would take too much precious time. "Isn't everyone?"

Most were, but I had a feeling she brought it to collegiate levels. "You're a junior in high school?"

"A senior." Her lips pursed even more. "Accelerated classes."

"Ahhh." I hoped to sound smart, because I had a feeling I was in the presence of an intellect that would make my own relatively impressive brain blush with embarrassment.

"I'm hoping to be accepted into Harvard for my undergraduate courses."

"How come?"

She scowled at me, just the slightest lowering of her brows. "What?"

"Why do you want to attend Harvard?"

"Education is the keystone to success." She said the words very succinctly. I had once seen *I, Robot* with Will Smith. Mostly in the hopes of seeing Smith sans shirt. Eureka! Not only had he been shirtless, there was a shower scene. I remember it vividly. I didn't recall the robots as well, but I believe they had spoken in a tone similar to Emily Christianson's.

"And how do you define success?" I asked.

She seemed a little confused. "The generally accepted definition, I suppose. A good career. A nice home. A decent financial portfolio."

She had a scant two inches of skin showing between her clavicle and the top of her blouse. Otherwise she was buttoned up tighter than Sister Margaret Mary on holiday. Even the cuffs at the ends of her long sleeves were secured over her narrow-boned wrists.

"What career are you considering?" I asked.

"I'll become a vascular surgeon." No equivocation. No "I hope" or "I might."

"So you're interested in medicine."

Her hesitation was almost imperceptible. "It's quite fascinating."

"So are crickets."

"What?"

I gave her a smile. This trying-to-act-intelligent stuff was already wearing on my nerves. "I've always thought crickets were fascinating."

She blinked. Her hands, white-knuckled with close-cropped fingernails, were clasped atop her lap. "You're interested in entomology?"

I didn't try to explain my sense of humor. She wouldn't be the first to mistake it for lunacy. "How long have you wanted to become a surgeon?"

She shook her head, an almost negligible toggle of her head. "For as long as I can remember."

I wondered how long her *parents* had wanted her to become a surgeon, but I wasn't quite ready to pose that question. "So your grades are good?"

"For the most part. I'm somewhat concerned about Physics."

Somewhat concerned. God save the children. "Ninety-two percentile?" I guessed.

Her mouth tightened a little more. "If I receive less than a seventy-nine percent I'm in danger of an A minus."

I nodded. There were no perfectionists in my family. In fact, there was some question regarding the actual *species* of a couple of my brothers, but I had seen enough self-inflicted perfectionism to recognize it when it sat on my couch and clasped its hands. "Is that why you cut yourself?" It was all guesswork. I knew almost nothing about her, but the signs were there if anyone wanted to see them.

I wouldn't have thought she could get any paler. Wrong again. She shifted her arms the slightest degree, but refrained from tugging down her sleeves. The epitome of self-control.

"They were only superficial incisions," she said. "And just once."

I nodded and settled in.

"Ms. Christina?"

I jumped, spun around, and jammed my spine up against the door of my humble domicile. Maybe that seems like dramatic behavior, but I'd had one hell of a day at the office, and sometimes I prefer to know ahead of time when people are planning to kill me on my front stoop.

In this case, however, my visitor was just my next-door neighbor, Ramla Al-Sadr. Her attire had changed somewhat in the past few years. She no longer wore the traditional robes and full-face veil. Now she favored pretty head scarves, and colorful gowns. Although, she had informed me years ago that virtually all Muslim women appreciated a nice G-string under their burka. Ramla had taught me a fair amount about Islam, but her very best attribute, in my own humble opinion, was the high unlikelihood that she would ever attempt to kill me. Still, it took some time for my heart to decide to remain in my chest.

"Yes. Hi. Ramla. Hi." I considered trying to shuffle the bag of lo mein and fried rice into my purse hand so as to hug her, but it was too bulky. "How are you?"

She stared at me, dark eyes somber. "I am not so very well."

"Oh?" Due to Shirley's early-morning long john offering, I had opted to skip lunch. Hence, the smell of lo meiny goodness was all but overwhelming. "What's wrong?"

"It is my sister."

I frowned, trying to focus on her words instead of noodles in white sauce. "I thought you said she was doing better. That she and her husband had made amends."

"That is what she told me."

I sighed and lowered the bag. Lo mein goodness would have to wait. "What happened?"

"I have no word from her in two weeks of time."

Damnit. I glanced toward her yard. It was, as always, groomed to gleaming perfection. Considering the wasteland of my own property, it was a small miracle she would even speak to me. "How often do you usually hear from her?"

"Once each week, without the exception."

"Maybe she's having phone difficulties."

"Then she would write the letter."

I was scrambling. "Maybe—" I began, but she shook her head.

"There is trouble."

There was something about the way she said the words that made the hair prickle on the back of my neck. "What makes you so sure?"

"Aalia and I, we are more than the sisters."

"Still—"

"She is my Elaine."

I scowled.

"Elaine, your friend, if she were troubled, would you not know?"

In fact, we had proven that to be the case on more than one occasion. There was a weird connection between us. A closeness I sometimes thought I couldn't live without. My soul mate of the wrong gender. "Yes," I said, and quite miraculously, forgot about the lo mein.

6

Hard work and talent are all well and good, but don't underestimate the power of trickery and deceit.

—*Gregor Gooding, Elaine Butterfield's most motivated agent*

*M*inutes later when I stepped inside, my vestibule was dark. Which probably meant that Laney was home. She didn't believe in wasting electricity. Which often meant that she also didn't believe in light. Elaine is a tree-hugger down to the sap-sucking little roots of her being.

I turned to close the door, still carefully juggling the lo mein.

"Babekins!" someone chirped.

I screamed as I spun around. And sure enough, there was Solberg. Short, balding, and barely human, he had burrowed into my home like an unwanted boll weevil.

"What are you doing here?" I was struggling to breathe

normally. He was lucky my instincts were such that protecting dinner was more important than fighting intruders.

"I came to adore my stunning bride-to-be," he said.

"Why?" I asked, and checked the side of the bag, making sure no yummy juices had spilled.

"Why?" He grinned at me. Or maybe he had colitis. I believe the results can be similar. "Because she's the air that I breathe. The wind beneath my wings. The light of my—"

"Try not to creep me out," I said, and pressing past him, made my way into the kitchen.

Laney was there, setting the table. It looked as if she was just recovering from laughing at my expense. "Hard day?" she asked, far too smart to admit she habitually finds my grouchiness amusing.

"I actually thought it couldn't get any worse," I said, and she chuckled. Somehow my aversion to her betrothed completely failed to upset her.

"Jeen just stopped by to discuss the floral arrangements."

"Buying the tropics, are you?"

"It *is* getting a little out of hand," she admitted.

"Uh-huh. So Solberg's leaving soon?" I tried not to sound jubilant at the idea, but I'm not much of an actress. There had been a time I could have said the same of Laney. But no more. She was now the darling of Hollywood and would start filming her first motion picture soon. But that wasn't entirely due to her thespian skills. She was built like a fairy-dusted goddess and smart as a firecracker. Not to mention she was the most adorable person on the planet.

"Sorry I can't stay for dinner," Solberg said, walking into the kitchen. "But I've got stuff to do."

Despite my better judgment, I glanced up at his mysterious tone. "What stuff?"

His lips jerked as his colitis acted up. "Stuff I can't talk about when Angel's here."

Which meant I would never know, because I wouldn't be caught dead alone with him. I'd made that mistake before. In fact, I had dated him once. But that was before he'd caught his first glimpse of Brainy Laney. As far as I know his jaw hasn't been located since.

"He's buying my wedding gift," Laney said.

"I didn't know there were still continents for sale," I said. Solberg was just a little bit richer than God, which, oddly enough, had absolutely nothing to do with why Laney was marrying him. It was anybody's guess what her mind-boggling reasons might be. But I suspect they might have had something to do with eye of newt and possible necromancy. Voodoo is still alive and well in the greater Los Angeles area.

"I'm not *buying* your gift," Solberg said.

Laney and I looked at each other. She shrugged. He grinned.

"I gotta go," he said.

I turned away as he kissed Laney's cheek. Why spoil my appetite now?

The door closed behind him.

"You really don't know what he's getting you?" I asked.

"Not a clue," she said, and reached up to fetch the glasses from the top shelf. She was wearing green canvas shorts she had gotten from Goodwill in junior high. There was not a molecule of cellulite on her thighs. The sight made me want to eat until I was catatonic.

I opened the carton of lo mein. It was as pretty as a picture. "What did he mean by he's not *buying* it?"

"Maybe he's making me something."

I fished out a noodle and tasted it. Asian ambrosia. "Or renting you a slave."

"Can you do that?"

I shrugged one shoulder. The other was on sabbatical. "I'd rent myself out for the right price."

"I'm going to have to think about that. Tell me about last night," she said, and sat down at the table.

I did the same, then scowled as I dished up the lo mein and passed it to her.

She only took some lo.

"A client called," I said, beginning slow.

"Here?"

I nodded and tasted the sauce. It made chocolate pale by comparison. I swear to you, I wasn't drunk.

"How'd he get this number? You didn't give him your home phone, did you?" she asked, and taste-tested an onion as I slurped down a skein of noodles.

"I'm not brain-dead."

"I was wondering but I thought it would be rude to ask," she said. "What did he want?"

I gave her a look, but the meal was singing its siren song, pulling my attention away. "He wanted me to take his son."

She raised one brow. "Take his son or *have* his son?"

"*Take* him. Which seemed like enough of a commitment."

"He must be pretty good-looking if you'd even consider the possibility of procreating."

"Think Don Cheadle face, Matthew McConaughey body."

"Wow," she said, then, "Did I tell you I might be doing a movie with McConaughey?"

The fork dropped from my hand as the image of McConaughey jumped into my psyche. And voilà ... suddenly I remembered what was better than chocolate. We'd been McConaughey fans ever since he'd played David Wooderson in *Dazed and Confused*. In fact, Laney and I had spent an inordinate amount of time sitting in the dark watching everything from bad sitcoms to award-winning feature films. It had eventually made her a star. It had only made me pale.

"A movie with Matthew McConaughey! Are you serious?" I asked.

"No," she said, and stabbed a mushroom. "I just wanted to see your reaction. So when did Micky call?"

"I didn't say ... what makes you think it was Micky?" I asked.

She didn't answer immediately. She was busy masticating. A sesame seed can take her half an hour. It could be morning before she finished up with the mushroom.

"How do you even *know* Micky?" I asked.

"When did he call?"

"Maybe it *wasn't* Micky," I said, and she laughed.

"You've got fourteen black clients. Three of them are under the child-bearing age. One is a grandfather, and nine are women. I don't know a lot of women with McConaughey's pecs."

"You've been talking to Shirley."

"Someone's got to keep you from getting yourself killed. And seriously, Mac, I don't think it's ever going to be you. What were you thinking, galloping out there at midnight?"

Galloping? "Have you been talking to Rivera, too?"

"Should I?"

"No!"

She grinned. "Then tell me what's going on."

I succumbed. Not that I wouldn't have anyway. But the idea of her and Rivera comparing notes made it easier to capitulate. Of course I swore her to secrecy first.

Fifteen minutes later I had consumed enough noodles to feed Cambodia. Laney's meal could have fit in my molar.

"So you think this Jackson guy was high?"

"I think so. He had just been shot and he acted as if he was floating on cloud nine. Crooning about rosewood and retribution."

"Retribution."

"It sounds better than revenge, doesn't it?"

"No."

"It's all so sad," I said, and sighed. "From what Micky's said in the past he's got everything—brains, education, money. He looks like a forty-year-old Jimmy Trivette."

"From *Walker, Texas Ranger*?"

"Yeah."

"You have a Texas Ranger swearing revenge?"

"I have a *nutcase* seeking *retribution*."

"Why don't I feel better?"

I shrugged. "I think you're a natural pessimist."

She gave me a look. "What makes him a nutcase?"

"According to Micky, it's mostly stuff he's done to past girlfriends."

"Physical stuff?"

"That, too," I said, scraping the last bit of sauce from my plate. "But probably more emotional. Psychological. Micky's been checking into Jackson's past. There's a girl named Becca. Says he'd make her call him 'Sir' and cook his meals in the nude."

"That's unusual?"

I jerked my gaze to her. Her expression was absolutely serious, but her eyes were too bright.

"You're so not funny," I said.

She laughed, apparently disagreeing. "So Micky's grandmother didn't know about Jamel?"

"I don't think so. As of Micky's last appointment he hadn't told her yet. He'd just gotten the test results back and needed some time to think things through."

"So how did she know to show up at Jackson's house?"

I shrugged and fished the last noodle out of the box. I needed it about as much as a bullet to the brainpan. "Micky said she can be spooky. Maybe she uses the same voodoo witch you do."

"Shirley? Would Shirley have told her?"

The noodle drooped from my fingers mere millimeters from my gaping maw. "She wouldn't."

"Why not?"

"Because she's my receptionist. It's her job to keep things confidential."

"What's *your* job?"

"You blackmailed me into divulging all that information about Jackson."

She didn't comment on her threat to contact Rivera. "I guess it would have been worse if no one showed up for Jamel."

"*I* was there."

"And what would you have done with him?"

I shrugged. One of my past boyfriends had told me I had the maternal instincts of a snail. "I would have worked something out."

"You and François?"

"François happens to be a very sensitive guy."

She didn't respond to that other than to roll her eyes. Maybe because François runs on batteries and lives in a drawer beside my bed. Laney rose to her feet and started clearing dishes.

"I take it Rivera wasn't happy about the situation, either."

I watched her work. "The François situation or the Micky situation?"

"He knows about François?"

"Probably not."

"Probably?"

"I don't even know how *you* know."

She grinned as she put the dishes in the sink. "What was the good lieutenant's major concern regarding the Micky situation?"

"Probably that he couldn't tell me what to do."

She turned, putting her ridiculously well-toned derriere against the counter. "Have you considered that maybe he worries about you?"

"I'm a big girl."

"Mac, a guy was shot. A woman was stoned. Not to mention armed. And Micky's been accused of rape on more than one occasion. Maybe he's not as innocent as he seems."

"He's had a tough road. And how do you know—"

She raised a hand. "Just be careful. Okay?"

"I don't intend to get myself shot," I said, trying for levity. "I mean, how embarrassing would that be?"

She glared at me. "Sometimes you're an idiot."

I gave her a hopeful expression for the "sometimes." "Things are looking up, then?"

"I'm serious, Mac. You just keep putting yourself out there. Looking for trouble."

"I do not."

"Really? What did Ramla want?"

I was pretty sure my earlier conversation with my neighbor wasn't something I should be ashamed of, but somehow I was. "What?"

"Ramla." Laney was adopting her combative mien. Generally, she's about as aggressive as a daisy. Other times she seems to think I need a mother. Which, by the by, I already have in spades. "What did she want?"

"Do you have spies out there or something?"

"Yes. I thought her sister was doing okay now."

A while back, I had told Laney about the Al-Sadr situation. She'd informed me that a friend of hers from the Middle East might be able to help. But before any plans were made, Aalia, Ramla's sister, had reported that all was well. Unlikely as that had seemed, there wasn't much I could do about it. "I guess she's not anymore."

Laney's brow puckered. I was glad to see it could happen. "Maybe you shouldn't get involved."

"Little Miss Fix It doesn't think I should get involved?"

"I'm serious, Mac. I have a bad feeling about this."

My stomach curled, but I forced a laugh. "Aalia's in Yemen. What could happen?"

"I don't know," she said. "But if it can I'm pretty sure it will."

7

Men . . . a sure cure for sanity.

—*Shirley Templeton*

On Wednesday I wore my favorite warm-weather ensemble: a cranberry shell that fit snug across my boobage and tucked neatly into a high-waisted skirt that hugged my behind like a perverted banana peel. The flirty ruffle at the bottom added interest, and the wide black belt cinched my waist into a neat little sphere.

Perhaps because of my clothing choice, the day went fairly smoothly. At least in comparison to the norm. Still, by 7:50, when my last client whistled out the door, I felt like I'd been dipped in battery acid and hung out to dry. Nevertheless, I felt it necessary to speak with my receptionist.

Shirley was just pulling her purse out of a big drawer at

the bottom of her desk when I stepped into her domain. Seven plants had come to live in the area since her arrival. I never knew where they came from or what they were called, but they glowed with green happiness. "Can I talk to you for a minute?"

"Sure," she said, and pulled the strap of her purse over her shoulder. "What's up?"

I didn't want to broach the subject of her speaking with others about my clients, but the Board of Psychology can get a little testy about that sort of thing, and the truth is, I'd rather take a fork in the eye than face an uptight shrink with nothing better to do than looking into my affairs.

"You know my clients' files have to be kept confidential, right?"

She nodded once, looking serious.

"I mean, don't get me wrong, you're a fantastic—"

"It was me," she said, brow furrowed.

I stood there with my mouth open for a few seconds. No thoughts flew in. "What are you—"

"I worry about you, girl. You gotta be more careful. Your clients, they love you. I know they do, but they ain't exactly comin' here 'cuz they got all their ducks in lock-step, you know. I have to talk to someone."

I was trying to think. Perhaps that wasn't apparent by the look on my face. "So . . . you've been talking to Laney?"

"Don't take this the wrong way, 'cuz I don't say this lightly, but . . . maybe you should get a man."

I managed to shake my head. "What?"

She broadened her stance as if ready for a fight. "A man."

"For . . ."

"I know, I know." She waved at me as she came around the corner of the desk. "I kind of implied they're worthless as a peashooter at a gunfight, but sometimes they come in handy. I mean, you drive out of here alone every night. Get here alone every morning. Pretty thing like you. What if someone's waiting?"

Why was everyone suddenly so concerned about my well-being? "What am I supposed to do? I can't just run out to the man store and pick up a sample." I thought about that for a second. The images were appealing. *I'll take one in brown, one in white, and one in nothing at all.* "Can I?"

She snorted. "Honey, if you wanted you could just walk out there and whistle. There'd be a dozen guys at your feet before you got done puckering."

"Umm." I shook the lovely image out of my head. "Thank you, but about confidentiality—"

"If you don't want me talkin' to Laney, I won't. You're the boss, and I'm grateful for the job, but I think you need someone in your corner. And you know Laney and me . . ." She shook her head once and tightened her jaw. "We got your back."

For some reason, the way she said it brought tears to my eyes. I cleared my throat. "Yes, well, as long as you don't talk about my clients to anyone else."

"You know I won't."

"Okay, then. I guess that's it. You probably want to get going."

It took her a moment to lose the pugilist stance. "No hurry."

"It's late."

"The next bus don't go through for another fifteen minutes."

"I made you miss your bus?"

"Don't worry about it, honey," she said. "Truth is, there ain't nobody makes me do much I don't wanna do these days. Besides, the 8:05 ain't near so busy as the earlier rides."

That was because all the commuters who worried about their continued survival were padlocking their doors as we spoke. "I thought you had a car."

"I do," she said, and didn't bother to expound.

"Then why aren't you driving it?"

"The boy needed it."

"Dion?" It was a wild guess. Shirley had had a butt-load of kids. Oddly enough, she still loved babies. If I had popped seven kids out of an orifice the size of a walnut I'm pretty sure I wouldn't love anything.

"Dion? You kidding? He'd only get in trouble with a set of wheels. But Vin, he got himself a job at Target. The graveyard shift. Ain't no buses running at three in the morning."

"So how far do you have to walk?"

"Not far." Turning, she straightened the Ansel Adams that adorned the wall above the tiny table that held two water glasses.

"How far's that?"

She looked at me, attitude personified. "Why you wanna know? Do I look like I'm getting too skinny to you?"

I gave her attitude back. "I was going to ask about anorexia. How far?"

"I ain't counted the blocks."

I snorted. "I'm giving you a ride."

"No you ain't," she said, and suddenly her eyes looked

all shiny and funny. "You're gonna get your scrawny butt to bed so you can help the next Micky that comes along."

I stared at her. "Are you crying?"

"You kiddin' me?" she asked, and swiped away the moisture from her cheek with the back of her hand. "I don't even have tear ducts no more."

"Then I think it's raining on your face."

She sniffled a laugh and while she was distracted I shuffled her out the door. To this day, I'm still surprised I won that argument.

By 8:30 I had dropped her off outside her apartment building. It was a three-story complex in a decent part of Eagle Rock. I made sure she was inside before I headed for the market. My usual store was Von's but Laney liked me better when I shopped organically at Trader Joe's. I considered just getting a Trader Joe's bag to make it look as if I'm conscientious, but then Laney would be disappointed that I didn't use the cloth bags she had given me.

In the end, I parked in Joe's lot, shut off the Saturn, and stepped outside.

It happened so fast, I barely had time to think. One minute I was walking toward the store and the next I was grabbed from behind. I tried to scream but a hand cut off my breath. I shifted my eyes, throat already closing up, trying to see my assailant. Something was poking me in the side.

"You here alone?"

It took me a moment to understand what he was saying over the hammering of my heart. I nodded before I thought better of it.

"You carrying Mace?"

I managed to shake my head, though my spray was

within reach, dangling from my key chain. If I could just reach it, I'd have a chance, I thought, but suddenly the hand slipped away.

"Well, why the hell not?"

I spun around at the sound of Rivera's voice. He stood not three feet away, glaring at me.

I slammed my palms against his chest with all the rage my pent-up fear allowed. He staggered backward, almost fell, then caught himself just in time for me to sputter into his face, "Are you out of your mind?"

"Me? Christ, woman, you're cruising around town like you don't have a brain in your—"

"You've been following me?" I was either starting to shriek or a car alarm had gone off in my head.

"I told you . . ." He held up his index finger. "Look around before you leave your office building." His middle finger rose. "Get in your car quick." By the time his ring finger popped up I was just about ready to lop it off with nail clippers. "Check your rearview mirror, your side-view—"

"You've been following me ever since the office." I'd gone from shriek to growl.

"I bet you didn't even check your trunk."

"My *trunk*?" From growl to rumble.

"Damnit, McMullen! We've gone over this. You know how easy it is to jimmy a car lock? Some bastard could get in there before you leave your office. Your backseats fold down. He could climb over your seat and put a gun to your head. Next time I see you taking idiotic chances I'm going to hide in your trunk and—"

"I swear to God, Rivera," I said, stepping toward him.

"If you hide in my trunk they won't find your dead body till Christmas."

"Listen," he said, and grabbed my arms, but someone had just exited Joe's.

"Hey!" He was already approaching. I turned my head. He weighed about a thousand pounds, was big, bald, and scary as hell. "What's going on here?"

"LAPD," Rivera said, and dropping my arms, pulled a badge from some unknown orifice. "Lieutenant Rivera. Everything's fine."

"Neighborhood Watch," rumbled the stranger. "Aaron Berkhouse. And I don't give a shit if you're the pope. He bothering you, miss?"

Miss? I considered batting my lashes at him, but decided to just go for Rivera's jugular instead. "He grabbed my arms," I said. My voice was as soft as whipped butter.

"You know this guy?" Berkhouse asked.

I bit my lip. "Kind of."

"You grab her arms?" Aaron rumbled.

"Listen, Berkhouse—"

"Did you grab her arms?" he asked, and stepped a little closer.

I thought, but I wasn't sure, that Rivera cursed under his breath. "Yes, I did."

"Apologize."

I looked at Rivera, crushed a smile, and tried to refrain from doing the "You better watch your ass" dance.

"I'm sorry," he said, but the words were hard to understand coming through his teeth.

"For what?" I asked, and added a lovely blink to my performance. So far it was one of my best.

"For grabbing your arms."

The big guy nodded. "That good for you, miss?"

"I suppose so," I said. "I don't think he meant any harm." I tried another blink. I didn't want to overdo it. There's a fine line between appearing helpless and myopic. "He's just so forceful sometimes."

Berkhouse scowled, then pulled a card from his back pocket and handed it over. "You give me a call if he bothers you again."

"Okay. Thank you, Mr. Berkhouse."

He turned and ambled away with a lot of lateral movement. I watched.

"You happy now?" Rivera asked.

I turned toward him. "I can honestly say that was the pinnacle of my day so far."

He snorted.

"I'm not helpless, Rivera," I said.

"I never said you were helpless."

"How about brainless?" I asked.

"Listen, McMullen, I know you're intelligent."

"Well, you don't act like it."

"Neither do you when you—" He stopped himself. "Is it too much to ask for you to be a little careful?"

I gave him a raised brow. "Check my *trunk*?"

"Just last week a Caucasian female was accosted by a man thought to have been hiding in her trunk."

"A Caucasian female?" I asked, and turned in a circle to search for my dropped keys.

"A woman," he said. "Not unlike yourself."

Spotting a glint of metal near the Saturn's right front tire, I bent to retrieve them.

"She probably wasn't helpless, either." Not five feet

away there was a quarter. I bent to retrieve that, too. "Or brainless. Or—"

A dime lay not far from the quarter. I bent.

"Jesus!" He sounded near to exploding. "Will you quit doing that?"

"What?" I straightened, honestly confused this time.

"Holy fuck, woman, could that skirt be any tighter? What if I really *did* plan to jump you?" he asked, and stepped up close.

I refused to crowd back. He smelled kind of good. "Didn't you?"

"If I have plans for you, you'll know it," he said, and nudged a thigh between mine.

"I believe Mr. Berkhouse is still within shouting distance," I said, but really my hormones were already getting pretty noisy.

"If he saw you bend down I'm pretty sure he'd sympathize with me."

"You mean like this?" I asked, and pivoting, bent away from him.

"Christ," he said, but just as he was reaching for my ass, I turned and raised my key ring to eye level.

He stared at it, deadpan. "I thought you said you didn't have your Mace."

"I didn't know I was required to be honest with rapists."

"You drive me crazy."

"Just an innocent passenger on the road to Nutville, are you, Rivera?"

He pressed up against me. "Not too innocent."

I could feel his erection as he slipped his hand behind my back, skin against skin, rucking up my cranberry blouse. Sneaky. I was sure it had been securely tucked into my stylish ivory skirt. But I was kind of glad it wasn't. His fingers felt warm and strong.

I moved in for a kiss.

"Promise you'll check the trunk," he said.

We were inches apart. "I'll scan the parking lot before I leave my office," I vowed.

"No deal."

"It's my best offer."

"Liar," he said, and slowly slid his hand up my spine. Hot slippery feelings shimmied through me. I was breathing kind of hard.

"I'll check the backseat," I promised.

"Maybe we could do that now," he said, and kissed the corner of my mouth.

"I'm pretty sure there's no one there."

"Good thing, 'cuz I'm the jealous type."

"It's my favorite thing about you."

"You sure?" he asked, and applied more pressure to my thigh. I could feel the hard length of him against my happy skirt.

"Maybe I'll reserve judgment."

"The backseat," he suggested again. His deep voice rumbled against my pheromones, but I tried to remain lucid.

"Isn't there some kind of law against that sort of thing?" My tone didn't sound very lucid.

"Only if you get caught. We won't get caught."

He was doing something tricky with his fingertips, stroking my back in a manner that rocked me to the tips of my toes.

"I'm a screamer," I said.

He eased back half an inch. "What's that?"

"When we do it," I said. "I plan to scream."

He murmured something. I'm not sure what it was but it sounded kind of naughty.

I swallowed and found a modicum of self-control. "And I don't plan to do any screaming in a parking lot. Not unless someone has a gun," I said.

"I could get my Glock," he offered, but I was already pulling regretfully out of his grip. Adjusting my clothing, I sashayed away, sure my little ruffled skirt was rocking. Just as sure he was watching.

8

Sometimes a cigar is just a cigar.

—*Sigmund Freud*

I felt kind of powerful as I shimmied through Joe's sliding doors. I didn't look back. Cool me.

The grocery carts were mating in the entryway. I rudely pried one from its partners and proceeded into the store. The produce section, as colorful as Mardi Gras, called to me. The peppers looked ripe and sassy, the lemons firm and shapely. I picked one up.

"Take two," Rivera said over my shoulder. "They're small."

I turned to him, *über*-controlled, one brow raised. "I was hoping otherwise."

He exhaled his derision and pressed the extra lemon into my hand. "I believe you saw me showering."

"Did I?" I said. "I hardly remember." I skimmed the bananas.

He reached for a plantain, long and dark and thick.

"Shall I attribute your forgetfulness to dementia or post-trauma?" he asked.

"How about to disinterest?"

"Not until you're dead," he said.

I gave him a look.

"And you're not dead."

I fluttered my lashes. "That may be the nicest thing you've ever said to me."

"Meet me in the backseat and I'll recite poetry," he said, and weighed a Bosc pear in his right hand. His fingers curled tantalizingly against the firm fruit.

"It would almost be worth it to hear the dark lieutenant spouting Longfellow."

"I was going to quote Browning," he said, "but if you think Longfellow more appropriate . . ."

Our gazes met. A fork of electricity sizzled through me, but I managed to pull my attention away and move on.

He followed. Like I said, stalking . . . titillating.

"How are you stocked for meat?" he asked.

I smiled to myself. "Laney's a vegetarian."

He lifted a link of sausages. "But you're strictly carnivorous."

"You don't know me, Rivera."

He snorted a little. "I've saved your ass too many times to be mistaken."

"There's more to me than my ass."

His gaze burned me. "You think I haven't noticed?"

"The possibility crossed my mind."

"I know where all the parts are."

"Hmmff."

"Climb in the backseat and I'll prove it."

"I think I'm noticing a recurring theme."

"I always knew you were brighter than you seemed," he said, and handed me a jar of honey.

I handed it back. "Too bright to play grab-ass in the backseat with Robocop."

"If you're worried about room, we could lower the seats, utilize the trunk."

"You *are* a romantic," I said, and wheeled my cart into the bakery department.

"I thought you should know," he said, and handed me a package of dinner rolls. They were golden brown, creased neatly down the middle, and sexy as hell.

I put them in the cart, but did not caress them.

He handed me a twelve-pack of vitamin water he'd gotten from God knows where.

I gave him a look.

"We're going to want to stay hydrated," he said, and I couldn't help but laugh.

It was then that my phone rang . . . a tinny little rendition of "Holding Out for a Hero." I paused. I can't tell you how many times I've been saved from the dark lieutenant's dubious advances by a phone call. Or how many times I've been pissed at my bad luck. Our gazes caught. He shrugged, pragmatic.

"Better now than when we're in the trunk," he said.

Pulling out my cell, I snapped it open. "Hello."

"Christina McMullen?"

I scowled. The voice was breathless and rushed. But it seemed too soon for another catastrophe.

"Yes?"

"Christina, this is Ramla Al-Sadr."

"Ramla." I focused on the conversation, momentarily forgetting how the lemons had felt against my palm. "What's wrong?"

There was a pause. Usually when there's a pause in one of my conversations someone drops dead. "I am not sure."

So far so good, then.

"I received a call from a strange man."

Getting worse. "There are a lot of them out there," I said, and shifted my gaze to Rivera. He was scowling. Maybe his coppie-sense was buzzing. Or maybe he was always scowling when he wasn't thinking about being naked in the backseat of a Saturn. As for me, I was struggling to keep things light, but I could already feel the muscles in the back of my neck cramping up.

"He said I must go to the airport at once," Ramla said.

"What airport? Why?"

"He said he would call with more information later."

"And you don't know who it was?"

"No. But I cannot go to the airport, Christina," she said. "My husband, Taabish, he is gone for the business. I am in Simi Valley with my children and cannot leave them."

"You think this has something to do with your sister?"

"I do not know what to think." There was a pause. "My sister, she has no passport," Ramla said, and began to cry.

I tried to console her, but the truth is that overt displays of emotion make me itchy. We Midwesterners are more comfortable with snot than with tears. It's a condition that conflicts almost constantly with the sappy Celt in me.

In the end I promised Ramla I would go to the airport in her stead and wait for the man to call her again. I snapped my phone shut and dumped it back into my purse.

Rivera's eyes were shooting sparks. "You don't have to try so hard," he said.

"To prove I'm nuts?" I guessed, and wondered rather dismally what I had gotten myself into.

"Give the lady a beer," he said.

I took a deep breath, gathered my keys, my nerve, a little bit of sanity. "Not right now," I said. "I'm driving . . . to the airport."

"Good idea," he said. "I'll head on home. Catch a rerun of *Friends*, maybe surf for porn. Then tomorrow I can enjoy your obituary with my morning coffee."

"I thought you didn't drink coffee." I turned away, but not before I saw him grind his teeth and follow me.

I drove as fast as the traffic on the 110 allowed.

"Tell me what she said." Despite Rivera's dissertation on how he planned to spend his evening, he was sitting beside me, in the Saturn's passenger seat.

"A strange man called her," I said.

"I got that part." He was using his patient tone. I hate his patient tone almost as much as I hate Brussels sprouts, which, by the by, barely deserve to be classified as food.

"Then you know about as much as I do."

"I've got to tell you, knowing some stranger has called my next-door neighbor rarely prompts me to rush to the airport."

I gave him a look. He gave it back. Grumpy as hell. Maybe he really *didn't* want to read my obituary in the morning paper. So I told him the whole story about how

Ramla had been worried about her sister in Yemen. How I had promised to look into things. How I had even farmed the problem out to Brainy Laney, only to learn that things were looking up for Aalia and her hubby. I didn't leave out any salient points. Hardly.

"So this guy's been knocking her sister around for years," Rivera said.

"I believe so."

"And your neighbor honestly thought the bastard had suddenly been canonized?"

There may have been a certain amount of carefully re-strained vitriol in the statement. I had to assume it was brought on by the thought of wife beaters. He had never seemed sexier. Except maybe in the shower. "I take it you don't think people can change."

"It generally takes a high-caliber handgun and a believ-able threat." He was glaring out the window.

"Maybe his conscience got the better of him."

He turned toward me, eyes flat.

I shrugged, seeing something in his gaze that suggested he had witnessed more of the seedy side of life than I had realized. "Or maybe Aalia owns a handgun," I said.

He sighed. "Then why the call from the stranger?"

"That's what I'm wondering."

"Couldn't we have wondered that from the backseat?"

I examined him. Someone honked his horn and shouted an obscenity as he sped past in a convertible, but I barely noticed. It's one of the many valuable skills I had learned since moving to L.A. "I think you protest too much," I said.

He lowered one brow.

"I think you want to help her," I said.

He snorted. "I'm just hoping to keep you alive until we test your backseat."

I snorted.

"What did she say about a passport?" he asked.

I blinked. As it turns out, that was one of the few salient points I had neglected to tell him. Damn him and his coppie-sense. "What?" I said. See how I did that? Smooth as glass.

He was watching me evenly. "At the end of the conversation, I thought she said something about a passport."

"Did she? Oh, yes," I said, and wondered vaguely if people were still struck dead for lying or if their noses just grew like willow branches. "She said she got hers."

"The sister."

"Yeah."

"Without her husband's consent."

I shrugged. "Things were better between them. Maybe they were planning to travel together."

His brows lowered even farther. But before they could descend into hell, my phone rang. I gripped it like a lifeline, grateful for the interruption.

"Hello?"

"Christina." Ramla sounded breathless. I was just wheeling into short-term parking at LAX. "She is here."

"Aalia?"

"I have just received the call."

I glanced nervously at Rivera. He was glaring again. Or still.

"From whom?"

"He did not say."

"Did you ask?"

"He did not seem to wish to tell me."

I heard Rivera swear. The same words zipped through my brain. I mean, I'm naturally the trusting sort, but folks have attempted to kill me a few times and that's put something of a damper on my optimism regarding the inherent goodness of the human spirit.

"Why?" I asked.

"What?"

"Why do you think he wouldn't tell you?"

"I do not know."

"How much do you know about Aalia's husband?"

"Ahmad? He comes from a favorable family."

The same could be said of Ted Bundy. "Anything else?"

"The Orsorios are a wealthy, intelligent people. We thought it a fine match when first he asked for her hand. We had no way of knowing of his cruelty."

I gripped my cell a little tighter as I pulled into a parking spot. "Do you happen to know if *Ahmad* has a passport?"

There was a long pause fraught with a butt-load of bad vibes. "He travels a good deal."

"Beyond Yemen, I suppose you mean."

"New York City. Washington, D.C. He is an important man with Sanaa Oil."

"I see." That in lieu of a bunch of bad language.

"And is not without friends among your government, I think."

A little of the bad language leaked out.

"You are worried that it is he who called. That he hopes to confront those who would assist my sister," she guessed.

"The thought crossed my mind."

She drew a carefully controlled breath. "I will find another to care for my children and travel to the airport myself."

It was tempting as hell to take her up on her offer, but her kids had eyes as big as softballs. They were like two-legged basset hounds at a sad movie. And besides, Ahmad wouldn't recognize me. I hoped. The same couldn't be said for Ramla.

"Don't do anything just yet," I said, then, "Did the stranger say what flight your sister is on?"

She told me.

"Can you describe her for me?"

There was a pause. "I cannot ask this of you, Christina. It is too big."

"Describe her," I said. My voice sounded gravelly, but when Ramla next spoke, her own was the reverent whisper of a terrified sister.

"She is beauty itself," she said, "when the bruises heal."

The butterflies in my stomach somehow morphed into land mines. My eyes met Rivera's. His sparked amber-colored flame. "If she's here, we'll find her," I said, and clicked the phone shut.

9

In this country, if one dresses well, it matters little if her soul belongs to the devil.

—*Ramla Al-Sadr, on*
American fashion

*A*s I stepped out of the car a moment later, I tried Elaine's phone. She answered on the first ring.

"What's wrong?" Laney rarely bothered with salutations. We had something of a language of our own. But most of it involved old movies and young men. As far as I knew Laney could recite every single line from all five seasons of *Scarecrow and Mrs. King*.

"Did you talk to your friend about Ramla's sister?"

"Ghazi? Not recently. Why?"

I skittered a worried glance to Rivera. He was still scowling. It's nice to know some things don't change.

"So he doesn't know Aalia is in trouble?"

"*Why?*" The question was pointed now.

I gave her the details in a few brief sentences as we breezed through the airport's automatic doors and into canned air.

"I left a message on his cell phone and his home phone after Ramla spoke to you last night," Laney said. "But I think he may have been out of the country."

"Does he have the kind of clout that would enable him to get a married woman out of Yemen without her husband's consent?"

She paused for a moment, thinking. It never took long. "His surname is Saud."

"Translate."

"I think he may be a prince."

"Like '*He's a real prince*' or—"

"A Saudi prince."

"And he works as a prop master for *Amazon Queen*?"

"I believe there are a couple thousand extra princes left in his homeland to take care of any royal duties."

"Really? How many are single?"

"Can we wrap this up?" Rivera asked.

I glanced at him and almost resisted grinning before a thought struck me. "How many times did he propose to you?" I asked.

Laney never hesitated. "Just twice."

He wasn't very serious, then. I had known men who would beg every single Sunday for most of a decade. "Does he hold out any hope?"

"I sent him a wedding invitation," she said.

"Some guys aren't easily discouraged." At least where Laney was involved.

"I think his other wives will console him."

"You wouldn't be his *numero uno*?"

"Not even his *numero dos*."

"So you'd be like . . . dessert?"

"Baklava."

Rivera muttered a curse. I almost laughed.

"I've got to go," I said.

"Mac?"

"Yeah?"

"If you're dead for my wedding I'll never forgive you, and I'm a very forgiving person."

"You are."

"Don't be dead."

I smiled. "This is the first time in my life I've got a bridesmaid dress that doesn't make me want to poke myself in the eye with a fork."

"We did well on that, didn't we?"

"It was a steal."

"And perfect for you."

"I do look kind of great in it."

"Like a mermaid princess."

"I was thinking of getting those sandals with the amber stones on the instep. What do you—"

"Remember anything about an abused Yemeni girl?" Rivera asked, and I felt a little guilty.

"Hey, Laney, when you spoke to Ghazi, did you mention my name?"

"No names. I just said Aalia was a friend of a friend."

"Okay. Thanks."

"Hey," she said before I could hang up. "Arrive home alive tonight and I'll treat you to ice cream."

"Mocha Moose?"

"Your choice."

"Can I get extra caramel?"

"We'll buy an economy-sized jar."

"And we won't have to drink a green hair-slop chaser?"

"I don't drink green hair slop."

"Well, whatever that stuff is that's supposed to make hair all glorious."

"I don't care if all your hair falls out."

"I love you," I said, and hung up.

Rivera was staring at me as we walked.

"What?" I said, but he just shook his head.

"Where are we going?"

"To pick up a friend of a friend," I said.

"The wife of an abusive Yemeni oilman with ties to our government?"

"Yeah."

"All right," he said, then gripped my arm, forcing me to a halt. "But you're staying here."

"Really?" I loved the idea. It may have been the best idea I'd ever heard in my entire life. But the fact that it was a direct order from Rivera made my back go up like a pit bull's hairy spine. "You bring your cuffs again, Rivera?"

A man glanced our way, but kept walking. I resisted flipping him off. The entire male population was *not* responsible for the fact that Rivera had once handcuffed me to his father's kitchen cupboard. Probably.

"Maybe Elaine's wrong," he said. "Maybe she let your name slip. Maybe this bastard knows more about you than I do."

I glanced at the hand that gripped my arm with mind-imploding arrogance. "That wouldn't take much."

"Yeah? I know you're wearing leopard print underwear."

"I . . ." I screwed up my face at him, but truth to tell, I

was kind of impressed. My skirt was high-waisted. "How did you know that?"

"I'm a cop," he said. "And you're staying here."

"The hell I am."

He drew a careful breath as if that would keep planet Earth from tumbling into chaos. "I'm *asking* you to stay here."

"And I'm telling you no."

He ground his teeth. Pretty soon he was going to be edentate. Which would make him decidedly less sexy. Damnit! Why do I find irritating men sexy? "Maybe you don't realize how dangerous these domestic cases are, McMullen."

"I'm a licensed psychologist."

He canted his head. "Was that a *psychologist* or a *psychotic*?"

"Huh!" I chortled, then yanked my arm out of his grasp, turned away, and marched through the airport like a storm trooper.

I heard Rivera swear again, then, "Damnit, McMullen, why can't you be just a little bit—"

"If domestic cases are as dangerous as you say—you being the lauded police lieutenant—then we don't have much time to waste."

"You don't even know if she's really here."

"Good thing I have eyes."

"You going to wave a sign? 'Abused Wife of Asshole Oilman, Over Here'?"

"I think the burka might give her away," I said, but when we reached the baggage claim there wasn't a respectable face veil in sight. Just your average mix of bad taste.

There was a baker's dozen of white folk as pale as myself, all dressed as if they were going slumming; a trio of black women heatedly discussing something obviously near and dear to their hearts, and an olive-skinned boy with low-slung jeans bobbing to the beat of the iPod plugged into his ears. His baseball cap was frayed and said I ♥ NY.

"You sure this is the right place?" Rivera asked.

"She said United—" I stopped talking as two men in turbans turned left into the area. They were tall and lean, with hungry eyes and handsome hooked noses.

"Wow," I said. I can't help it, there's something about those haughty Middle Eastern men that makes the animal in me want to take a bite out of their dark-meat flanks.

The taller of the two shifted his sexy dusk gaze toward me and my breath caught in my throat. He stood very straight, shoulders drawn back, somber mouth even.

"Looking to be wife number six?" Rivera asked, and I snapped myself back in line, silently reprimanding the lazy-ass feminist in me.

"Do you think they're looking for her?" I asked, and turned my gaze casually away, but Rivera was still glaring at me.

"Are you looking for *them*?" he asked.

"I don't know what you're talking about," I said, and skimmed the growing crowd.

"You look like a hyena in a herd of wildebeest."

I gave up my perusal. "Maybe you could be jealous and insecure later," I said, and he snorted.

The boy with the New York cap adjusted his backpack, then touched a finger to his iPod, and in that moment I noticed something odd. I scowled and turned toward Rivera, not wanting to seem conspicuous.

"Don't they usually light up?"

"Would it be too much to ask you to make sense?"

"iPods," I said, frustrated. Laney would have understood my question, and had an interesting TV-related anecdote seconds ago. "Don't they light up when you touch them?"

"Do I look like Sean Diddy?"

"Just the attitude," I said, and turned momentarily back to the boy. His eyes were large, dark, lipid, and gorgeous. His black hair was cut short. In a second he looked away and tugged his tattered baseball cap lower over his forehead. His backpack looked heavy and his wrist was bruised.

Our eyes met, and in that moment he lowered his arm, letting the sleeve of his jersey fall back in place, but it was already too late.

I had found Aalia. Unfortunately, there was no reason to believe the turbaned men hadn't done the same.

10

Red lace garters have their appeal, but naked's pretty much a showstopper.

—Lieutenant Jack Rivera,
while perusing Chrissy's
Victoria's Secret

I sucked in a gasp and yanked my attention back to Rivera. "It's her."

"What are you talking about?" He was still scanning the crowd, but I touched his arm and laughed, at which time he glanced down as if I'd lost my last viable marble.

"Don't look," I said, but he lifted his head, and in that moment I did the only possible thing I could do. I kissed him, openmouthed and no-holds-barred.

One thing I'll say for L.A. cops, they can rise to the occasion. I felt it happen against my thigh, in fact. Felt his tongue slip into my mouth. Felt my libido amp up like an old rocker's subwoofers.

My hand was still on his arm when I pulled away. His eyes were smoky. His voice the same.

"Where?" he asked.

I almost said "backseat," but I caught myself just in time and remembered the moment at hand. "Kid in the baseball cap," I said.

He pushed the hair from my neck, caressing my skin with his fingertips. I shivered. It was probably just part of the act. "And the iPod?" he asked.

"I don't think it's turned on. Are the turbans still watching us?"

He pulled his attention from me, but his fingers remained on my neck. "Yes."

"Maybe you can delay them while I speak to Aalia," I said. She had turned away and was already leaving.

He kissed me again. There was a good deal of tongue. "Sometimes the mayor gets kind of pissed when we harass foreigners with friends in high places."

"I'm not asking you to shoot them."

"My mistake," he said, and slipped his hand down my bare arm.

It was all for show. I knew that. But someone had failed to inform my endocrine system. I was starting to drool a little. His hand skimmed the ribs just below my breasts.

"This isn't illegal, is it?" he asked.

I was breathing hard. "I'm of age."

The corner of his mouth hitched up in that way that made my own go dry. "I meant getting involved with this girl. She's legal, right? All documents cleared and everything? I'm not going to get my ass thrown in jail, am I?"

I shook my head, though I wasn't really sure why. "I have other plans for your ass."

"Promise?"

"You bet your ass," I said.

"Figuring out jurisdiction here is hell," he said, and kissed the corner of my mouth. "I might as well have left my badge at home."

Which was about as likely as leaving his dick in the kitchen drawer.

"Do you think you can just distract them for a while?" I asked.

"Hell, I might even be able to offend them."

"*You?*"

"Never know until you try. Get Aalia to the car. I'll catch up to you later," he said, and gave me a sizzling grin, up close and sexy, before he turned away.

I managed a nod, but he was already sauntering toward the men in turbans, narrow-hipped, loose-limbed, and smoking hot. "What are you looking at?" he asked. His voice was just loud enough to hear from my position. The tone was abrasive, arrogant, and as irritating as a toothache.

Perfect.

The two straightened even more, immediately affronted and entirely forgetting about me.

"You fucking camel jockeys," Rivera said. "Don't you have women where you come from?"

I heard one of them mutter a response.

"Yeah?" Rivera said. "Well, that one's mine, so back the hell off."

I almost fainted before remembering it was all an act. At which time I corralled my humping hormones and turned casually in the direction Aalia had taken. In a moment I was out of sight and speed-walking down the corridor, but she was nowhere to be seen. I broke into a trot, rounded a corner, skipped between suitcases and surfboards and little girls with pigtails, then came to a halt . . . glancing right and left down the row of luggage carousels. Still nothing. But then I saw her, heading away. She was wearing blue jeans and a red sweatshirt now, but she'd kept the cap.

Damn, she was good, I thought. Rushing toward her, I caught her arm.

"Aalia," I murmured.

The man who turned toward me wore a Fu Manchu beard and aviator glasses.

"Damn, girl!" he said. "You scared the shit out of me."

I stepped back a pace, stammered an apology, and turned toward the crowds again, but if Aalia was amongst them I didn't see her. Where, then? I zipped my attention back toward the carousels and caught a glimpse of restroom doors.

My breath caught in my throat. She was in there. I knew it. Probably had a change of clothes in her backpack and would come out looking like Halle Berry at the Oscars.

I rushed into the ladies' room. A woman stood at the sink. She was stout, blond, possibly albino. Glancing under the doors I saw that only two stalls were occupied. "Aalia?" I called.

No one answered, but she would be wise to be cautious, and judging by her disguise, I assumed she was not only wise, but clever. I bent to look under the first stall door and was just straightening when a woman stepped out. She was six feet tall and missing one of her premolars. Her hair was going gray, but muscle rippled across her shoulders and her hands were the size of catchers' mitts. She could have bench-pressed a trailer if she had put her mind to it. Still, I studied her a moment, making sure she wasn't a five-foot Yemeni beauty.

She wasn't. I was sure of it when she glared at me.

"Sorry," I said, and moved on. Pretending I had to pee, I scampered into a stall, closed the door, and bent double to look under the partitions. Three stalls over, there were a pair of sneakers peeking out from under blue jeans. Straightening abruptly, I waited for the vertigo to pass, then hurried out to tap on her door.

"Aalia."

"Who is there?" The voice was small and uncertain.

"I'm here to help you," I said. "We don't have much time."

"Who are you?"

A handsome woman in a yellow suit entered the restroom, eyeing me like I was some underworld oddity.

"My name's Christina. Your sister sent me."

There was a pause. I gave the suited woman a smile to indicate I wasn't about to murder her if she turned her back on me. She didn't look like she was buying it, but it didn't matter because just then the stall door clicked open and the occupant stepped out.

Her hair was red, short, and spiked into little meringuelike peaks at the top of her head. Her blouse seemed to be made of aluminum foil and her skin was just a shade lighter than the albino's. Not an easy feat.

"Damnit," I said, wondering where Aalia had gone.

The woman scowled. I seem to have that effect on people. "Why did my sister send you?" she asked.

"Sorry." I was already hurrying away.

"Is she still living with that jerk, Jerry?" she called, but I didn't have time to waste on explanations that might make me look like an idiot.

Instead, I skedaddled out the door and glanced to the right. The first thing I saw was the two men in turbans. They were looking at each other as they approached, deep in conversation, possibly discussing what assholes Americans are.

I only had a fraction of a second before they turned toward me. In that harrowing instant I scurried into the men's room.

There's something about the sight of urinals that always gives me pause. I mean, it's not like I see them every day and when I do I'm momentarily distracted. But I quickly got back on the job, scanning the stalls. Three of them were occupied. One showed blue jeans under the door.

"Aalia," I whispered, but the door of the restroom was already opening. I yanked my attention in that direction as Middle Eastern accents floated toward me, then jumped into the stall next to the blue jeans.

The two men entered the room. Still talking, they seemed to split up. I heard their shoes squeak as they opened stall doors to the right and left. Biting my lip, I dropped to my knees and gazed at the jeans in the next stall. They seemed to be about the right shade. Tennis shoes peeked out the bottom of the pants legs. Another stall door opened and closed. I had no choice.

Dunking down, I pushed my head under the partition.

The woman inside jerked her gaze toward me. She still wore the battered cap extolling her affection for New York. Her eyes were wide, her lips parted in fear. She jerked back a few scant inches, but made no sound as she stared at me.

I put my finger to my lips, then shimmied under the partition. It was tight inside. I was careful not to hit my head on the toilet stool as I straightened.

The men were approaching from opposite ends of the room. A stall door squeaked open to my left. We jerked our gazes toward the noise in unison, both breathless as I grabbed her arms. She dragged her attention back to me and we waited. Three stalls to the right, another door opened. Her eyes were steady on mine, sharp with focus, bright with terror and intellect and hope. I pointed toward the floor. She stared a moment longer, then, without a word, dropped to her knees, where she remained, gazing up at me. I held up one hand, heart pounding. The door next to us was pushed open. The man's footsteps came toward us. I pointed. Aalia rolled silently into the stall he'd just checked. At the same moment I stepped out, adjusting my skirt.

"I don't like to use those nasty urinals," I said, and sashayed to the row of sinks. An old man with a goatee hobbled in, looked at me, and backed out. It took all of my restraint to keep from searching for Aalia. Instead, I made a great show of lathering my hands.

The second Middle Eastern man reached the first. In the mirror, I watched them confer. My fingers were beginning to chaff, but finally, after glancing once more in my direction, they left.

I dried my hands with a paper towel, then tossed it in the nearly empty basket, just as Aalia slipped from hiding. Ramla was right. She was gorgeous. All smooth mocha skin and soft eyes.

Her wide gaze skittered to the door. "They will return," she whispered.

My mind was bouncing like an overinflated balloon. What would a cocky man do to keep a woman like this? "You know them?"

She shook her head. "But my husband, he has many friends."

"Do you think they recognized you?"

"I am not certain."

I contemplated that for a moment, then, "Get undressed," I said.

She stared at me. "I do not think it proper—" she began, but I interrupted.

"Your husband has many friends," I said. "You have me."

She stared at me a moment, then nodded curtly and disappeared into the nearest stall.

Yanking the plastic bag from the garbage can, I emptied the few contents, then tore a hole in the bottom.

In a moment Aalia opened the door, wearing nothing but her underwear. The bra, white and lacy, did good things to her modest boobs. The panties were a floral pattern and the size of a midget's handkerchief.

"Victoria's Secret?" I guessed.

"Orchid V-string."

"Nice," I said, but just then a noise sounded from outside. I crowded her back into the stall and closed the door behind us.

She took the garbage bag from me and popped it over her head without a question asked. It just reached the middle of her perfect thighs. Whipping off my belt, I handed it over.

The restroom door opened. We both froze but in a moment a stall door creaked open and shut.

We exhaled in tandem, then she cinched the belt around her waist.

I glanced at her. She looked like a high-fashion model with poor taste. Perfect.

We traded shoes in a matter of moments. She teetered a little in mine, but managed the altitude. It was the *attitude* that was problematic.

"You've seen Gisele Bündchen?" I whispered.

"The model super?"

I nodded. "Be her."

It took her a moment to assimilate my meaning, but then she transformed, pulling her shoulders back, letting her eyes go mean. By the time we stepped back into the bustle of LAX, she looked angry enough to be anorexic and we'd been inside the restroom less than five minutes. I glanced in both directions but the turbaned men were nowhere to be seen. Aalia was walking straight and true on my three-inch heels as we made our way toward the parking lot. All seemed well. But as we stepped past the nearest carousel, three men caught my attention. Their nationality was uncertain, but they wore Italian suits like they had been born to them. Their black hair was peppered with salt, and their dark eyes were narrow and cautious as they glanced at us.

We kept walking, and though I didn't turn toward Aalia, I could feel her falter.

"Aalia."

"Yes?" Her shoulders were still pulled back and somehow she had learned to lead with her hips, but her pace had slowed the slightest degree, and her voice sounded vague.

"Do you know what a lesbian is?"

"In my country they are put to the death."

"In mine, they get their own talk shows."

She shook her head, but her attention was on the suits. "It is a mortal sin."

"We kind of frown on wife-beating here," I said.

A degree of color seeped from her face. Then, reaching out, she took my fingers in hers. They felt as cold as Popsicles. Our gazes met and stuck. I swung our hands between us and forced a smile. It took her a moment to reciprocate, but when she did the world lit up like a carnival. Just when we were even with the suits, she leaned over and kissed me.

I stared, agog, and she laughed. Slipping her arm through mine, she toted me outside.

"Give me the keys."

I jerked toward the speaker. Rivera was right beside me, face hard, body language unspeakable. I hadn't even heard him approach, but he was matching my stride.

"The keys," he said again.

"I can drive," I said.

"She needs you."

"She's fine . . . and amazing," I said, but he was already slipping my purse from my shoulder.

"Hurry up," he ordered, and it wasn't until that moment that I realized Aalia was crying.

11

It is better to be a coward for a moment than to be dead for the rest of your life.

—*Irish proverb*

E ven though the traffic was atypically light, it was still a long ride home from LAX to Sunland. I sat in the backseat with Aalia. For the first few miles I just stared out the back window, but if anyone was following us, I couldn't see them.

I was able to coax almost nothing out of Aaila. In the end, she fell asleep, head resting against the cushion behind her. I tried to call her sister, but my message went instantly to voice mail.

By the time we reached the 101 I had given up, but Ramla was out her door before Rivera had pulled the Saturn to a complete halt. Instead of rushing toward us, however, she stood absolutely still, waiting on her stoop, hands clasped in front of her mouth, brows drawn painfully together in the sweep of her porch light.

Rivera turned off the car and glanced back at me. Aalia came awake slowly and blinked, then started slightly as she saw us staring at her.

"It's okay," Rivera said.

"We're here," I intoned, and nodded toward the Al-Sadrs'. "Your sister's waiting."

Aalia lifted her beautiful face toward my neighbor's house. "Ramla?" She said the word strangely, almost like a prayer, and then she was fumbling for the door handle. Ramla was running toward us. I sat perfectly still, watching as the two women met and clasped, cried and hugged and cried some more. Sitting in the backseat, I felt my eyes well up as Ramla and Aalia turned, still hugging, toward the house. One hot, fat tear slipped down my cheek.

The night went silent. Even Rivera seemed beyond complaints.

"I'd join you back there," he said, "but I'm probably in enough trouble for harassing strangers without being found in the backseat with a weeping woman."

"I'm not weeping," I said, and inconspicuously wiped away the tear.

It was very dark, but I could still make out his cut-granite features in the dimness. "Is that an invitation?"

"No," I said, but truth to tell, I did kind of need a hug . . . or something.

"You okay?"

"Sure," I said. "It was easy peasy."

He raised one brow. "You dressed a Muslim woman in a garbage bag."

I sniffed a little. "There were Muslim men nearby."

He nodded.

"I'm getting a kink in my neck," he said, twisted around in the seat. "We should get you inside."

I didn't say anything. The memory of Ramla wrapping her sister in her arms still made my throat feel tight.

"Or I could join you back there."

"Geez," I said, and shedding the melancholy mood, clambered out of the car. He followed me to the door, where I put my key in the lock.

"I'll call you in the morning," he said.

I turned toward him. "You're not coming in?"

"I've got some things to take care of," he said.

I winced despite myself, remembering the part about Aalia's missing passport, my *lies* regarding Aalia's nonexistent passport, and the fact that Rivera probably knew all along I was lying. "Any of those things going to get me incarcerated?"

He glanced at me. "Would it matter?"

"What are you talking about?"

"You might enjoy the company in Sing Sing."

I gave him a look that may have suggested I thought he'd lost his last vestige of good sense.

"But maybe they don't kiss as well as Aalia."

I felt myself blush. "That wasn't my idea," I said, and he laughed as he stepped up on the stoop and slipped an arm around my waist.

"So you think you'd prefer the companionship in Lompoc?"

"I don't know what you're talking about."

His mouth was still slanted up at a cocky angle. "Looks like *nobody* can resist you," he said.

I considered pushing him away, but didn't really want to. "You're doing okay."

He snorted and slipped a loose lock of hair behind my right ear. "She even got in your backseat before I did."

"There was no tongue," I said.

"Jesus, McMullen," he said, and pulled me closer. "I'm having a hard enough time remembering you two kissing without thinking about . . ." The length of him felt hard against my thigh. He shifted uncomfortably. "Jesus."

"So you're one of *those* guys," I said.

His eyes were like dynamite. "One of those guys who wants to screw you?"

I swallowed. "One of those guys who gets turned on by the thought of two women together."

"Oh, you mean a guy with balls. Yeah," he said, "I am. But I'm not sure mine are as big as yours."

"What are you talking about?"

He shook his head. "Sometimes I don't really know if you're gutsy or just stupid."

"Gutsy," I said.

He chuckled a little and touched my cheek. "What the hell were you thinking?"

The events of the evening were beginning to take their toll. The palms of my hands suddenly felt sweaty. "Do you think they'll figure out where she's at?"

His eyes were dark and seemed to be whispering sexy secrets about abandoned beaches and breakfast à la him. "There's no way to be sure if they were even after her."

"They checked all the bathroom stalls."

His fingers paused on my cheek. "What's that?"

I swallowed. I felt a little shaky suddenly. "They came into the restroom and checked all the stalls."

"Muslim men went into the women's bathroom?"

"Um . . . no."

He swore, but it was quiet, so I wasn't too concerned.

"I didn't *make* her go in the men's," I told him.

He shook his head. "You are something else, woman."

"In a good way?" I asked. "Or in a way that'll get me five to ten."

"That's yet to be determined," he said, and slipped his hand lower.

"What determines it?"

He shrugged. "Care to bribe an officer of the law? I think the backseat's still empty."

I laughed a little. "I think the Middle Eastern guys were shocked enough."

"After that kiss, they're probably home beating off right now."

"Is that what you plan to do?"

His lips hitched up a notch. "I've still got hope here."

"No, you don't," I said, but my voice was kind of squishy.

He chuckled, low and hot. Then he leaned closer. All my juices rushed to the forefront. All my inhibitions swooshed away like rain down a storm drain, but he reached around me and opened the door.

I scowled. He nodded me inside, so I stepped in, and he followed.

"Elaine." He called her name and she was there immediately, eyeing me, eyeing him.

"What happened?" She was wiping her hands on a towel. A frown had dared venture onto her perfect brow.

"I want you to make sure McMullen doesn't leave the house tonight," he said.

"Okay."

"If someone comes to the door, call me immediately."

She nodded.

"If you hear a strange noise, call me immediately."

"All right."

"If you're nervous—"

"Call you? Immediately?"

"Right."

Reaching out, she pulled me farther into the vestibule. Rivera turned, closing the door behind us, leaving us alone.

Laney tugged me into the living room. "Sit down," she said, and urged me toward the La-Z-Boy.

I sat.

"I'm going to make you some tea, then I'm going to ask you, again, what happened."

"You said we could have ice cream," I said. I wasn't whining, but . . . Well, maybe I was whining a little.

"You need something to calm your nerves first. Ice cream will just make you sick."

"Slander," I said, but she had already left. "Ice cream has never made me sick."

I leaned my head back against the cushiness of the chair and contemplated the cosmos. Laney was back in a moment. Sitting on the couch close to the 'Boy, she took my hand.

"You found Aalia," she said.

I managed a nod.

"Rivera went with you."

Another nod.

"Someone tried to stop you."

I considered that for a moment, but I wasn't sure of the

answer so I changed the subject. Or maybe I changed it because I have the attention span of a gnat. "Rivera thinks I'm a lesbian."

She sat looking at me. "Is that a good thing or a bad thing?"

"Not sure."

"Did he say 'ick' or did he try to get you into the backseat of your Saturn?"

I frowned. Or maybe I had already been frowning. "I really don't understand how you know these things."

"You don't understand how I know that men try to get women into the backseats of Saturns?"

I stared at her. She was, without a doubt, the most beautiful person in the world. Probably the universe. Yup, even counting possible extraterrestrials, she was the best. And I'd been kissed by *Aalia*.

"I guess I understand that one," I said, and dropped my head back against the cushion.

She patted my hand and rose to fetch the tea. In a minute she was back. I don't really like tea, but it was a prelude to ice cream, which I love more than French-kissing.

I took a sip of my tea and made a face. "What is this?"

"Ashwagandha."

"It tastes like cat pee."

"The fact that you know that begs so many questions," she said, then moved on. "Aalia's with her sister?"

I nodded.

"Did you have to put her in some kind of disguise?"

"How did you know that one?"

She shrugged. "You love disguises. Hey, I brought home one of my old wigs."

"I never have understood why they would have you

wear a wig when your own hair is like . . . well, like that." I motioned toward her mustang's mane. Maybe mine would have looked similar if I drank her Green Goo, but some things aren't worth the trouble.

"They still have me wear hairpieces sometimes," she said. "But Nadine likes to work with her own creations."

"Nadine? The set's hairdresser?"

"Yeah. She creates her own wigs, so they throw the old ones out. I thought of you."

"You make me sound like a two-year-old," I said, although, actually, I couldn't wait to play dress-up.

"A two-year-old superhero," she said.

I smiled a little and took another sip of cat pee. "I *was* kind of amazing," I said, and she laughed.

"You always have been," she said, and sighed as she rose. "That's why I don't want to take advantage of you. You ready for ice cream?"

"Is there caramel?"

"More than you can eat," she said.

"I'll place wagers," I said, and stood, but something wasn't quite right. I suspected it as I followed her into the kitchen. Knew it as I watched her reach for bowls, retrieve spoons, get out the blessed ice cream.

"What's going on?" I asked.

"We're celebrating your continued survival," she said.

I nodded. "A serendipitous occasion."

"And unexpected."

"What did you mean by 'you don't want to take advantage of me'?"

She smiled. "Neither do I want to offend you with the truth," she said.

"Since when?"

She laughed. "You're a good person, Mac. Have been since the moment you were born."

"That's not true at all."

"Well, you did a good thing tonight. So let's eat a toast." She'd dished up the ice cream. Two big scoops for me. A molecule for herself. She pushed my bowl across the kitchen table, lifted her own. "To Christina McMullen."

"Ph.D.," I added.

"Ph.D.," she agreed. "May all her acquaintances appreciate her marvelousness."

"Here, here," I said, and tasted my dessert. Laney had added cashews and caramel. The woman's practically a genius.

"How is it?" she asked.

"Almost as marvelous as me."

"They could use that in their marketing."

"Call it Christina's Caramel."

"Or Mac's Madness."

I gave her a nod and set my bowl down. Sometimes I'm not only marvelous, I'm disciplined. But usually I'm just marvelous. "What's going on?" I asked again.

She stared at me for a long second. "I don't want to get you involved."

"With what?"

For a moment I almost thought she was going to lie to me. But Brainy Laney is practically physically incapable of fabrications. I don't have that problem . . . except where Laney's involved.

"I've been getting some unusual mail," she said.

"Define unusual."

She drew a careful breath and cocked an almost-hip

against the counter. "An adjective. Meaning uncommon. Rare."

"I wasn't asking for Webster's opinion."

"And I'm not asking for your help."

"Why?"

"Because I like eating ice cream with you."

"You haven't eaten any."

She smiled. "You tend to get too involved."

"I'm funny that way. I prefer for my friends to have pulses," I said, and picked up my bowl again. Laney had gone through the trouble of dishing it up after all.

"You had never even met Aalia before you went charging off to her rescue."

I took a bite of ambrosia and gave her a look.

She glanced away, frustrated. Worried. "I didn't think it was anything to be concerned about."

"The unusual mail."

"It was just an odd letter here or there."

"But now?"

"They're getting odder. I'm thinking of moving in with Jeen before the wedding."

"So that if it's a murderous fan, Solberg'll be the first to go?"

She gave me a disgusted scowl. "So you don't get hurt."

I nodded. "We're sacrificing *you*, then, I take it?"

Her scowl took on a little more attitude. One would think as pretty as Laney is, she wouldn't be very good at angry, but that's not true. She could drive a Navy SEAL to his knees if she put her mind to it. Of course it might have less to do with anger and more to do with the size of her boobs. "We're not sacrificing anyone," she said.

"Have you talked to the police?"

"On location," she said.

"Not here?"

"I just opened the letter today."

"It's been a big day," I said, and took another bite of ice cream. It had lost of little of its scrumptiousness. I resented that.

"I'm sorry," she said.

My spoon paused halfway to my mouth. "You're apologizing? Seriously?"

"Very seriously."

"Did *you* send the letter?"

"You're such a dirt wad."

"A dirt wad?"

"Don't make me swear," she said, and I laughed, but in that moment I saw that her eyes were teary.

"Elaine." I set my bowl down. Laney had learned to sob from the virtuosos on daytime television, but in real life she was a silent crier. She never made a sound when she was truly upset. "What's wrong?"

She scrunched up her face and glanced away. "You are always taking care of me."

I couldn't possibly have been more surprised to hear that. "Are you kidding? What are you talking about?"

"I don't know. I'm living here." She flapped a hand sideways toward my threadbare carpets, my scuffed walls. "Mooching off you, and I'm never here. Always planning for the stupid wedding that's been blown way out of . . ." Her voice trailed off.

Stupid wedding? "Yeah," I agreed, voice cautious and hopeful, "the wedding's a lot of stress. Maybe you should call it off."

She laughed even as she wiped away a tear with her knuckles. "I'm not calling it off. It's just . . . it's gotten out of hand."

"So take it back in hand."

She shook her head. "Solberg wants . . . spectacle."

I refrained from informing her that Solberg was an idiot. "It's *your* wedding, Laney. You should—" I began, but she was shaking her head.

"It's not that. Please don't worry about that. I'm sorry I'm whiny. I just . . . I just feel badly that I'm taking advantage of you. Hiding out here like a frickin' convict."

"Well . . . you could deliver truckloads of cash to my front door."

"Would you take it?"

"Absolutely."

She laughed again. "I'll call the cartage company immediately."

"They're probably closed now. Better wait till morning."

"You're so practical."

"Yuh-huh," I said, and watched her wipe her nose with the back of her hand. "Show me the letter."

"Mac—"

"You want me to tell Solberg?"

"Oh, man, it would kill him."

"Exactly."

She sighed, then turned and trotted upstairs. Returning moments later, she handed me a business-sized envelope. Her expression was somber.

"Do you think I should wear gloves or something?" I asked.

"You're the detective."

"Psychologist," I corrected, and going to a drawer, came back with tongs and a pair of mismatched rubber gloves.

"Very professional," she said.

"CSI: L.A.," I said, and pinching the envelope with the tongs, put it on the counter. The handwriting was blocky and perfect. There was no return address. "Nice penmanship," I said.

"I was impressed, too, before I thought he might intend to kill me."

"How many letters have you gotten?"

"It's hard to say. I'm not exactly sure which ones are from him. There have been five that seem very similar. But I have other mail without signatures, too."

"When did they start?"

"Back in May. About one a month."

I glanced at the envelope again, finally read the address, and felt myself pale, felt the world slow like an unwinding top.

"They sent it here." My voice was almost entirely without inflection.

Hers was the same. "Yes."

"I didn't realize . . . I mean, I thought you got it with your latest mail bundle. I . . ." The floor beneath my feet felt oddly tilted. "So they know you're living here."

"I'm sorry."

"No. It's . . ." I began, but suddenly I was shaking too hard to continue. My skin felt clammy and my stomach queasy.

A hundred ugly scenarios bloomed in my mind, and as I imagined men in turbans floating down on a sea of oversized envelopes, I made a beeline for the bathroom.

12

Not every Prince Charming has a full head of hair.

—*Brainy Laney Butterfield,*
being brainy, and a little
depressing

"*H*ow long has she been sleeping?" Rivera's voice rumbled softly through my sluggish system. I was lying on my side in my own bed, with no idea what time it was. In fact, I was entirely uncertain of the day. I glanced toward the window. It was dark.

"Half an hour," Laney said. "Maybe more. I was worried. She was pretty upset before she fell asleep. I'm sorry to bother you."

"It'd be more of a bother to find your decaying bodies three days after the event."

"Sensitive," she said. "That's what I love about the L.A. Police Department."

"To protect and serve," he said, and she laughed. "Is this

the letter?" I heard him move away, heard his volume lessen.

"Are you in love with her?" Elaine's voice was barely audible now.

My ears perked up. I glanced furtively toward the kitchen but was foiled by a couple of walls.

I could imagine him looking at her. "You a spy?"

She said something I didn't hear.

He answered. Also unheard.

I swung my feet quietly to the floor. Standing carefully, I stepped into the bathroom adjacent to the kitchen. Quiet as an Apache.

"She drives *everyone* crazy, but that's not what I asked," Laney said.

"She takes too many idiotic risks."

"She's plucky."

"Plucky!" He snorted, then sighed. I could imagine him rubbing his eyes. Sometimes I seemed to make him tired. "I haven't gotten a full night's sleep since I met her over Bomstad's dead body. She's like a damned commando."

"Can I tell her you said that?"

"If you want to spend a night in lockup," Rivera said.

She laughed again. "There's no one more loyal."

"Or with a better ass."

"Whoa," Laney said, but in that moment, Rivera peered around the corner. His face was inches from mine, his expression absolutely unsurprised.

"Did you hear that one, McMullen?"

"What?" I stumbled back a step, then stretched, awkward as hell. "I just woke up. When did you get here?"

He chuckled and disappeared. I didn't have much

choice but to follow him. He was already peering at the envelope on the counter when I arrived.

"Nice penmanship," he said. "I assume none of them have a return address."

"None that I can identify as his," Laney said.

"Are they all postmarked from L.A.?"

I felt myself pale again.

"The others were from Montana," Elaine said.

"Where you film?"

"We're actually in Idaho, but the border's just a few miles away."

"How many letters?"

"Five altogether, I think."

He nodded, then glanced at my hands. One was garbed in a pink rubber glove. One in blue. I was hardly surprised that I had fallen asleep with them on. As a teenager, I'd once slept still wearing my tuba. "That to eliminate fingerprints?" he asked.

"Maybe," I said, and he shook his head as he held the envelope up to the light.

I crowded closer as he pulled out the letter. The handwriting inside was just as neat as on the envelope. Perfectly spaced and uniformly sized. I read it through.

Dearest Ms. Ruocco,

I write again to caution you to use your gifts wisely. Your God-given beauty will eventually fade. Make certain when that day arrives you have not foolishly squandered your time and talents nor spent your days with those unworthy of you. I do not deny that your betrothal is disconcerting to me. But perhaps it is not his money but his wretchedness that draws you to him.

*Perhaps you are being charitable in that regard. And
in charity we find peace. I hope you will take my words
into consideration, as I have no desire to take further
steps to ensure your future happiness. I prefer that you
find that path on your own.*

"Is this typical of the others?" Rivera asked.

"Pretty much. The threat in this one seems more overt.
Or maybe it's just that it was delivered here."

"Today?"

"Yes."

"Regular mail?"

"It was in the box when I checked this afternoon."

"But the others were threatening also."

"In a nebulous sort of way."

"Any idea who it might be?"

"None."

He glared silently at the letter. If I were a nasty missive,
I would have turned tail and run . . . if I weren't so damned
plucky.

"Do you know anyone who holds a grudge?" he asked.

Laney shook her head.

"How about you, McMullen?" he asked, glancing at me.
"Anyone you can think of who might be angry with her?"

I shook my head, too.

"Do you owe anyone money?" he asked.

"Mac," she said.

"Really?" he asked, looking curious.

"Truckloads," she said.

"You write this?" he asked, glancing at me.

"Just the part about Solberg," I said, and he snorted as
he turned toward Laney.

"Any disappointed men in your past?"

She blinked.

I laughed out loud. "Are you serious?"

He turned toward me. I raised a hand to indicate her perfection. "Look at her. She's the most gorgeous woman on the planet. Every man in the world is disappointed. Except Solberg, and he obviously made some sort of pact with the inhabitants of the underworld."

Rivera stared at me all stormy-eyed and there was something in his expression that almost seemed to refute my opinion. It made me feel a little breathless, but he turned his laser-vision away in a moment.

"The first letter arrived about five months ago?"

"I believe so."

"Was there anyone new in your life at that time?"

She shook her head. "People come and go all the time on location."

"Did you work with any new men?"

"Yes."

"Can you give me a list?"

She paused for a moment. "I don't think it's any of them."

"We're going to have to assume this isn't obvious."

Her frown was back in place. "I'll see what I can do."

"I'd like to take all the letters to our analyst."

"I can have the others sent to me."

He nodded. "In the meantime, I don't want you living here alone."

I blinked. "She's not alone," I said.

He turned toward me, jaw muscles already jumping as if itching for a fight. "I meant the two of you. I don't want you here alone."

"Oh?" I was calm. Like the eye of the proverbial storm. A tornado maybe, with the rest of the world swirling around me. "What do you have in mind, Rivera?"

He pulled a hard breath into his nostrils. "It would be best if you lived somewhere else for a while."

"So I should just shut down my practice and hike out to . . ." I felt anger beginning to bubble up a little in my gut, but I just let it simmer. "Do you have somewhere specific in mind?"

His eyes were dark and low-browed. "You should get out of L.A. Schaumburg might be—"

"You think I should go crawling back to Chicago?"

"Don't be juvenile about this. I'm sure your parents would love to have you stay—"

"Before you continue, I want you to think of Harlequin," I interrupted, smiled, unclenched my fists. "Where will he live if I'm incarcerated for shooting an officer of the law?"

"Are you *threatening* me?"

"Yes."

He shook his head. "Your family isn't that—"

"My brothers put bugs in my rice." I was coming to the boiling point.

"I didn't say they were—"

"Pete called it fried lice. Said it was an Asian delicacy." I was starting to snarl.

His frown deepened. "I'll ask them not to do that anymore."

I paused, trying to get adequate air. Turns out there wasn't enough to accommodate my lungs while thinking of living with my parents. Holly had kicked Pete out of the house again. Which meant he would be crashing with the folks. "You'll ask them—"

"I'll *tell* them not to."

"I'm not running back to Schaumburg like a—"

"That's because you're too fucking stubborn to realize—"

"Jeen can move in," Laney said.

We turned on her as if she'd just been diagnosed with mad cow disease.

"What?"

"*What!*"

"I think he'd be happy to look after us," Elaine said. "Besides, if the letter-writer found me here, what's to stop him from following us to Chicago?"

It took a moment for my brain to form intelligent thoughts, a little longer to articulate them. "I'm sure Solberg would be tickled pink," I said. "But I'm not going to—"

"It's not a bad idea," Rivera said.

I jerked toward him so fast I could hear my neck snap. "Do you hate me that much?"

"Only when you're acting like an adolescent—"

"I'm not an—"

"Then don't act like one. Would you rather be killed in your sleep or spend a couple weeks with Solberg?"

I stared at him.

"McMullen—"

"I'm thinking!" I snapped.

"Well . . ." He chuckled, shook his head. "I'm thrilled to know you're still capable of such—"

"Hi."

We turned back toward Elaine. She had a cell phone pressed to her ear. I was already holding my breath.

"I miss you, too," she said, and smiled past the little receiver at me.

I could hear Solberg's whiny tone on the other end of the line. I would have snarled something but I felt too sick to my stomach, and I wasn't naïve enough to blame the ice cream.

"I know," she said. "Just a couple more weeks." She paused, listened, then, "But how many seconds left?" she asked, then laughed. "Maybe you can recalculate later."

More whining. Another laugh on her part.

"Listen, Jeen, I have a favor to ask you."

Mumble, mumble, whine, grovel.

"I don't actually *need* your liver." She glanced at me, grinning a little, knowing I was about to puke, and enjoying it immensely. "But I was wondering if you could come stay with us tonight."

There was stunned silence from the other end of the line. Maybe if I was really lucky he'd die of shock. So far as I knew, and I knew pretty far, Elaine and Solberg had never shared a mattress.

"Honey?" she said.

I heard a croaking noise from the other end of the line. Some frogs turn into princes. Some frogs will forever remain frogs.

"You don't have to—"

Even through the phone, I heard him slam his door.

"Honey, I need you to pack some clothes. Get a toothbrush. Stay a few days."

But his car was already starting. He owned a Porsche. A cobalt blue Turbo Cabriolet. Laney didn't particularly care for it because it got about a half an inch to the gallon. But I had driven it once and determined without delay that I'd trade thirty-seven Solbergs and his mansion in La Canada for that car.

There was silence for a moment, then, "Oh, okay, then. Love you, too," she said, and hung up.

We stared at her.

"I take it he's coming?" Rivera said.

"You'd better open the door or he'll drive straight into the living room to save time," I warned.

"He loves me," Laney said, and laughed when I threw up a little bit in my mouth.

13

As a rule I'm against capital punishment. But I know a
few boys who could benefit from a little public flogging.

—Linda Griffin, Chrissy's new
neighbor, and single
mother of a teenage
daughter

*T*he next couple of days went by with relatively few ca-
tastrophes. Over the weekend I picked up my mermaid
princess gown from the tailor, took Harley to the dog
park, and placed my vote on what flavor frosting Laney's
five-tier wedding cake should have.

Monday rolled around, and although I hadn't yet been
attacked by either an abusive Yemeni or a whack job letter-
writer, I still felt jittery.

Temporarily losing my mind, I opted to go for a run.
Not because I wanted to. Not because it was safe to, but
because exercise sometimes helps me relax. Of course,
high doses of calories will generally put me into a lovely
catatonic state, but I had left all of my would-be calories at

the grocery store when Ramla called. So I did my three miles of perdition, showered, then locked myself in the bedroom lest Solberg groggily stumbled into the wrong room. After that I got dressed and rushed off to work.

When I say "rushed," I mean that I drove twenty miles per hour in head-pounding traffic since the 2 was reminiscent of Macy's parking lot. I actually think I saw some guy serving lemonade from the back of his pickup truck.

Eventually I arrived at the office. Shirley was manning the desk.

"Whoa," she said as I rushed in the door. It was two minutes before my first client was scheduled to arrive.

I teetered to a halt on wedge cork heels.

"What happened to you?"

"What do you mean?"

"I mean you look like you slept hanging upside down last night."

"I didn't."

"What happened?"

I considered telling her the whole story, but I had a client due to tell me his/her problems in approximately ninety seconds. It probably wouldn't be good if I was crying about my own. "Just a little trouble in the neighborhood."

She stared at me. "Umm-huh," she said finally. "Anyhow, you rushed off without breakfast again, didn't you?"

"I appreciate—"

"Didn't you?"

"Yes."

She shook her head. Reaching into her bottom drawer, she pulled out a white bag and handed it to me. I peeked inside. A breakfast burrito smiled up at me.

"Get in there now," she said, and shooed me away. "Hurry up."

"But don't I have—"

"I don't care what you have," she said. "Nobody can't do no good on an empty stomach. I'll keep your first appointment busy until you give me a buzz on the phone."

I tried to argue, really I did, but in a moment I was alone with the burrito and then it just seemed rude not to eat it.

I'd like to say I felt guilty for my caloric transgressions, but really I felt much better afterward, almost ready to meet my first client of the day.

Mr. Howard Lepinski is a mousy little man with a mustache and a thousand neuroses. He is also one of my greatest successes, someone who had gone from being a patently unhappy man who constantly obsessed about every minute detail of his life to a relatively happy man who only occasionally worried about every minute detail of his life. It had taken a good deal of harsh reality, a divorce, and a new relationship with a woman who didn't criticize his every breath to reach that pinnacle of sterling sanity.

"How was your weekend?" I asked as he took a seat on my couch.

He wobbled his scrawny neck, a mannerism indicative of his newfound relaxation. When I'd first begun seeing him he'd been as stiff as a kayak paddle.

"So-so. The stocks are still in the pits, my accounts are down by eighteen percent thanks to this danged recession, and I think I'm allergic to raspberry compote," he said, itching madly at a tiny rash on his arm.

"Raspberry compote?" I said.

He nodded.

"Raspberry compote that your lovely wife made?"

"Uh-huh."

"Raspberry compote that your lovely wife made because she *adores* you?"

"Yeah," he said, and grinning like a contented little spider monkey, forgot all about the stocks and the recession and the tiny rash.

By the time Emily Christianson arrived I almost felt worthy of the psychology license matted and framed on my office wall.

She looked as crisply thin and tightly strung as the first time I had seen her.

"How are you today?" I asked, and settled in for the long haul.

"I am well," she said, and sat down on the couch.

I watched her. Most people are okay. Some are good. A few are awful and actually know it. But not many are "well."

"Did you get that A minus taken care of?" I asked.

"Mr. Brickman allowed me to do extra credit."

"So you're still on track for an A plus?"

She nodded. Her lips were pursed. I wondered how she saw herself. If she realized she exuded tension like an open wound.

I watched her for a moment while neither of us could think of anything to say. "I wasn't sure you would return," I said finally.

"As I said, my parents asked that I speak to someone."

"I'm surprised they didn't accompany you."

Her left thumb, resting just so atop the right, jerked. Just a little. "They're extremely busy."

"Oh?" I gave her my best "Talk to me" smile. "What do they do?"

"My mother is a cellist with the Philharmonic Orchestra."

"Here in L.A.?"

"Yes. Gustavo is quite demanding."

"Gustavo?"

"The director." She seemed to be doing a decent job of containing her disdain for my ignorance. I couldn't help but feel grateful. "I don't believe he appreciates Mother's drive. She also teaches at Thornton and plays with Sawallisch in the Johannes String Quartet."

"I see." I didn't really. "And your father?"

"He's an anesthesiologist at the Palmdale Medical Center."

"In Palmdale?"

For a moment I thought she didn't intend to honor that little piece of genius with a response, but finally she nodded crisply.

"It's a long commute, and a high-stress occupation. As you can imagine, my parents are hoping for something better for me."

Holy crap. Better than that? Even *I* had heard of L.A.'s legendary orchestra. And anesthesiologists make a butt-load of money. Three years ago I had discovered I was fostering a baby kidney stone. After a fair amount of projectile vomiting, I had checked into Oakview's emergency room. The ensuing bill had made me consider leaving my spleen as a down payment.

"And you're their only child?"

Her lips pursed a little more. "Perhaps that's why they expect so much of me."

"What *do* they expect?"

She shrugged. The movement was stiff. "Responsible behavior. Good grades. Respect."

I smiled and wondered if she would crack if she did the same. "There's a difference between good grades and straight A pluses," I said.

"Father says it is a shame to waste one's gifts."

"And what happens if you *do* waste them?" I asked.

"They are disappointed."

The session went on like that for a while. Except for the scars on her left wrist, she was, it seemed, the perfect daughter. She was also perfectly miserable, all but seismic with angst.

People should be required to take a test before becoming parents. If the standards were up to snuff we would not only see fewer traumatized children, we'd probably lick that overpopulation problem within a generation. If I had my way, there would be about one kid born every fourteen years. But so far Congress hasn't asked for my opinion.

Micky Goldenstone was my fifth client of the day. He looked somber but steady as he entered my office.

"Micky." I rose to my feet and took his hand. A few phone calls had assured me that he was well and free, awaiting a trial. "How's Jamel?"

He exhaled through his nose as he sat. His eyes looked grim. "I took him back to Glendale yesterday."

"To Lavonn's?"

He snorted a laugh. "She was awarded guardianship, but that place ain't hers. Jackson'll make sure she never forgets that. Sold her damned soul for rosewood flooring."

"How's she doing?"

"She's still pissed."

I wanted to ask what the chances were that she and her boyfriend would come to my house and shoot me in my sleep, but I didn't think it would sound professional. "What about Jackson?"

"They think he'll be out of the hospital in a couple of days."

I didn't know whether to cheer or mourn. "Back to Lavonn's?"

"Yeah," he said, and after staring out the window for a moment, covered his eyes with his palm. "Shit. I should have left things alone."

"You don't think you should have tried to prove paternity?"

"I don't know," he said, and dropping his hand, leaned back against the couch's ivory cushions.

"Do you still want custody?"

"It doesn't matter what I want. I fucked up."

"How so?"

"By losing my temper." He shook his head. "I should have kept my ass home. Now I'll be lucky if my son gets to visit me in *jail*."

"But there must have been drugs in Jackson's system. Don't you think that will weigh in your favor?"

He half laughed. "Shit, Doc, this is L.A. There's probably crack in the fucking ventilation system."

I almost wished that was true. I could use a little something to dull the aches and fatigue that plagued me. "Isn't crack supposed to make you feel good?" I asked.

He looked at me and grinned a little. "You *do* kinda look like you been hit by a train."

I resisted checking the little round mirror stashed in my purse.

"Do you still hope to gain custody of Jamel?" I asked.

He watched me with solemn regard, then rose and walked to the window. I have a tantalizing view of the coffee shop next door. "He's my son," he said.

"There's no law against saying no to that question." I kept my tone soft. Emily Christianson carried her stress in the tight clasp of her hands. Micky wore his on his face.

"He's not safe where he is."

"But if he were . . . if he were safe and happy, would you still want him to live with you?"

He didn't answer immediately. "You know what he said this morning?"

I shook my head, even though he couldn't see me. A patron had exited the coffee shop. He'd tip the scale at a solid three hundred. It almost made me regret my breakfast burrito. At least I should have refrained from eating the bag.

"He said he wanted to grow up to be president. That Barack Obama did it, so he knew he could, too."

"Big goals."

"Yeah, I told him that would take a lot of work. That he'd better do well in school."

I waited.

"He gave that some thought, then said maybe he'd just marry one of Obama's daughters, then, 'cuz they're hot."

I watched as he turned toward me. There were tears in his eyes. My heart tied itself in a tricky little knot in my chest.

"Yeah," he said. "I want him."

* * *

The rest of the day slipped by. Trying to make recompense for breakfast, I had a late lunch, which consisted of nothing but yogurt, and made it through the afternoon without falling asleep or dying of malnutrition.

Ramla called at 3:20. I hadn't heard from her since Thursday when she'd left a voice mail saying all was well. Shirley put her through to me.

"Allah blesses you," she said.

I wasn't sure how to respond to that. My first reflex was to ask her to thank him for me, but that might sound kind of cheesy and I needed all the blessings I could get. "So Aalia is doing okay?"

"She is resting and healing. Safe and whole. Because of you. Already, though, she becomes impatient to be out on her own. To see this new country."

I thought I heard a little worry in her voice. "There's a lot to see, and maybe she feels she's been told what to do long enough."

"This is just what she says. But I have no wish for her to reject the ways of our people. It is . . . how do you say . . . who she is."

I wondered to myself if poor little Aalia had any idea who she was. When a man promises to love and honor, but ends up abusing and debasing, it tends to mess with a girl's head.

"She has some decisions to make," I said. "But I'm sure she'll figure things out. She's very clever."

"She has always been so." Ramla's tone was rife with that deep maternal pride some older sisters develop. I wondered what it would be like to have a sibling who adored you instead of three bothers who consistently tried to make you spew Jell-O out your nose.

"Has she said anything about the men at the airport?"

"She said that you should be very careful."

My heart slowed dramatically. That wasn't exactly what I had been wanting to hear. I had hoped that after she was able to relax she would realize there was nothing to fear.

"She still doesn't think she recognized any of them?"

"No. But she said that her husband . . ." Ramla made a spitting noise. I waited patiently until it ended. "She said he has many friends she was not allowed to meet."

I called Elaine a couple hours later. She answered on the third ring.

"When will you be home for supper?" she asked.

"You're cooking?"

"Jeen is."

That was not good news. It meant that Solberg was in my house. Touching my worldly possessions. But at least it meant that Laney *wasn't* cooking. Laney's meals generally consisted of something that slurped out of her juicer and had a high likelihood of being nutritious. God help us.

My last client left my office at 8:57. Outside the strip mall where I work, it was almost as dark as the inside of my head. I hadn't gotten a lot of sleep the previous night and the early morning jog had only made me more tired.

My little Saturn was one of the few cars left in the parking lot. It sat like a quiet sanctuary under a tall light. I had strategically parked there in case of an attack of turbaned men, irate junkies, or old flames. But suddenly the asphalt stretched in front of me like a desert. The night seemed abnormally quiet. There was not a person in sight. Had there been a music reel to my life it would be playing the kind of spooky stuff that makes moviegoers hold their breath and wait for the blood.

As for me, I stood frozen, also waiting for the blood. A noise clicked off to my right. I turned, ready to scream, frozen. A marmalade cat trotted around the corner, tail tweaked at the end, looking jaunty.

I put my hand to my chest and said a little prayer just as a man stepped into view. He lurched toward me. I squawked like a chicken and jerked up my Mace, fumbling madly for the button, ready to spray, but at the last second, a few commonsense cells filtered erratically into place.

"Ms. McMullen! Don't shoot!"

It was then that I recognized Willard Benson from the office three doors down. I lowered my weapon and tried to do the same with my blood pressure. No go. It was off the charts and rising.

I slumped back against the building. "I'm sorry. I didn't—"

"Holy cow! Are you okay?"

"Yes. I'm sorry. I didn't mean to . . ." *Be an idiot.*

"That's okay. No problem. Best to be careful," he said, but there was a little more hustle in his step as he scurried away.

I remained as I was, still breathing hard, hands still shaking, until I felt I could convince my knees to do my bidding. Taking a deep breath, I shook my head at my own foolishness and headed for the Saturn.

All was well. I realized now that there were half a dozen patrons in the nearby coffee shop. I strode across the asphalt almost like a normal person. I was not abandoned to the miscreants of the world. I had my Mace and my cell phone close at hand.

I popped the locks on the Saturn and rounded the front bumper.

I felt his presence, even before I heard the rustle of his movements behind me. Even before he spoke.

"Don't scream," he rasped, and I didn't.

14

Conscience . . . nature's way of making sure we don't have too much fun.

> —*Officer Tavis, who didn't actually believe there was such a thing as too much fun*

"What do you want?" My voice sounded like the croak of a waterlogged bullfrog.

The man behind me pressed a little closer. I swallowed and tried to breathe. "What are you offering?" he rumbled.

"My wallet's—" I began, but in that instant my memory clicked into place. This same scenario had played out just a few days before. I took a deep breath through my nose, straightened slightly, and shifted my gaze cautiously to the left. "If you're Rivera I'm going to kill you," I said.

There was absolute silence, then, "What if I'm not Rivera?"

Something thumped in my chest. I think it was my heart hitting the light pole. I turned slowly, then glanced up.

Officer Tavis stood not three feet away. Tall and handsome and as innocuous as flan. He was eating an ice-cream cone that he held in his left hand.

"I take it you and Rivera aren't quite ready to tie the knot," he surmised. The words were a little muffled as he licked his cone.

"What the hell is wrong with you guys?" I asked. Tavis was a cop for a McTown nestled quietly up against the mountains a half a lifetime to the west of L.A. I'd met him while checking into a grisly murder that had taken place in sleepy little Edmond Park. He'd propositioned me within the first ten minutes. I wish I could say I resented that.

"Me? I just brought you an ice-cream cone," he said, and shoved his right hand forward as proof.

"An ice-cream cone? An ice-cream cone?" My voice had risen into the range where only gerbils and cockroaches can hear it. "I don't want a damned ice-cream cone. I want to be able to walk into a parking lot without having the bejeezus scared out of me by some hulking—"

"You don't want it?"

"No, I don't . . . Oh, give me that," I said, and yanked it from his hand. It was starting to drip.

I licked the perimeter. Chocolate vanilla swirl.

"So I scared you?" he asked.

I gave him a glare. "What the hell were you doing lurking like a . . ." I searched for the proper words. ". . . gargoyle between the damned—"

He laughed. Golden-haired and beautiful, he looked like a happy angel. "I didn't think you *got* scared, Chrissy."

The ice cream was beginning to chill my nerves and restore the usual munificence I reserve for all mankind. "I didn't think *you* were an idiot."

"Really?" When he smiled his dimples popped out. It was like trying to stay mad at Buddha.

"But I was obviously wrong," I said.

He put a palm to his chest. It looked broad and capable. "That's the meanest thing anyone's ever said to me."

"Yeah, well . . ." I opened my car door. "Stick around," I said, and he laughed.

"I was *hoping* for an invitation."

I scowled over the driver's door at him. "What are you doing here?"

"Me?" He could look as innocent as a choirboy when he wanted to.

I gave him a look. He dimpled again.

"I came in for the premiere of the new Jonas Brothers movie."

I stared, waiting for him to crack a smile. Nothing. "You're a Jonas Brothers fan?"

"Don't you think they're dreamy?"

I canted my head at him.

"I have two nieces living in Covina," he explained finally. "They assure me the Jonas Brothers *are,* in fact, dreamy."

"You came all this way to see a boy band?" I was going to have to readjust everything I knew about this man . . . which, admittedly, wasn't much. But maybe I shouldn't have been surprised. This was, after all, California. Half the population was invited to red carpet shindigs. Westwood Village was always shining with starlets.

"Well, for that," he said, "and to ask you to have sex with me."

I shook my head and put my foot inside the Saturn.

"Chrissy?"

"Yeah?"

"Yeah, you'll have sex with me?"

I snorted and lowered myself toward the seat. I had almost quit shaking.

"Don't you even check your backseat?" he asked.

Sometimes I truly hate men. "Thing is," I said, "I find that the real crazies are in the parking lots."

"Hey," he said, and stepping forward, crouched in my open doorway. "I have a question for you."

"No sex in the backseat!" I snapped.

A woman walked past holding a little girl's hand. She scowled through the windshield at me. We watched them go by in silent tandem.

"Wow," Tavis said as they disappeared from sight. "That was embarrassing. Anyway, I was wondering if you've heard anything about something called Intensity."

I scowled, licked off my cone, and watched him. "Is this some sort of lead-in to more sex talk?"

"Do you want it to be?"

I put my key in the ignition, but he put a hand on my arm, and even that little touch did something odd to me. Fear sometimes heightens my libido. I know it's weird. But so are emu.

"I'm serious as a heartache, here, Chrissy. Intensity . . . you heard anything about it?"

I lowered my hand and stared at him. He did, in fact, look serious. And ridiculously handsome. "What is it? A new form of Russian roulette or something?"

"I was hoping you could tell me."

I shook my head and he sighed.

"Meth's a problem in Kern County, but I think there's some new shit hitting the fan."

"How do you mean?"

"We had two kids die in the past month."

"Teenagers?"

"Yeah."

"From overdose?"

He shook his head. "Nothing showed up in the tox reports."

"And there were no other signs of trauma."

"Coroner says they died of asphyxiation."

"Some weird sex thing?"

"There was no sign of anything sexual."

"So you thought of me?"

He laughed. "I was wondering, you being a psychiatrist—"

"Psychologist."

He grinned. "Thought maybe you'd heard something."

"Why do you think there are drugs involved?"

He shrugged, heavy shoulders lifting and falling. "There was some erratic behavior reported concerning the girl."

"Erratic?"

"Friends say she was doing great for weeks. Happy. Good grades. Then one day she became aggressive. Thought everyone was out to get her. The next morning she was dead."

"Did she have a history of drug abuse?"

"Not that anyone knew of."

"Lots of kids are good at hiding their addictions."

He nodded and backed away so I could close the door. "Well, call me if you hear anything, will you?"

I agreed.

"Or if you change your mind about that backseat," he said, and I drove away, squirming a little.

* * *

By the time I got home, I was dreading seeing Solberg, but the house was notably sans irritation.

Laney smiled as she took a casserole from the oven. Domesticity in blue jeans. "How was your day?"

"Weird," I said. "Where's Solberg?"

"I didn't think you'd feel too neglected if he ran a few errands while we ate."

"I'll try to survive."

She had the table neatly set. The pile of reading material I usually keep atop the place mats was M.I.A. Every woman should have a wife.

We were eating in a matter of minutes. The casserole was something involving broccoli. Which normally would be a bad thing, but there was cheese and crunchy onions and some kind of noodles.

"Solberg made this?" I asked.

"Full of surprises, isn't he?" she asked.

"I hope not," I said, and finished off my plate. "I've been thinking about those letters."

She scowled. "You shouldn't have to worry about that."

"I wish we had copies."

"And you assume we don't?"

I gave her the eye. "You've kept copies?"

"Mac, seriously, did you think I wouldn't know an obsessive-compulsive like you would need to pore over them?"

"You think I'm obsessive?"

"And compulsive."

"Oh," I said, and helped myself to a second serving. But just a little one since I was on a low-broccoli diet.

* * *

"So the length of each letter hardly varies at all," I said.

"Two or three are a few sentences longer." Elaine was standing upright, gazing at the letters laid out in chronological order across her mattress. Hers had been a better option than mine, as it didn't look as if a humpbacked monster were lurking beneath the scattered covers.

"And each begins with Dearest Ms. Ruocco. Your stage name." I scowled. "Very formal."

"So maybe he's an older man," Laney said.

"But not so old that he's shaky. The words are extremely well formed."

"His speech is quite proper, so I would guess he's educated."

"And it's written with . . ." I leaned down, putting my face close to the papers. "A fountain pen?"

She shrugged. "Maybe. Does that mean he's . . . Catholic?"

Even though Elaine is decidedly un-Catholic, we had attended Holy Name Catholic School together for more years than I care to remember. The nuns there thought ballpoint pens were instruments of the devil. "Or he just really likes fountain pens."

"He must have some resources," she said.

I nodded. "Either he followed you here to L.A. or he lived here in the first place and traveled to Idaho."

"Every loop is approximately the same size as the last. And the spacing between the words is uniform. He's very careful."

"So he wants to impress you," I said, and scowled. Laney had never met a man who didn't hope to make an impact in one way or another. I wasn't surprised one would finally stoop to penmanship. More than a few had tried poetry. Several had sung ballads. Three love-struck fellows had tattooed her name on some part of their anatomy and one particularly inventive chap had christened his prize-winning bull after her. Butterfield wasn't really that bad a name for a dairy animal.

"His letters are narrow and vertical," she said. "Suggesting a need to control."

I looked at her.

She looked back. "I was paying attention during *Murder, She Wrote.*"

"Seriously?"

"Are you saying I'm wrong?"

"It's bound to happen once." I scowled. "But I think the fact that you believe Solberg to be Homo sapiens has covered that eventuality." I was chewing my lip. We were both staring at the letters, considering our findings.

"So, in review . . . he's probably past middle age," she said. "Judging from the phraseology."

"But not yet old."

"He's relatively wealthy."

"And educated."

"Possibly Catholic."

"Repressed."

"*Definitely* Catholic," we said in unison.

"Formal," I said. "Yet with each letter he seems to become increasingly familiar."

"As if he knows me," she said.

"Or *feels* that he knows you."

She nodded. The paparazzi had been pretty busy lately. As far as we knew, none of them had yet realized she was slumming in Sunland with her dearest friend. So Letter-Writer must have gotten his information elsewhere. I wondered if it made him feel important to have obtained knowledge that others would have paid money for.

"He's controlled," Laney said.

"Neat."

"Polite."

"Obsessed."

We scanned the letters. Each one was almost identical to the next. "Methodical," Laney said. The salutation was the same, the body of the letter was short, direct, and adoring.

"And infatuated," I said. "Which probably brings the possibilities down into the millions."

15

Apparently a large number of people are extremely bored.

—Patricia Ruocco, aka Elaine
Butterfield, after hearing of
Amazon Queen's
phenomenal viewership

The next week was a whirlwind of activity. I saw a zillion clients, shopped for shoes, and finally perused Laney's list of cast members, aka potential whack jobs. The sheer numbers were daunting. Who knew it could take that many people to make a cheesy, international hit?

It was Monday night. I glanced up from the kitchen table at Laney, who stood beside me, reviewing the same list. "Yikes," I said.

"I know."

"Anybody you have any bad vibes about?"

"I'm not feeling great about judging people on a passing whim," she said.

"How do you feel about me getting shot in my sleep?"

"Iffy," she said.

"Good to know. Anyone?" I asked again.

She skimmed the list, scowling a little, then pointed to a name. "He's kind of . . ." She shrugged a shoulder. "Different."

I read the name. Benjamin Vanak. "What kind of different?"

"I don't know. He's . . ." She shook her head, thinking. "Aloof maybe."

I raised my brows and looked over my shoulder at her. "Are you saying he's not smitten?"

"Shocking, isn't it?"

"And refreshing. How long has he been with the *Amazon Queen* team?"

"A year or so, I think."

"And he hasn't asked to sire your children yet?"

She wrinkled her nose at me.

"How about poetry. Has he written any sonnets in your honor?"

"Not even a haiku."

"I'm calling the police," I said, and she banged my shoulder with her almost-hip. It was like being bumped by a fly.

"I don't want to get anyone in trouble," she said. "Jobs are hard to come by. Especially in this economy."

"So who could I call to feel Vanak out?" I asked.

"Why would *you* do the calling?" she asked.

"Who else?"

"I can still speak, you know."

"Don't you hire someone to do that for you these days?"

"Here's the thing," she said, ignoring my cleverness, "I think Derrick would be most knowledgeable about the cast."

"Derrick. The producer?"

She nodded. "Yeah, but—"

"You're afraid he'll immediately fire everyone on the set if he thinks someone's causing you trouble."

"Not *everyone*."

"Everyone except you?"

"Could be."

"Because he's *not* aloof."

" 'Aloof' isn't the term I'd use for him, no."

"What *is* the term?"

She thought for a moment. "Jittery? Short? Friendly?"

"Uh-huh. How many times has *he* proposed?"

"I'm not that good at math," she said, and I gaped.

"*That* many?"

"He's kind of a flirt."

"A flirt who has a wife and four dozen kids."

"Approximately."

I nodded, thinking. "Anyone besides Vanak give you weird vibes?" I asked.

"Are we talking male *and* female?"

"We're talking interspecies."

"Agatha once said she'd kill to have my body."

"Do you think she meant it literally?" I asked, scanning the paper until I found her name with my right index finger.

"Supposedly my death would not actually give her my body."

"Is she bright enough to know that?"

"A Rhodes scholar."

"So was President Clinton. He wasn't smart enough to keep his pants zipped."

"I've never seen Agatha in pants."

"Ever?"

"Always wears dresses."

"Hell, that alone makes her suspect."

"I'm glad to see this is a scientific system."

"You know it," I said, and turned back toward the paper. "Who else do we have?"

She pointed out three others with whom she felt skittish. Out of more than two hundred people, that didn't seem like a staggering number.

"What now?" she asked.

I shrugged. "I'll find out what I can about them."

"Promise you won't do anything stupid."

"I'm insulted."

"I mean it, Mac, promise."

"Of course I promise."

"You won't call any gangsters, will you?"

"If you're referring to D, he prefers to be called a collection engineer." Dagwood Dean Daly lived in a high-rise on the Gold Coast in Chicago and had some kind of odd crush on me. In fact, he had once challenged Rivera to a duel, winner take *me*.

I had left the two of them bloodied and stupid outside the Mandarin Hotel. Oddly enough, I hadn't seen D since. I couldn't say the same of Rivera, though he *had* looked a little chagrined when he'd finally showed up at my door, scabs healing.

"I don't think any collection engineers will be necessary for this," I said, and scowled. "I thought I'd just ask some questions."

"Okay," Laney said, obviously dubious, "but let's not get anyone in trouble."

I glanced once more at the letters spread across her perfectly made bed. "I think someone's already troubled," I said.

"Christina McMullen." Officer Tavis answered on the third ring. He must have caller ID at the station in Edmond Park. He also had a very nice voice.

"Are you busy?" I asked.

"Absolutely," he said. "We've had two jaywalkers and a prank call."

"Just this morning."

"This isn't L.A," he said. "I'm talking all week."

"Well, I'd better let you get to interrogating them. Maybe you can call me back when you're not so frazzled."

"No hurry," he said. "Our thumbscrews won't be here until tomorrow. We share them with the next county."

"And they're being used right now?"

"They've had a problem with littering."

I huffed a laugh, then, "I have a question for you," I said. "It's—"

"I don't care what color your underwear is," I said, and he chuckled as he settled in.

"What can I do for you?"

"Last week you said something about a drug called Intensity."

"It's just a theory."

"What are the effects?"

"That's the thing, the kids who died didn't seem to have any symptoms in common."

"What do you mean?"

"Jerome, the boy, was happy and well adjusted. Didn't seem to have a care in the world. At least according to friends and family."

"Would friends and family tell the truth?"

"Hard to say. The girl's behavior was entirely different. Aggressive and loud. What's up?"

"I have a . . . acquaintance who's been getting some funny mail."

"Funny ha-ha or funny—"

"Funny disturbing. I'm wondering if they might be drug related, but there are no restricted substances allowed on . . . my friend's workplace."

"Drugs aren't exactly welcomed into the public school system, either, Chrissy. But I can't think of another excuse for the blue haze in the bathrooms."

"I think my friend's . . . manager . . . actually insists on blood tests," I said.

"Uh-huh."

"You think traces of Intensity wouldn't show up in the reports?"

"Nothing's been flagged so far. And we're not the only county in California that's losing kids."

"Any idea where the drug came from?"

"Are you asking for my hypothesis?"

"Why not?"

"I think it's an offshoot of meth. Cheap to make, but without the usual side effects."

"Except for death, of course."

"Except for that one."

I asked a few more questions, but learned nothing concrete.

"Thank you," I said, and prepared to hang up, but he stopped me.

"What's it worth to you?"

"What's that?"

"The information I gave you is rather sensitive."

"Really?"

"No. But I think it's worth something."

"What do you have in mind?"

"Seriously?"

"I'm not going to have sex with you."

"How about some heavy petting?"

"Why haven't you been fired yet?"

"Because I'm a nice guy."

"To whom?"

He chuckled. "Necking?" he asked.

"No."

"Can you talk dirty to—" he began, but I was already hanging up.

A few hours later, still alone in my office in Eagle Rock, I gazed morosely at the list of people employed on the *Queen* set. Generally, when I need to know something that can be found on the Internet, I call Solberg. And although Laney had finally told him about the letters, she was downplaying their significance and *I* wasn't going to be the one to tell him the truth.

"Lieutenant Rivera." He answered his phone like Robocop on steroids. It made me rather desperately want to mock him, but I resisted. Such is the way of maturity.

"Ph.D. McMullen," I said. Okay, maybe I was mocking him a little.

"What?" he said, and I immediately felt stupid. Go figure.

"This is Christina," I said.

I heard his chair squeak as he sat down.

"Being a smart-ass?" he asked.

"Let's keep in mind that I'm very brave," I said, and could almost hear him relax on the other end of the line.

"Has someone threatened your life yet today?" he asked.

I resisted glancing toward the door. "It's still early."

"Most crimes occur during daylight hours."

Now I did glance. "Really?"

"Do you have your doors locked?"

"Wouldn't that be bad for business?"

"You're still at work?"

"I'm brave and *ambitious*."

"You should consider changing your hours."

"Maybe I could counsel the neurotic and paranoid just until noon. In case it gets dark."

"There's a reason for paranoia."

"Too much time talking to you?"

"I'm only . . ." he began, then sighed as if giving up. "Did you have a reason to call?" The "other than to irritate me" part was implied.

"I was wondering if you had learned anything about those letters yet."

He paused. I realized I was holding my breath. "The analyst has a suicide letter, two ransom notes, and five bomb threats ahead of you."

"You're kidding."

"Unfortunately, there's no overt threat implied in those letters."

"Unfortunately?"

"It would still put them behind the bomb threats

and the ransom notes, but might boost them ahead of the suicide."

"Any idea when things might be happening?"

"A week maybe. If no one else feels the need to blow up anything or talk about offing himself."

"Laney's right," I said. "You're overly sensitive."

"Occupational hazard," he said.

"I've got some info on the Overo case." Someone was speaking from the background of the precinct.

"A minute," he said, partly covering the mouthpiece, then to me: "I'll try to hurry it up, but no guarantees."

"Do you think Laney's in danger?"

He exhaled softly. "I'm a cop."

"Ergo everyone's in danger?"

"Check your trunk," he said.

I snorted and moved to hang up, but he spoke again.

"Who are you planning to call next?"

"What?"

"To ask 'bout the letters. Who else do you have on your list?"

"No one."

"No one owes you any favors?"

"Besides you?"

"What do I owe you?"

"I saved your father's life."

"And I'm trying to forgive you for that," he said, and hung up.

I sat there for a while, fidgety and fretful, reminding myself that, as Rivera had said, the letters weren't overtly threatening. But sometimes danger isn't obvious. I thought of a dozen such scenarios. Scenarios regarding people who thought they had been perfectly safe.

Rivera's father, for instance. Rivera himself, paranoia personified, had thought the senator was safe. But that hadn't been the case. In the end, I had found the senator held at gunpoint on his ranch in the Santa Monica foothills. And from there things had gone downhill. The gunman had gotten angry, the police had revved their sirens, and I had been shot.

On the upside, the senator had sworn his eternal gratitude.

The thoughts spun to a halt in my head.

Of course, Rivera and his father were barely on speaking terms. Hence, I shouldn't get senior involved in junior's affairs, namely police work. That would be wrong.

Then again, I wouldn't feel all that great about letting my best friend get killed, either, I thought, and picked up the phone.

16

I believe in sex and death, two experiences that come only once in a lifetime.

—Woody Allen

That night I was lying in bed, surrounded by tasseled pillows and gorgeous, half-naked guys. One was massaging my lower back with a scented oil that smelled like man. Another was giving me a foot massage. My toes were nestled up against his warm, muscular chest when a bell rang.

The foot man sucked my baby toe into his mouth and I moaned. The bell rang again. Probably summoning the dessert-bearer. But perhaps I would forgo dessert this once. At least until the pedi-masseur was finished . . .

"Hello," crooned a voice. I smiled and snuggled a little deeper into my pillows. "Yes," he said, but the voice had morphed from the sexy rumble of a good man-slave to the high, jittery tone of a nerd.

Damnit! I had been dreaming. Or maybe I was dreaming now. If memory served, and history was repeating itself, I had gone to bed alone.

But the voice spoke again. I reached out, groggy, hair in my eyes. And sure enough, my hand met the body of another human being.

Unusual. I slipped my hand over what felt like a shirt.

"What? Oh." There was relief in the voice, which, now that I was marginally coherent, sounded a full octave higher than that of any self-respecting sex slave. I scowled and slipped my hand down my visitor's spine. It was conspicuously devoid of heaving muscle. And his ass . . .

"You're going to want to wake up now, Mac," Laney said.

I opened one immediately paranoid eye.

Solberg turned toward me, his Woody Allen face illuminated by the diffused light of the hallway.

I jerked upright. Harlequin lifted his head, offended that I had yanked my foot out of his tongue's reach.

Laney was staring at me from beside the door. "The man-slave dream?" she asked.

I snapped my gaze from her to Solberg. "What's going on?"

"Phone. I thought it might be important," Elaine said. moving nearer.

Solberg nodded and handed over the receiver. "It's for you."

I scowled, still hoping I could chalk up this late night interruption to just another good dream gone bad. "Is it a mass murderer?"

"Don't think so," Solberg said. "But it's probably not a sex slave, either."

I shot a jaundiced glare toward Laney, reminding her that best friends keep secrets, but she just shrugged. "Would you rather have him believe you were coming on to him?"

I said something suitably nasty and took the receiver.

"Hello?" My voice sounded like a cross between a rusty hinge and a water buffalo.

"Ms. McMullen?"

I glanced around the dimly lit room. There were four articles of clothing on the floor, six half-read novels beside the bed, and a dehydrated philodendron wilting by the window. Probably my house. "I believe so," I said.

"This is Renee Edwards."

I patted the top of my head. The snarl quotient felt about the same as mine usually does at this time of night. Evidence was rising that I was, indeed, Christina McMullen. "Who?"

"I'm a handwriting expert," said Edwards. She had a tough, impatient voice. "I work for the Los Angeles Police Department."

"Oh, yes." I shot my gaze to the twosome near my bed and tightened my grip on the phone.

"I'm told your case is of an extremely urgent nature."

I bit my lip, feeling the slightest twinge of guilt. After some soul-bending deliberation, I had called Rivera Senior. Subsequently, the senator had worked his usual magic. But as with any genie's lamp, there were always repercussions. I was still waiting to discover what they would be.

"Yes," I said again.

"Ergo, I've reviewed the letters in my free time," she continued.

Ergo, she sounded a little miffed about it. "All of them?"

The affirmative seemed to be implied. "And worked up a preliminary analysis."

I was trying to get my ducks in a row, but there were a couple little buggers that kept popping out of line. "What time is it?"

"Four hundred hours."

My mind worked dizzily on that for a while only to realize it was an ungodly time of the night when no one in her right mind should be conscious. What on earth did this gal owe the senator?

"I'll send you a written transcript of my findings, as well, of course, but thought you might like to hear an expedited opinion of my conclusions immediately."

At four hundred ungodly hours? Was she kidding? "Yes," I said, trying to wrestle my hair out of my eyes. "Please."

"It is my estimation that the author knows Ms. Butterfield personally."

"How personally?"

"An acquaintance."

"A man or a woman?"

"I can't ascertain that with any accuracy at this time. But for the moment let's assume he is male."

"Okay."

I could almost hear the military-crisp nod. "He has strong feelings of inferiority and an intense need to be accepted."

So he was human, I thought, and tucked my wet foot under the blankets. Harlequin looked bereft, which might mean that the letter-writer could also be canine. Or Great Danish.

"In your opinion is this person dangerous?" I asked.

There was a long pause. For a moment I wondered if she had fallen asleep. It was, after all, Ungodly Hour. But she spoke finally.

"That's impossible to say for certain."

"Let's say for uncertain, then."

"In the wrong circumstances, I believe he may be."

I glanced at Laney again. "What circumstances would those be?" I asked.

"If there was a situation that was pushing him to act, perhaps violence would be imminent."

"What kind of situation?"

"Something that needed immediate attention. My evaluation suggests that he is not a person who likes to be rushed."

There were a few more salient pieces of information, but I hung up shortly afterward.

I couldn't help but notice that Solberg was now sitting on my bed. The sexy man-slaves were notably absent. For a moment I questioned the existence of a loving God.

"A handwriting expert," I said.

Laney nodded. "Who keeps odd hours."

"Maybe she's a night person."

"Or you called in favors," she guessed.

I didn't comment. "Why is Solberg on my bed?"

"I thought maybe you were comatose," Solberg said.

"Get off," I said. "Or someone will be."

He grinned and rose to his feet.

"Rivera's not going to be happy if he finds out you contacted his father," Laney said.

I scowled at her psychic weirdness. "I didn't know who else to call."

"We could have hired our own analyst," she said.

"Or bought one," Solberg suggested.

"Most of those analytic slaves don't work around the clock like they used to in the good old days," I said.

"Plus, doing it this way had the added bonus of irritating the lieutenant," Laney said, watching me.

My first instinct was to brush off her statement, but even at Ungodly Hour, it made a certain amount of sense. So I filed it away for later analysis of my own before recapping my recent phone conversation.

"Inferiority and an intense need to be accepted," Solberg said, ruminating.

"Yeah." I stared at him. "Can I see a sample of your handwriting?"

He watched me for a second, then threw back his head and laughed.

I resisted rolling my eyes as I returned my attention to Laney. "Any ideas?"

"I don't think I've ever met anyone who *didn't* feel inferior," she said.

"Besides yourself."

"I would hate to spoil your delusions, Mac."

"Thank you. Can you think of anyone who might fit that description?"

She shook her head, then stopped abruptly.

"What?" I asked, and she adopted my scowl.

"I have a stunt double. I never even considered him before."

"Aren't stunt doubles built like . . . well, like *you*, thereby making her immune to inferiority."

"I'd give an Oscar for his legs."

"It's a man?"

"Emery Greene." She grinned. "We'll discuss Santa Claus later."

"Leave Santa out of this," I said, then, "So why would you suspect Greene?"

"He hasn't . . ." she began, then looked surprised and laughed at herself. "Nothing."

I caught the drift. "Maybe he just hasn't gotten around to proposing yet."

"Not everyone has to like me," she said, but there was something in her voice. It almost sounded like insecurity. I hadn't seen that in Laney since she was buck-toothed and built like a chopstick.

"If that's true we have no supporting evidence," I said.

"I love you, Mac," she said, then shook her head and waved away her previous thought. "Come to think of it, Emery just came on board recently. After Stevie broke her arm."

"Stevie?"

"She was my other double."

"Stevie's a girl."

"Bending the genders," she said. "Anyway, the first letter arrived before Emery."

"Which doesn't necessarily rule him out."

"But doesn't put him at the top of the list."

I scowled, hating to agree, but if the truth was told, I didn't even *have* a viable list. "Who's the king of the heap?"

She considered that for a minute, then shook her head. "I just can't think of anyone who would threaten me."

"We're not talking out-and-out threats, remember. We're talking skin prickles."

She thought some more, then did a little head tilt.

"What?" I asked.

"Do you know Morab?"

"It's the language they speak in Morabia, isn't it?"

Her brows lowered, etching tiny creases in her forehead. "There is no Morabia."

"Then I don't know it."

"Morab," she repeated. "He's one of the characters in *Queen*."

I shook my head, feeling guilty for my lack of time spent devoted to her rising success. Some say the Catholics have taken guilt to an art form. I would say it's more like a science. "I haven't had much time lately to watch—" I began, but she was already shushing me.

"Mine is not a series you should apologize for missing," she said.

"Not everything has to be the History Channel," I said.

"You're too good to me," she said, but before we got sappy, she continued. "Morab . . . he's one of the Withians. His name is hardly ever mentioned, but you'll see him in the background periodically, looking . . . shiny."

"Shiny?"

"These guys could keep Chevron in business."

I thought for a moment. "Ahh, they're oiled."

"Like the Tin—" she began, but suddenly I remembered my wet dream.

"Are you talking about the guy in the loincloth?"

"All the Withians wear loincloths," she said. "It's to denote their lowly status." Her voice was deadpan. Despite her well-fought climb to success, she was not one to overemphasize the importance of pop silliness.

"Yeah, but the guy with the . . ." I took a deep breath and tried not to burst into spontaneous orgasm. This guy had probably prompted my current fantasies. "The guy with the brand on his . . ." I motioned vaguely toward my right hip.

"Shall I get you a paper bag?" she asked.

"I'll be fine as soon as my vision clears." I shut my eyes for an instant and shook my head. "Yeah," I said finally, making my tone perfectly matter-of-fact. "I think I might have noticed him." I glanced at Solberg. For his own self-preservation, he rarely watched *Amazon Queen*. Thinking of Laney surrounded by beautiful people tended to make him depressed. I figured there wasn't enough Prozac in all of L.A. County to offset the effects of seeing Morab in a loincloth.

"He has talent, classical training, and an accent," she said.

"Not to mention the fact that he's hotter than tamales," I added, and thought I could actually *feel* Solberg pale. I liked this Morab guy better by the moment.

"And he's intelligent. Still, he was cast because of his physique, more than anything else. He exercises like a machine. Cross-training, weight lifting, tria—"

"I think he's the culprit," Solberg said.

Laney and I each raised a brow at him.

He shuttled his gaze back and forth between us. "You can't trust those bodybuilder types. Obsessive-compulsives."

I blinked.

"Neurotic," he added. "Maladjusted. *Weird*."

I smiled a little and turned back toward Elaine. "Why didn't you think of him earlier?" I asked, and she shrugged.

"Generally, he seems really secure." She paused, mouth quirking. "In fact, sometimes he seems a little *too* secure."

I considered that for a second. Thought about Emily Christianson, the self-destructive girl who had everything; Micky Goldenstone, uncertain he would make a better parent than a violent crackhead; and Howard Lepinski, still obsessing about sandwich options after umpteen years of therapy. "I rarely see that in my line of work," I said.

Elaine shook her head and sighed. "I mean . . . the chances of getting a successful show . . . they're astronomical."

"So?"

"What determines an actor's success? Besides luck?"

"Tiny pores?"

"Sergio happens to *have* tiny pores."

"Sergio?"

"Sergio Carlos Zepequeno. Aka Morab. He's Brazilian."

"A Brazilian who you think is hiding his jealousy?"

"*I* would be if the situation were reversed."

I stared at her. Laney . . . jealous? I hadn't seen that since the neighborhood boys had started an all-male clubhouse. "Please don't tell me the Easter Bunny's fictional, too," I said.

She gave me a bland expression. "He once told me there was no one more deserving than I. And he said it with absolute conviction."

"The Easter Bunny?"

"Sergio."

I shrugged. "I concur. With both of them."

She was stellar at ignoring me. "What about the Dalai Lama."

"I wasn't even aware he belonged to the actor's guild."

"You know what I mean," she said.

"Maybe he just admires you. This Morab guy, I mean. Not the Dalai Lama."

"The point is," she said, "no one's completely secure."

"And you think if his act is too convincing . . ."

"He's an excellent actor. Worked on Broadway to sold-out crowds."

"Then maybe you can't tell if he's acting or not," I said.

"Or maybe he thinks he deserves more," Solberg said.

"But getting rid of Laney won't help him. It's not as if he can take her place."

"Maybe he's so bitter he doesn't care," Solberg suggested. "You know what those good-looking guys are like.

"Baby," he turned to Laney with panic in his eyes. "We should get you a bodyguard."

We stared at him as if he'd just grown a second head.

"*What?*" he said.

"A bodyguard," I repeated.

"Yeah."

"Someone big and burly and manly to shadow Laney's every move?" I said, and watched him pale some more.

Laney shot me the kind of look she used to give bullies who were picking on the skinny kids.

"I didn't say Sergio wanted to get rid of me," she said. "It was just . . . I thought of him, the unfairness of this business. That's all. He's a nice guy."

"And extremely good-looking." I glanced at Solberg. Sometimes I *am* kind of a bully.

17

I'd rather be happy than be president.

—*Jamel Blount, weighing*
options

"How's Jamel doing?" I was back at work. Neither talk of Morab the man-slave nor dead of night shall keep me from my appointed tasks.

Micky Goldenstone sat on my couch. "All right, I guess."

"Is Jackson back home?"

Micky nodded stiffly, then glanced out the window toward the coffee shop. "Back home, filling my son's mind with shit."

"What do you mean?"

He shook his head. "Lavonn thinks he's some kind of damned savior. Bought that house in Glendale, and a big-ass Cadillac."

"Where'd he get the money?"

He shrugged. "Not all assholes are morons. I heard he got a scholarship to some Ivy League school. Made a shit-load of money in biochemistry or something, then came back here to save us poor niggers."

"How do you mean?"

"He got some investors together, bought up a bunch of property on the east side. Tried to . . ." He made air quotes . . . "save the culture."

"Didn't work?"

"Place is a fucking wasteland."

"He must have lost some money in the deal."

"You'd think, wouldn't you?"

"So how'd he recoup?"

"I have no idea."

He drew air slowly through his nostrils, thinking as he scowled. "Turns out he wasn't on drugs."

"The reports came back clean?"

"And they didn't find anything in his house."

"Which means you may have more trouble getting custody than you had hoped."

"It means he's a fucking bastard!" he said, and clenching his teeth, ran his palms down his black denim pants legs.

I gave that some judicious consideration, but couldn't quite make sense of it.

"At least if he was high he would have had an excuse," he said.

It seemed like there was some problem with that logic, but I couldn't quite put my finger on it.

"What about Lavonn?" I asked. "Was she tested?"

"Clean, too," he said.

I remembered the woman's wide pupils, her erratic behavior, juxtaposed against her beau's dreamy persona. I also remembered a possible drug called Intensity, but I wasn't ready to mention that to Micky. "Maybe Jackson's frightening behavior will convince her to ditch him."

He looked at me, dark face inscrutable. "You believe in the Tooth Fairy, too?"

"Please don't," I said, then continued without explaining Laney's threat about Santa Claus. "People change, Micky," I said. "You did."

"Did I?" There was tight anger in his tone.

"Yes."

"Then why was it my first instinct to shoot?" he asked.

"Is that why you went to Glendale? To kill Jackson?"

"I went to see my son," he said, and rose jerkily to his feet. "Shooting that asshole was just a bonus."

I watched him pace. "If it was so much fun, why the guilt?"

He shut his eyes. A muscle danced taut and jittery in his jaw. "She never cried," he said, and stared out the window, fists deep in his front pockets.

I waited for him to continue, but Micky always had more patience than I.

"Lavonn or—"

"Kaneasha. When I . . ." His jaw jumped again. "When I raped her," he said. "She just looked at me. Like Jamel does sometimes. Like they expect more. Like they expect better."

I let those words steep in the air for a moment. Seconds ticked away, thick with regret, sticky with self-loathing.

"Then give them better," I said finally.

"I can't!" He turned on me like a snarling Rottweiler.

"Don't you see that? This is what I am." He thumped his chest with stiff fingertips and took a terse step toward me. "You can't change what you are."

Rottweilers are scary as hell, and I didn't like being intimidated in my office by wild dogs, so I raised my chin and gave him my best bad-ass glare. "Not if you stand there and whine about it, you can't," I said.

He glowered at me for half of forever, then snorted his disdain. "Where did you grow up? Disneyland or something? I bet you had yourself a daddy who thought the world revolved around your pinky finger."

I gave that a moment's thought. On my good days, Dad had referred to me as "the girl" and treated me as if I had a chronic case of the pox, but that was hardly the point, was it?

"You deserved better," I said. "No one's denying that."

"Damned right, I did," he snapped. "I deserved—"

I closed the trap with hardly a tickle of guilt. "And so does Jamel."

He paused, eyes gleaming, then gritted his teeth and sat down. Seconds ticked away like time bombs. "You think he's better off with me?"

"Than with Lavonn and Jackson?"

He nodded.

In my own little mind, I thought living with a pack of man-hungry hyenas would be preferable to living with Lavonn and Jackson, but I smugly kept that opinion to myself. "What do you think?"

He glanced toward the window, expression solemn, dark eyes so sad they would have made a weaker woman cry. "A boy needs a mother," he said.

"Even if she's a mother on drugs?"

The muscle jumped in his jaw again. "I don't even have a girlfriend."

I refrained from asking if he wanted one, even though the sight of him, introspective and broken, weakened some part of me that was generally as hard-assed and grumpy as a curmudgeon. "You have a grandmother."

He gave me a look from the corner of his dark eyes. "I'm hard up," he admitted, "but I think Grams is a little old for me. And aren't incestuous relationships still frowned upon?"

I didn't honor his facetiousness with a response, though high-sarcasm often garnered awards in a clan as obnoxious as the McMullens. "How did she and Jamel get along?"

"She made him eat All Bran. For roughage," he said. "All Bran tastes like sidewalk chalk."

For a moment I almost asked just when he had become aware of the similarities. He'd never mentioned having brothers like mine—inclined to "encourage" siblings to try new delicacies.

"And she smells funny," he added.

"Is that your opinion or Jamel's?"

"Both." He said the word with some feeling, but I contained my laughter. My grandmother had smelled funny, too, but she could still make my mother grovel, and for that I would be eternally amazed.

"I don't think odor precludes a person from parenting," I said.

"How about great-grandparenting?"

"Probably not," I said, but he was already shaking his head, leaning his close-cropped skull against the couch's cushion, sighing.

"You have any idea how old she is?" he asked.

"How old?"

"I don't know," he said, and looked at me with wide, frightened eyes. "Fuck. You don't think I'm ballsy enough to ask her, do you?"

I liked this woman more every moment. "Maybe age doesn't preclude a person from parenting, either."

He exhaled heavily. "She gave up her life for me," he said, and winced, remembering. According to his stories, he hadn't made it easy. "I couldn't ask her to do more."

"Are you sure you'd have to?"

He glanced at me.

"Are you sure you'd have to ask," I explained.

He said nothing. I changed tack.

"I thought you had decided not to tell her about Jamel yet," I said.

"I *didn't* tell her. I planned to introduce them. But not like that. Not . . ." He paused, grimaced. "I didn't want her to think I was a fuckup. Not again. Not anymore." He chuckled. Humorless. "All grown up and still trying to impress my grams."

"Maybe it's admirable," I said.

"Yeah." He snorted, then scowled at me, curious. "How about you, Doc? You still trying to make your parents proud?"

His question spurred some hidden part of me, because deep inside I was pretty sure I had given up even before I had yanked my proverbial roots and escaped to the desert.

"You don't think your grandmother is proud?" I asked.

"She didn't cry, either," he said. "Not when she saw Jackson on the floor. Not when she came to see me in jail. She didn't even look surprised. Just disappointed. Just . . ."

He exhaled, sliding into the black hole of self-recrimination. "Like Kaneasha. Like—"

"Did you lie to me about the events that night?" I asked, tugging gently at the rope that kept him swinging above the bottom of the abyss.

"What?"

"About how Jackson was shot. You said it was his gun. You implied that he would have killed you if you hadn't stopped him."

He looked away, face hard. "Maybe that's how it should have gone down. Maybe he *should* have shot me."

My stomach churned like a cement mixer. Some people believe therapists shouldn't get involved with their clients. Obviously I'm not the only one who believes in fictitious characters.

"So you think it would be good for Jamel if his aunt's boyfriend killed his father?"

He looked at me, eyes solemn. "Fuck," he said finally, but softly.

"Did you lie to me?" I asked. "About that night?"

He stared at me, eyes angry and strangely accusatory, but I continued.

"Was the gun his?"

His face was devoid of expression. "He pulled it out of his waistband." He swallowed, reliving. "He had that look," he said. "That cocky-ass 'I'm invincible' look. I've seen it before. Seen it. Lived it." His lips jerked spasmodically.

"What should you have done differently?"

"I don't know." He dropped his eyes closed for a moment, then shook his head. "Shit! I . . ." He exhaled a laugh. "Lavonn had bruises on her throat. You see that? I swore at him. Called him a fucking coward." He laughed again, but his eyes showed his agony. "You know what you shouldn't do?"

"Call a man names when he's holding a gun?"

"See." He flipped a tense hand at me. "Normal folks know those things."

"Are you referring to me?"

He almost grinned, though the sadness never left his eyes. "If it had been you, Jackson wouldn't have been in the hospital."

I considered telling him that if Jackson had pulled a gun on me there was a fair chance I would have peed my pants and swooned like a debutante, but I'm a professional. "Jamel wouldn't be better off with Lavonn than with you," I said.

He raised his brows in surprise. "You actually giving me your opinion, Doc? I thought that was against shrink code or something."

"They'll probably forgive me if they find out I'm suggesting that you have something to live for."

He watched me for a moment longer, then nodded. "Jamel," he said.

"I think a boy needs a *father,* too."

He sighed, frowned. "I fucked up."

"Sometimes there are no perfect options."

"Well, there should be." He rose to his feet again, restive. There had been a time, early in our relationship, that I thought he might be using, but I had learned since then that thoughts of his past made him jittery. "There *should* be choices: education, consideration, kindness . . ." He paused, all but breathless.

I let the silence swell around us for a moment.

"Is that what you want for Jamel?" I asked.

"Fuckin' A," he said, but his tone was chagrined, as if embarrassed by his emotion.

"Then give it to him," I said.

"And how the hell am I going to do that? I work full-time. My apartment's the size of your . . ." He waved wildly. ". . . shoe. And . . ." He laughed. ". . . I just shot someone."

"Not to mention the fact that you're kind of whiny."

"Jesus, woman!" he said, turning toward me, aghast. "Do you drive everyone this crazy?"

I thought about avoiding that question, but the answer seemed so obvious. "I believe I do."

He stared at me for several seconds before his mouth quirked up a little. "Want a ready-made family?" he asked.

"I'll think about it," I said, and he laughed.

18

The good thing about dating an ex is that they already know you're a moron.

> —Donald Archer (Mac)—a
> man who has never been
> particularly adept in social
> situations

*L*ater that afternoon, I sat alone in my diminutive kitchen. Laney and the Geekster had gone to extinguish yet another wedding fire. Elaine had, in fact, passed up the opportunity to attend the afterparty for *Jungle Heat* to do so. It wasn't exactly the norm for a television spin-off to have such an event, but this party was expected to be quite a blowout, mixing financiers, minor celebrities, and shining stars into one intoxicating brew. Laney, however, had opted to see to her wedding instead. Sometimes I don't know where I went wrong.

As for me, I had expected to put in a full day at the office, but my last two clients canceled, which meant I had time to go for a run . . . or to eat a supper rich in saturated fat and fall into a lipid-induced coma. After some nasty internal warfare, I lost my mind and chose running, but as I slipped out of my business clothes, I noticed my bridesmaid dress. It was a thing of rare beauty. Made of a coppery fabric that caressed every curve, it was the equal to anything seen on the red carpet. In fact, it would look great at the *Jungle Heat* party, the party where Laney's peers would be gathered, where people like Colin Farrell and Gerard Butler might well stroll past in tuxedos while sipping intoxicating beverages. There was a rumor circulating around town that Colin had gotten smashed at the last shindig and danced the jitterbug wearing nothing but a cummerbund.

My imagination reared like a wild stallion, but I reined it down because, obviously, Colin wasn't the reason I was interested in *Heat*'s party at all. It was because Laney had been receiving threatening mail and it was conceivable that the author of that mail would be commingling with the likes of Colin Farrell and Gerard Butler, who would stroll past in tuxedos while sipping . . .

I closed my eyes and tossed my skirt on the bed. Insanity. That's what it was. I was not going to crash some party just because there was a mermaid dress hanging on the back of my closet door. I was more mature than that. Besides, I didn't have any passes . . . and after a fairly exhaustive search, I realized Laney must have taken hers with her. Which was just as well. I was going to go for a run, get to bed early, and never tell Elaine I had entertained any idiotic thoughts to the contrary.

I was set on that course for all of thirty-four seconds, but the temptation of seeing Colin in nothing but a cummerbund and a burr was more than I could resist.

"Mac?" I was gripping the receiver in both hands.

"Christina?" said the voice on the other end of the line.

I closed my eyes for a minute and wondered if I was out of my mind. "Yeah. How are you doing?" I asked. I had met Donald Archer while investigating a murder. He was his father's heir apparent and would someday inherit a boot manufacturing company called Ironwear. Originally I had thought he might also be a murderer. Now I believed him to be a genuinely nice person. Does it seem odd that a licensed psychologist can't tell the difference?

"What's up?" he asked.

I cleared my throat and reminded myself that although Mac was extremely wealthy and undeniably sweet, he had always been more interested in me than I was in him; I had no right to play with his emotions, but I needed a favor and told him as much.

He paused for a minute. "Is this the kind of favor that's likely to get a guy killed?"

As it turned out, he was also a pragmatist. I considered his query for a second. "I don't think so."

"Wow," he said. "That's not quite the answer I was hoping for."

"Looking for more of a thrill?" I asked and he chuckled, inexplicably charmed. Poor guy.

"What's the favor?"

"There's an . . . event that I'm hoping to attend. A Hollywood event. I know you sometimes get invitations and was wondering if I could maybe be your escort."

He paused a moment. "That might actually be worth getting killed for."

A little more guilt seeped in. I fought it off. I'm frickin' amazing at fighting it off.

"What's the event?"

"The afterparty for *Jungle Heat.*"

"*Jungle* ... Hey, I think I *do* have an invitation for that."

"Yeah?" I couldn't decide if I should be thrilled or terrified.

"When is that again?" he asked. Mac was, it seems, the kind of unassuming bazillionaire who gets so many invitations to stare at Colin that he can afford to forget about them.

I bit my lip. "Tonight."

"*Tonight?*"

"Yes."

"Man, I wish I were a girl," he said.

"Ummm ..."

"*I* have to start looking for a date a full month before the actual event."

"Does that mean you'll do it?"

"Is it in Cincinnati?"

"What's that?"

" 'Cuz that's where I am."

"Cincinnati, Ohio?"

He considered that a second. "I don't think they'd make another one."

"Oh."

"But maybe if I head straight to the airport, I could hop on a plane and get into LAX before—"

"That's okay, Mac," I said. The guilt was becoming a little more invasive. "It was just a whim."

"It wouldn't be any trouble," he said.

"If you like to be strip-searched for trying to rush through airport security."

"I *have* been pretty lonely," he said, and I laughed.

"I'm not sure a strip search is the way to start a lasting relationship."

"Probably not with a belly like mine."

I remembered now why I liked him. It wasn't for his body. "We can talk when you get back," I said.

"I could make this work if it's important to you," he said. "I don't think Dad would disown me or anything if I left the convention early."

"What's the convention on?"

"Shoelaces."

"Strip-searching is sounding better."

"I could tell him I just found out I'd knocked someone up and had to go home to take care of things."

"And that wouldn't make him upset?"

"I think he might actually be proud. Hard to say, though. He's been kind of surly lately. I think marriage number five is on the skids."

"I'm sorry."

"She's twenty-four."

"I'm even more sorry. Listen, Mac, don't worry about this. I'll call you later."

"Really?" He sounded desperate. I opened my mouth to spout . . . something. "That sounded desperate, didn't it?" he asked.

"No."

"Yes it did. Sorry. I meant to say, of course you'll call me. I'm very rich."

I laughed. "And nice," I said. We hung up a few moments later. I dialed the phone again barely three seconds after that.

"Eddie?"

"Chrissy McMullen, Ph.D.," Eddie said. I could hear him settling into his easy chair, oozing muscle and charm. Eddie and I had dated briefly. The fact that he was as interested in men as I was had eventually put something of a damper on our relationship.

"I need a favor," I said.

There was a pause. "Is this the kind of favor that will get me killed?" he asked, and I scowled into the phone.

"Why do people keep asking that?" I said, and he laughed.

"What do you need?"

"A date. For tonight."

In the end it was a no-go.

After that there was a long procession of additional calls. I may have, in the past, mentioned my impressive number of old flames. I'm closing in on four score. I think I called most of them . . . excluding the convicts and the guy who had died after trying to jump the train tracks on his motor scooter.

By five-thirty I was feeling a little desperate. Because, although crashing a Hollywood afterparty might seem like a stupid idea to the uninitiated, I had made up my mind. And once that happens it's hard to unmake it . . . at least if it involves Colin Farrell and cummerbunds.

"Officer Tavis?" I said.

"You must be calling to tell me you can no longer resist my charms," he said.

"I'm calling to see if you have an invitation to the *Jungle*

Heat party." In my zealot's quest for tickets I had almost forgotten his propensity for sexual harassment.

He paused a moment. "Sure," he said, "and after that I'm going to have tea with Angelina and Brad."

"So you're in L.A., then?"

He chuckled. "I was just there. Why would I go back?"

"I thought you might be stalking me."

"Well . . . I'm a little busy right now. But maybe this weekend."

I stifled a sigh. "So that's a no?"

"Yes," he said. "But I could maybe buy a couple theater tickets if you promise to show me your boobs."

For a moment I considered a couple snappy comebacks, but in the end I just hung up.

After that I sat staring at my address book and biting my lip until insanity got a good firm hold on my psyche. I dialed a moment later.

"Yeah." Vincent Angler had once been a defensive lineman for the L.A. Lions. Big and black and as aggressive as sin; even his voice was scary. But maybe it was all a cover-up. Maybe he just *acted* scary to hide his sexual orientation. When I'd last seen him, years ago, it hadn't been widely known that he was gay, but I had a sixth sense about such things. The fact that he had eventually begun to pursue an acting career had added credence to my theory. Not that every actor was gay. There were several whose sexuality I absolutely refused to call into question. Once again Colin Farrell sprang nimbly to mind. But he was quickly displaced by the thought of Angler, who had kindly confirmed my suspicions by coming out of the closet some months ago.

"Mr. Angler?" My voice sounded as if my sphincter were being squeezed in a winepress.

"Who is this?"

"Christina McMullen." I had met him, too, while investigating a murder. Apparently felonies are an excellent way to expand one's circle of acquaintances.

"Who?"

Generally speaking, it is not a good sign when your prospective date doesn't recognize your name. Even worse when he sounds irritated by your presence on the planet.

"We met a few years ago. I was Andrew Bomstad's psychologist."

There was a prolonged pause. Andrew Bomstad had once been my most illustrious client. But that was before he'd ingested enough Viagra to arouse a pachyderm and chased me around my desk like a hot-footed cheetah. After scaring the bejeezus out of me he had dropped to the floor, deader than an alligator handbag.

"The white chick with the great legs?" Angler asked.

Ummm . . . "Maybe."

"We had drinks and shit at the Hole?"

"Yes." I cleared my throat. "That's me."

"Huh. What do ya want?"

"I was wondering if . . . possibly . . . you had invitations to the *Jungle Heat* afterparty."

"*Jungle Heat?*"

"It's a spin-off of *Amazon Queen.*" I paused. He said nothing. "Patricia Ruocco's show."

"Yeah?"

"I know you've been doing some acting lately, and thought . . ." I shrugged, hoping his career was going better than I suspected. So far as I knew he had gotten about thirty seconds of screen time, most of which was shared with a half a dozen other extras. "Maybe you had access to the party."

The pause was deep enough to sink a battleship. "I could maybe get my hands on a couple of invitations if I had me a reason."

My heart was lodged somewhere in my esophagus. "After we met . . . at . . . the Hole . . . you said I should call if I ever needed help."

"Was I high?"

"Not so you were incoherent," I said, and he listened as I gave him the details.

*F*orty-five minutes later I was cleaned, partially dressed, and marvelously coiffed. If marvelous coiffing involves a strawberry blond wig that one borrows from one's BFF.

I had told Vincent I would meet him at the coffeehouse on Rosemary and Pine, so I had to get a wiggle on.

My bridesmaid gown boasted one broad shoulder strap and a back that plunged down to no-man's-land, or at least very-seldom-visited-land. At the very bottom of the valley a rhinestone pendant made my caboose more noticeable than was probably absolutely necessary. I was just mourning the passing of the girdle when the doorbell rang. With one last glance in the mirror, I trotted barefoot through the living room.

Harlequin rumbled two deep-throated barks, then rested on his laurels and watched the door with a cocked head.

Probably Ramla with a concern about her sister, I thought.

But gazing through the peephole I saw a man. Big, black, and bulging with muscle, he was scowling at my disheveled front yard with what looked like an equal mix of awe and contempt.

For a moment I considered hiding behind the wall and pretending I wasn't home, but chances were good that he was actually my date.

It was a testament to my courage ... or my stupidity ... that I opened the door.

"Vincent Angler?" I said. I was holding Harley back with one knee, stretching the mermaid dress to its coppery limits.

The man on my stoop skimmed me with his dark-syrup gaze. "White chick with the great legs?" he asked.

"I thought I was going to meet you at the coffee shop."

"I was in the neighborhood," he said.

"In Sunland?"

"In California."

"Ahh." I nodded stupidly. Harley was leaning heavily against my leg, trying to get a whiff of our guest's genitals.

"That is one big-ass dog," he said.

"He used to be a linebacker," I said.

It was then that Ramla stepped onto her stoop. She was eyeing Vincent like he was a wolf and I a mutton chop. "Is everything with you okay, Christina?"

I gave Vincent a smile I hoped looked charming instead of apologetic. "Yes." I gave her a little wave. "Everything's fine."

She was scowling above the gauzy swirl of her head scarf. "I should not call the 911?"

"Yes," I yelled.

There was a pause. "Yes, I should call them. Or yes—"

"Don't call them," I said.

She paused for a couple more seconds, then nodded briskly and returned to her house.

Angler was watching me with brows cliffed low over his eyes. "The 911?" he asked.

"I, ahh . . . thought I saw a suspicious character earlier this evening," I lied. There seemed little point in admitting some people were still inherently terrified of big black guys with muscle. Even more pointless admitting that one of those people was *moi.*

"Suspicious character?" he asked.

"Yes," I said. "Skinny little white guy."

He was glaring at me. Or maybe he was just looking.

"White. Very white," I added, and he chuckled finally.

"You gonna let a nigger in or what?" he asked. "It's hotter than shit out here."

"Oh, yes, sorry," I said, and grabbing Harley's collar, pulled open the door.

It wasn't until then that I noticed the limo parked behind my Saturn. It looked like a thoroughbred humping a Shetland pony.

"Is that yours?" I said.

"You said it was black tie."

"I didn't say black car."

He grinned crookedly and stepped inside. "I had something else planned."

I closed the door behind him. "I'm sorry if I disrupted your evening."

He shook his head, eyes gleaming as he skimmed my sleek, sausage-casing dress. "Not a problem."

I cleared my throat and managed not to squirm. "Do

you mind if I turn him loose?" I asked, nodding toward Harley.

"He going to eat me or something?"

"You're awfully large."

"You ain't seen nothin' yet," he said. I let Harley go and turned. I was starting to blush, and truth to tell, I wasn't sure why. He may have been referring to the size of his ego, for all I knew.

"Do you want something to drink while I finish getting ready?" I asked, but privately I wondered what I would give him. Generally, real people aren't thrilled about the prospect of drinking the magic Green Goo Laney serves, and it had been a while since I'd ventured into Trader Joe's for nutrients.

"You fill out that dress pretty good," he said.

"Umm." I resisted running my hands down my body like Zsa Zsa or tittering like a tween. "Thank you." *Steady now*, I thought, and put on my professional face. "But perhaps we should *clarify* this evening."

He straightened a little, pushing out his chest and filling his nostrils. It was pretty impressive. "Clarify away."

"This isn't really a date."

His brows rose a little. "So that rag is just something you wear 'round the house?"

I thought of a dozen snooty answers to that, then decided on, "Yes."

His eyes gleamed as he glanced at the gown's train. "Good for sweeping the floor and such, I suppose."

"The point is . . ." I drew a deep breath. "A friend of mine is in trouble."

"I know I'm black and all, but I didn't do it."

I opened my mouth, then recognized the jest. "She's been getting odd mail."

"This friend, she have a name?"

"None that we bandy about."

"Do you talk like this to everyone or just us niggers?"

"I can't tell you her name," I said.

He nodded. "Okay, so you got yourself a friend getting some spooky mail."

Succinct. "Yes."

"And you want to go to this bash, why?"

"I thought I could maybe ascertain who's been sending it to her."

He nodded. "So you want to see what's shakin'."

I thought about that for a moment. "Yes, but I . . ." I took a deep breath, and now I *did* run my hands nervously down my body. "I don't want anyone to recognize me."

"You do that a couple a times, nobody'll get their eyeballs above your tits."

I actually didn't know if I should be offended or flattered. Inside me, there is sometimes an odd mix of the lady and the tramp.

"So you'll help me?" I asked.

He shrugged, a casual lift of linebacker shoulders. "I'm here, ain't I?"

"Yes, you are."

"You well known at these Hollywood gigs?" he asked.

"Not really, no. But I don't want anyone to associate me with my friend, so I'm . . . I'm kind of going in disguise."

"Disguise."

"Yes."

"Are all you white chick psychologists so crazy?" he asked.

"Maybe," I said, and he nodded.

"Okay," he said, and after an elongated moment of discomfort, I turned away. I didn't look back as I crossed the living room, but I was pretty sure his gaze never left seldom-visited-land.

19

*I don't want any yes-men around me. I want everybody
to tell me the truth even if it costs them their jobs.*

> —Samuel Goldwyn—neatly
> summing up the
> entertainment business

I had been to a number of Hollywood afterparties with
Laney so I thought I knew what to expect. But upon retro-
spection, I realized the events I had previously attended
had come about before she had reached stardom, before
she had begun truly mingling with the rich and bizarre.
She was on a whole new level of weird now.

As the limo pulled up to the curb near the almost cir-
cular DGA Complex, I realized that instead of discussing
a game plan, Vincent Angler and I had been reminiscing
about our native lands. As it turns out, Vincent had grown
up in Cicero, not far from my own roots, and had visited
my old place of employment, the Warthog, on more than
one occasion. The entire conversation had helped me

relax. But as I glanced out the window at the milling crowds confined behind a roped-off section of sidewalk, I felt my nerves crank up. Vincent grinned at me, then stepped out of the car. Flashbulbs flashed. He waved a hand as if he were a prodigal princeling, then reached inside for me. My mouth felt dry as I stepped into the strobe lights and hot-fired questions.

"Mr. Angler, which is worse, directors or coaches?"

"What do you think about the new Lions roster?"

"How's your knee?"

"Who's your date?"

One reporter pressed in a little closer than the others.

"What's your name, honey?"

I opened my mouth for my latest lie, but nothing came out. I realized, rather belatedly, that I hadn't covered this eventuality with my escort.

"This is Jessica," Vincent said.

Reporters were scribbling wildly.

"Jessica who?"

"Jessica Rabbit," Vincent said, and putting his hand on my back, ushered me through the pandemonium. He towered over me. Not an easy feat with me in four-inch stilettos, but one I appreciated considerably more than the new nomenclature.

"Jessica Rabbit?" I said, tone dry as a martini.

"I panicked," he said.

I glanced up at his face. Panic was nowhere to be seen. In fact, his expression was totally unchanged. Probably the same when he was napping as when he was being targeted by a four-hundred-pound nose tackle. But maybe there was a little something in his eyes. His fingers were now spread across my back. My notably *bare* back.

"Mr. Angler!"

"Mr. Angler!"

Reporters were still slavering like junkyard dogs, leaning in, snapping pictures, yelling questions. It was then that the truth dawned on me.

"You already planned on coming here," I said.

"What's that?" He leaned down without taking his attention from the salivating paparazzi.

"This was the event you were planning to attend all along," I said, and for reasons quite unknown to me, the idea made me angry.

One corner of his mouth jerked up a little. "The producer's a fan," he said. "We're talking movie deals."

"Are you serious?"

"Do I look serious?"

As a Michael Moore documentary. But that seemed to be his only expression. "You could have told me earlier."

Ushered into the inner sanctum, the first thing we saw was a movie poster featuring Wesley Donovan wearing little more than a fine sheen of sweat and a grim expression. But I wasn't given much time to appreciate the marketing genius. A moment later we were milling in a sea of bling, angst, and beautiful faces. A place where cellulite was treated like the Black Plague and silicone was as common as the proverbial cold.

Fake trees hung with vines were interspersed through the cavernous lobby. Jungle music throbbed in the background, and near the distant wall was a buffet table, spread with every possible delicacy, but there seemed to be an invisible shield around it. There was not a soul in the vicinity except a waiter who stood as stoic as my escort, hands clasped behind his back. I wondered a little aimlessly if he was serving the food or guarding it.

I was starting to drool in earnest. *Note to self: When attending a Hollywood event with starlets the width of my pinky finger, do not wait to eat until you get there.* That would be an erro—

Just then, someone approached from behind.

"Hey, Vinny. How's the knee?"

I glanced up, bug-eyed.

As it turns out, George Clooney *is* a god. He stood to my right, talking to Angler as if they were bosom buddies. But in a moment it was all over. Or maybe his smile had made me disoriented.

"See anyone you know?" Vincent asked.

Clooney was walking away. I blinked and glanced up at my escort. His expression was as animated as an apricot's. I tried to match his stoicism, but my tongue felt a little blocky.

"I think I recognize a few faces." I was going for that admirable apricot attitude, but the saliva dripping from my chin might have given me away. Still, I scanned the crowd in the hopes of remaining upright.

Angler chuckled and slipped his hand a little lower, hovering over the swell of my too large ass as my mind did a little exploration into reality. It's a state I don't often visit, but I was beginning to wonder if he had lied to the media about his sexual orientation. Before I could inquire, however, he spoke.

"You okay if I leave you alone for a while?" he asked. "There's someone here I've been meaning to terrorize."

"Sure," I said. "I'm a big girl."

"Noticed that," he said, and smoothed his palm over my behind.

"Vincent?" I glanced up. It was now or never.

"Yeah?" He was glowering into the crowd.

"You *are* gay, right?"

"We'll see," he said, and almost smirking, glided away.

I pondered that for a while, but the sea of beautiful people was so intimidating I felt the need to eat. In fact, they seemed to be washing me toward the buffet table. I hadn't had anything but a dry bagel all day, and even though the other women in the room probably hadn't eaten since their tenth birthdays, I, for one, was hungry. I was also pretty sure I could take the waiter if his task really was to keep the buffet safe from all comers.

I scanned the table, keeping an eye on the hovering waitstaff. The stuffed shrimp looked fantastic. I could do without the escargot, but the bruschetta called to me. My stomach spoke eloquently of missed meals and the coming seven years of drought. I was just about to fulfill my biblical obligations to store up when a woman approached the other side of the table. She looked vaguely familiar and though I couldn't put a name to her, she had that sleek, starved look so popular in our overfed part of the universe. She took a radish cut like a rose and two pretzels before moving away. I scowled, wondering grouchily if I was expected to do the same. When in Rome and all that crap . . .

But just then I saw the kabobs. I would have passed them by as too fattening and potentially mermaid-gown messing, but the center of the friendly little skewer held a pineapple chunk and I hadn't yet had my daily dose of antioxidants. Fetching a plate, I delicately put the skewer in the center, but it looked a little lonely there so I added a little dab of hummus and a splayed stick of celery. My ensemble then seemed to lack color. It was, therefore, my duty to add flare to the palette. A trio of chocolate-dabbed strawberries did that nicely. Their little green caps looked saucy beside the tiny cream puff I added. Then there were small clusters of red grapes. They had been sprinkled with something. Maybe fairy dust. Maybe sugar. Both were good. I popped one directly into my mouth.

"It's nice to see a woman eat," my date said, appearing behind me.

Still masticating, I added a triangular sandwich to my plate. "It's nice . . ." I began, but in that moment a memory tripped in my mind. I turned slowly, and sure enough, the newcomer wasn't my date at all. It was someone blond and yummy with a little boy smile and dimples deep enough to drown in. ". . . to eat," I finished numbly.

His grin cranked up another notch, then, scanning the buffet, he snagged an unassuming carrot from the assortment, and tossed it into his mouth. "Enjoy," he said, and ambled away.

I watched, slack-jawed.

"Yeah, it's the shits," someone said near my elbow.

"Was that . . . ?" My voice sounded funny, then gave up altogether.

"Brad Pitt?"

I managed a nod.

He chuckled. "Yeah. For the rest of your life you'll remember that the only words you ever uttered in his presence were 'It's nice to eat.' " He chuckled. "Look on the bright side, though. He probably hasn't heard that line before."

I turned numbly toward him. He was young and short and as cute as a baby chick.

"I'm Ethan," he said. "Ethan Engles."

I blinked, numbly wondering what the hell my alias was supposed to be.

I guess he misunderstood my silence for star shock because he said, "He's not *that* good-looking," in a somewhat insulted tone.

I was going to object, but someone beat me to the punch.

We turned toward the newcomer in unison. He was lean and pale with long-fingered hands and a hooked nose.

"I don't think we've met," Ethan said to him.

"Kenny Vogue." They shook hands. "I worked with Pitt on *Troy*. He spent half the time in nothing but a metal skirt. Trust me—he *is* that good-looking. And he kept us in stitches half the time."

"Looks and personality . . . there ought to be a law," Ethan said.

"Amen," I said.

They looked at me.

"Are you in the business?" Kenny asked.

I swallowed, then daintily wiped my mouth with a napkin the size of a plantar wart. "Ummm . . ."

"Wait. Don't tell me," Kenny said. "Didn't I see you in—"

Ethan snapped his cute little fingers. "You were in Morel's movie, weren't you? *Taken*!"

"The prostitute," they said in unison.

I choked a little on the first bite of my strawberry. "What?"

"The prostitute that Neeson talks to in Paris."

"What's your stage—" Kenny asked, but Ethan interrupted.

"No. Don't tell me. I never forget . . ." He paused, then, "Fani," he said. "Fani Kolarova."

I gave a laugh and a modest little shrug. I had no idea what they were talking about.

"So you're French."

I covered a ladylike cough with my hand. *"Oui?"* I said.

"Too bad you didn't get more screen time," Kenny said.

"You did a nice job with the part," Ethan added.

I cleared my throat. I meant to deny it all. I really did, but my plate was piled up with enough food to feed Indonesia and I suddenly felt the Hollywood angst like a cancer in my throat. "Just a . . . *petite* part," I said, demure as a kitten.

"You know what they say . . . there are no small parts," Ethan said.

"It's true," Kenny agreed.

"I disagree," someone said. We turned. A woman stood beside me. She was dressed in a red, floor-length sheath that skimmed her well-honed body like a crimson wave. Her hair, dark and glossy as a pampered seal, nearly reached her waist. She brushed it behind one shoulder. Slim muscles flexed gracefully in her arms. "I worked on *Gigli,* remember?"

They laughed. I did, too, even though Ben Affleck was another actor I would be happy to watch gargle. So what if the film had offended half its viewership and put the other half to sleep?

"Nadine, have you met Fani?" Kenny asked.

"No." She skimmed her gaze up my coppery form and

raised her brows when she reached my strawberry blond mane. "I don't believe I have."

"Fani Kolarova, this is Nadine Gruber, hairdresser to the stars."

"And philanthropist," Ethan added.

She pulled her attention from my lion's mane. I wondered uncomfortably if she recognized it from *Queen*'s set. "You're too kind," she said.

"Nadine is single-handedly saving the California condor."

"Any publicity is good publicity," she said, then grinned wryly at herself. "I'm just kidding. I love those ugly birds. I'm just trying to do my part. Those of us in the entertainment business, with a few exceptions, of course, aren't nearly as self-centered as people believe. Many of us feel the need to give back."

I watched her. "You are an actress as well?"

She turned toward me again, smiling prettily. She was not a young woman, but she had been as carefully preserved as Grandma's sweet pickles. I couldn't even begin to imagine the kind of exercise regimen it would take to keep every muscle so perfectly toned. She'd probably spent half her life in warrior III pose.

"I was for a time," she said, and laughed. "Until I was cured."

The guys laughed with her. I managed to look confused. It wasn't that hard.

"Cured?"

"Acting is a brutal business," she said. "The mad rush followed by hours of boredom drains body and mind of its natural vitality. Far better for me to work in the background, where I have time to hone my craft properly."

"You do a beautiful job at *Queen*," Ethan said.

"Well . . ." She shrugged. "I have excellent people to work with. Patricia, especially, has glorious hair."

"Only made better by your care."

"I *am* developing an excellent earth-based hair care . . ." she began, but suddenly her words were swept into a soundless abyss, because just then I spotted Adonis. He wasn't wearing the usual tux. Instead, he had donned an open-necked poet's shirt. Black jeans hung low on his hips. His skin was dark, his eyes as blue as God's heaven. He glanced toward me. Our gazes met. His grin was sparkling white and a little wicked.

I believe I said something like, "Ugga," and then he was sauntering toward me, big shoulders drawn back, all chest and smolder and beard stubble. The rest of the room seemed to fade to gray, evaporating into smoke until he stood before me like a mermaid's wet dream.

"Hello," he said, nodding toward my companions. For reasons unknown, their names had scattered like frightened poultry from my mind. It might have been the fact that Adonis had an accent. Or a chest. Or a smile that could light up the Getty Center.

"Sergio," they said, and then he turned toward me.

"We've not met," he said, and held out his hand. It was in that instant that I recognized him. Give him a loincloth and a hip brand and he was everyone's favorite slave.

Morab.

20

What can I do to pleasure you, my queen?

—*Morab the man-slave, just
before Chrissy awoke*

I fumbled with my plate for a moment, wondered wildly who I was, what I was doing there, and if my underwear was on fire. "I'm . . ." I glanced at Kenny. "Fani."

Our hands met. A little dab of sugar/fairy dust had somehow been sprinkled on my knuckles and subsequently smeared up against his pinky finger.

"Oh." The word sounded oddly breathy from my lips. "I . . . Sorry."

"Not to worry," he said, and sliding his fingers from mine, sucked the offending digit into his mouth. Swear to God, my own went dry. Every ounce of moisture drained from my head like water down a drain.

One of the other guys cleared his throat. "Well," he said. "I seem to have become invisible."

"Gay," said the other, raising his hand.

I think the three of them eventually drifted away together. Or maybe they evaporated.

I knew I should feel badly about ignoring them, but seriously, I didn't have a choice. It was like contemplating sauerkraut when you have cheesecake on your plate.

"Fani." Sergio purred the name. "How is it that we've not met before?"

"I have been . . ." Foolish. What had I possibly been wasting my time on that I hadn't met him? I mean, he was alive, in this universe. "Busy."

He was staring at me, possibly waiting for me to continue. Possibly just giving me time to stare in return.

"With work," I added, remembering belatedly that I was an actress . . . and—dear God in heaven—foreign.

"Ahh, on location?"

My mind was rattling around in my head like a walnut in a hamster ball. "Ahhh . . . *oui.*"

"And where is it you've been?"

Jesus, oh Jesus, oh Jesus, I thought, and searched wildly for some remote locale we would not have to discuss in a million millennia. "Minsk?"

"Yes?" He looked thrilled. "I, too, have worked in Minsk. Ahh, I lost my heart to the Svisloch. And the Belarusian theaters. Have you yet visited the Bolshoi?"

Jesus God. I'd never been to Minsk. I'd be lucky as hell to find it on a map. "*Non.* I have been quite busy while in . . ." Holy crap, what country was Minsk in? Or *was* it a country? "Minsk. Though I do not have a large part in the film."

He smiled and skimmed his gentian gaze down my now steaming body. "Well, I am certain with a figure such as yours that will not be true for long. *Sim?*"

I wondered vaguely if swooning had gone out of style. But maybe it was a moot point. The gown had been pretty tight to begin with—adding the dusted grape may have been more than my lungs could accommodate. "And what of you?" I asked. As if I didn't know. As if he wasn't featured in every dream where Rivera didn't make an appearance.

He shrugged. "I have been on location also."

"Yes? For a film?"

"A series. It is called *Amazon Queen*."

I leaned away and widened my eyes. "You joke!"

"I do not. I am Morab," he said, and grinned as he hooked a thumb into his jeans. "Would you care to see my brand?"

"Yes."

His dark brows rose. "Truly?"

I gave myself a mental shake and followed it with a hard slap. What the hell was wrong with me? I was a known actress. Fani. Or something like that. "I mean to say . . . *oui*, I recognize you now. You are one of the manslaves, are you not?"

"I am so flattered that you have seen my work," he said, and removed his thumb from his jeans.

I didn't even cry.

He shrugged, still grinning. "The scripts . . . they are not so wonderful. But there are many fans and I am hoping . . ." He gave me a lopsided grin. He looked as tasty as a Fudgesicle. "I am hoping what we all hope. *Sim?*" he said, and laughed at himself.

"To be discovered," I guessed.

"I know . . . it is not likely."

With his looks? Was he kidding? I'd pay full box office price just to watch him blink. Who needs a damned script? Put him in his loincloth . . . or not. An image of him naked zipped like a naughty Tinkerbell through my mind, but I shook my head and focused on the subject at hand. Opportunity was knocking.

"And what of Ruocco?" I asked, remembering Elaine had said he seemed too accepting of her success. "It is said she is not the easy one to work with."

"Elaine?" he said.

I nibbled on a celery stick. "That is her true name?"

"Some call her Brainy Laney."

I scowled. "Brainy?"

"It means . . . ahh . . . *inteligente.* Smart."

"Ahh, this is American humor, yes? Because she is not smart?"

"I, too, thought there must be something wrong with her when we first met, but . . ." He shrugged.

"Well," I said, not giving up, "I have seen her act."

He eyed me skeptically, reminding me that on more than one occasion men had seemed willing to sacrifice their lives for Laney's honor. Sacrificing mine would maybe be no sacrifice at all. I waited, breath held, for him to stab me with my own skewer, but he only sighed.

"For a while I, too, was envious. I thought . . . why not me? You know? But she is a good person. Everyone . . . they adore her."

Now we were getting somewhere. "Everyone?"

"Well . . ." He leaned closer. He smelled like sea foam

and orgasms. Try concentrating with those scents titillating your olfactory system. "There is a rumor."

"Oh?"

"I do not think anyone is to know this."

Just tell me, goddamnit, I thought, and made a crossing-my-heart motion.

"Last spring the whole of the cast got a raise in pay. Some say it is because of Elaine. That she asked for less so that each of us could receive the more."

Oh, Laney, I thought. *Have I taught you nothing?* "And this you believe?"

"It is something she might do."

"Where did you hear this rumor?"

He shrugged, snagged a nearby broccoli floret, and popped it into his mouth. "Even Ghazi is wild for her, and he is the Muslim."

"Ghazi?"

"The master of props. It is said that he is a prince and has two wives already. But perhaps his God does not care if he adds a nice Christian girl to his collection."

My ears pricked up. "He hopes to marry her?"

He smiled. "He would have to join me and . . . how do they say . . . the remainder of the club."

I felt my heart crack a little but tried to be strong. The show's viewership was off the charts. The fact that most men watched it with the volume off didn't make Laney any less appealing.

"Everyone, they adore her," he repeated.

"That can't be true," I argued, and he scowled.

"Why do you say this?" he asked, and suddenly he almost seemed menacing.

I resisted taking a step back. "No reason," I said.

He stared at me a moment, then shook his head. "I apologize," he said. "I have been somewhat worried for her of late."

"For *her*? Why? She has got what each one of us wants. *Oui*?"

"That is how it would seem, is it not?"

"I am wrong?"

He shook his head. "You have not seen the man she is to marry?"

As a matter a fact, I had. There was a reason I cried myself to sleep every night. "*Non*."

"The man . . . he looks like . . ." He shook his head, exasperated. "A chimpanzee with bad hair."

Thank you! I was beginning to think I was the only one who saw the resemblance. "Perhaps he is very nice," I said, and almost—*almost*—felt a niggle of defensiveness.

He took a drink from his flute. "There is none so nice as *that*," he said.

"Is he here now?" I asked, keeping the conversation flowing.

"I do not believe Elaine is to come this night."

"And what of Ghazi?" I asked, glancing about, but at that moment someone spoke from near my elbow.

"Sergio," she said, and I jumped, already paling as I pivoted wide-eyed, to find Laney within spitting distance. She glanced at me, smiled vaguely, and turned back toward her man-slave. Ethan Engles was at her side, looking happy as a clam just to be in the same universe. "It's great to see you."

"My queen!" he said, and leaning in, kissed her on both cheeks. It was like watching birds of paradise mate, but she pulled away after a moment, only holding his hands, looking completely nonplussed. She was wearing blue jeans. She'd left her tawny hair loose to fall over her frayed T-shirt, immediately making every woman in the room feel underdressed. But none of that mattered, because my head was spinning. Was it possible she hadn't recognized me?

"I did not think you planned to come this night," Sergio said.

"I didn't," she admitted. "I've been crazy busy with wedding plans. But I wanted to pop in for a minute to wish everyone well." She turned toward me then.

"*That* is an amazing dress."

I gave her a sick look and tried to think of something to say, but she only smiled.

"And it looks great on you," she added.

I shot my attention to Morab. His brows were somewhere in his hairline.

"Do you two know each other?" Ethan asked.

"I . . ." I began, and ran out of words. Laney just stood there, smiling benignly.

"Patricia Ruocco," she said finally, and offered her hand.

"Fani," I breathed, not daring to try the last name, and Ethan laughed. "You should have seen her with Pitt."

I glanced at him, guessed his misconception, and ran with it.

"You are the Amazon Queen." I managed inadvertently to sound breathless, but in that moment I saw wicked recognition gleam in Laney's eyes. What the hell had I been thinking? Laney would probably still be able to out-think me postmortem. I gave a mental sigh. "I very much enjoy your show," I said, and wanted, rather badly, to hide under the buffet table. But I could hardly give up the accent now.

She smiled. "And I'm always amazed at your talents."

Sergio glanced from Laney to me, then lit up like a Greek god in a bonfire. "Ahh yes," he said, beaming at me. "You were in Morel's film. The one with Liam Neeson."

Laney was frowning, but then she brightened. "Of course," she said. "The prostitute."

I gave her a look.

"A very well-cast movie," she said. "But I'm even more impressed with your current role."

"Current role?" Ethan asked.

"Fani is working in Minsk," Sergio said.

Oh, dear God!

"Minsk," Laney repeated. "I didn't hear about that one. I've always wanted to go there. I hear it's beautiful. But how do you feel about the Belarus Democracy Act, Fani?"

I resisted gritting my teeth at her. "I did not have a great deal of time while there," I said.

"Busy, were you?" She said the word kind of funny, as if she might burst out laughing at any moment.

"Quite," I said.

"Film or television?"

"Television."

"HBO?"

"Lifetime," I said.

"Who's the producer?"

So she wanted to play. I tightened my grip on my overloaded plate and lobbed back a name I'd heard bandied about at such parties. "Terrence Riglio."

"The director?"

"Madeline Futone."

She raised one brow a tiny amount. "How about the set designer?"

"François," I said, remembering the good friend I kept in my bed-stand drawer. "François Desmarais," I said.

"Really? I thought he was dead."

"He's not," I said.

She did laugh now. Sergio was looking puzzled. But Ethan was just tripping along. "What's Riglio like to work with? I heard he can be kind of an ass."

In for a penny, I thought. "He is like the Hulk Incredible when he is angry."

"So he's a monster?" Laney asked.

"*Oui,*" I said.

She nodded. "I've known a couple of those. Even created a few."

I gave her a nod for her wit.

"Who's the cinematographer?" Ethan asked.

Laney was smiling, happy as a songbird.

"Georgianna Winstead," I said easily. 'Cuz, shit, I was in too deep to back out now. Might as well employ another woman while I was making crap up.

"I don't think I know her," Ethan said.

"She is young," I said. "But has much talent. Do you not agree, Ms. Ruocco?"

"I think I'm feeling a little nauseous."

"Perhaps it is the champagne," I said.

"I think it's the baloney," she countered.

"They're serving baloney?" Ethan asked, and Laney broke eye contact, calling an unspoken truce.

"I think it might already be gone," she said, and smiled. "I heard they—" she began, stopping abruptly, and I knew immediately that I was in big-ass trouble, because her eyes were shining with manic happiness. I stiffened even before she spoke. "Look who just arrived."

"Who?" I asked. I had lost my accent, and possibly my mind. I was scared to turn around. Terrified to look.

"Rivera," she said.

"You're lying," I hissed.

She raised her perfect brows. "I don't lie, Fani."

"It is true. She does not," Sergio said.

But I was already clasping Laney's arm. "You've got to get me out of here."

"Out of here? Don't be silly. The party's just started," she said, and patted my hand like I was a wayward child. "You've already met Brad without swooning. Mr. Rivera will be a piece of cake."

"I'm serious, Laney," I said, but just then I felt someone approach from behind and knew beyond a shadow of a doubt that my remaining minutes were limited.

21

Of course I hate her. I just don't know why yet.

—*Christina McMullen, on*
more than one occasion

I felt the hairs creep up on the back of my neck. Felt my face redden and my pulse fire up like a rocket ship. Lieutenant Rivera was right there, behind me. Why? I didn't know. Maybe Laney had suspected I would come here and worried for my safety. Maybe Murphy's Law was simply overactive during this particular phase of the moon. Or, for all I knew, Rivera might be invited to all the Hollywood shindigs. It wasn't as if I knew every intimate detail about him. Then again, it wasn't as if we were complete strangers, either. We had indulged in a little heavy petting, a bunch of long-winded kisses, and that one memorable shower situation. Not to mention the airing of a basketful of dirty laundry. Certainly we'd developed enough of an emotional connection to allow him to see through a cheap wig and a phony accent.

Unless he was so enthralled with coppery boobs and fake hair that he wouldn't even recognize me. In which case I'd kick him in—

"Senator," Laney said, and smiled.

Senator! My heart did a hard thump in my fish-skinned chest. The senator was here? The dark lieutenant *hadn't* arrived to blow my cover and drag me off to the slammer? It was his political sire? I gave Laney a wild-eyed stare but she was busy beaming at the newcomer and studiously ignoring me.

"It's good to see you again," she said, and reached for his hand.

I turned, feeling hopeful and desperate and sick to my stomach all at once, but he was already kissing her knuckles and beyond noticing me.

"Your Majesty," he said, and gave her his trademark slicker-than-snot smile. Miguel Rivera had charmed women from puberty to menopause with less. "You look as regal as ever."

For a moment I considered slinking into the crowd before he could withdraw from Laneyland, but even as the thought flittered through my sizzling brain, Laney turned her spiteful gaze on me.

"Senator, I'd like you to meet a friend of mine."

He straightened, and even as he shifted his attention toward me, I saw his eyes spark with Latino interest. It was then that my heart began pounding in my left ear.

"Senator Rivera . . . Fani," Elaine said.

He caught my eyes with his. The world receded around us. For an instant I considered passing out before he demanded to know why I was playing dress-up, but then he spoke.

"Fani," he repeated. His accent rolled over me like a tide washing me out to sea. "What an unusual name. You must be the queen's lady-in-waiting." Reaching for my hand, he bowed over it. "As lovely as Her Majesty herself."

I gritted my teeth at Laney, then smoothed it into a smile as he straightened.

"And what is your family name, lovely Fani?"

Oh, my hell! What was Fani's last name? I didn't have a clue. Not an inkling. Not a flippin'—

"I'm afraid she's not fluent in English, Senator," Laney said.

"Oh, my apologies," he said, and switched to Spanish.

I could literally feel the blood rush from my left ear to my cheeks, but I managed to shake my head.

He pulled back slightly as if surprised. "*¿Hablas español?*"

I shook my head harder.

Laney actually laughed. If she were any giddier she might very well burst into song. "I believe she is . . ." She thought for a moment, eyes glowing with glee as she tried to place my weird-ass accent. "French?"

"Ahhh . . ." said the senator, then, "*Quel est votre nom de famille?*"

For several moments I hoped the world would end. Or, if not that, perhaps a bomb could explode under my feet. Wasn't L.A. supposed to be a dangerous city? What the hell were all the damned crazed bombers doing this time of night?

I realized suddenly that I was holding my breath.

"Fani?" he said.

Shitski, I thought, and opened my mouth.

"I must . . ." I paused, face burning and wondering frantically if there were still other people in the room. ". . . practice my *anglais.*"

"Ahh." He was still holding my hand. "A laudable effort. When first I came to this country I, too, found the language problematic. But that was back . . ." He stopped and laughed. His gaze never left my face. "Listen to me, rambling on when you must be famished." For a moment he flickered his attention to my overstuffed plate. "But you have no champagne." He drew back as if shocked. "As a gentleman and a Latino I feel it my duty to rectify the situation." He raised a hand without ever slipping his gaze from mine. A server appeared as if snatched out of the sky. Rivera retrieved two glasses from his tray. "Please, eat," he said. "Seeing a woman indulge brings me great joy. There is something almost sexual about the act when you are truly hungry, is there not?"

I stared at him. *Oh God, oh God, oh God,* I thought. He was coming on to me. Wasn't he? Yes, I was sure of it. Wasn't I? Rivera's father. The ex-senator was making a play for me. I was in purgatory and . . . Looking over Laney's shoulder, I saw Solberg hurrying toward her and felt myself drop into hell, heart rumbling like a freight train in my restricted chest. Every muscle was tensed for impact.

Sensing my mood like a mean-spirited clairvoyant, Laney raised one brow a quarter of an inch, then turned to follow the direction of my horror. She flickered her gaze over the crowd for a moment before her face lit with newfound joy.

I wanted quite desperately to plead for her silence, to waylay Solberg, to . . .

But time had run out. He was beside her in an instant. Fortunately, he failed to do so much as glance my way. Laney was all-consuming. "I didn't see you at the door," he panted. "I was worried."

"I'm sorry," she said, turning toward him with a smile that melted all comers. Sergio and the others seemed to be gone. Perhaps they had dissolved in her effervescent presence. "I saw that Fani had arrived and wanted to say hi before she disappeared." We watched his face in tandem as he turned toward me. "I don't know if you two have met."

He glanced at me distractedly. "Hi."

I didn't bother to respond, but it hardly mattered; he had already turned back toward Laney.

"You didn't have any trouble with the doormen, did you, Angel?" he asked.

"No," she said, smile beatific. If I hadn't known her better I would have thought she didn't have a mean bone in her stunning little body. "Everything was fine. No problems. You've met Senator Rivera, haven't you, Jeen?"

"Sure." He gave the senator a brief nod before turning back to his obsession. "But I think there may be a bit of a miff with security," he said, and glanced behind him.

Laney's smile faltered a little. "What's that?"

"I, umm . . . I'm not sure they believed I was with you," Solberg said, and just then I saw two burly guys in suits striding toward us. Solberg looked as pale as an anemic onion but stood his ground.

Burly One and Burly Two slowed slightly as they saw Elaine, then stopped six or so feet away, looking as if they didn't know if they should salute or pass out.

"Ms. Ruocco!" said the first one, eyes wide, jaw lax.

The other was slightly more controlled. "I'm sorry, Ms.

Ruocco. Security's usually tighter. But this guy's so skinny. He slipped in between us and dashed off before we could—"

"Kevin," Laney said, and smiled at the speaker. "And Greg, isn't it?" she asked, shifting her gaze from one to the other. They stared at her in immediate infatuation. Laney never forgot a name. She probably still sent birthday cards to the midwife who had brought her into the world. Solberg, on the other hand, frequently forgot who *I* was.

The bouncers were still staring at Laney. The larger of the two looked as if he was going to cry.

"I'd like you to meet my fiancé," Laney said.

For a moment the oversized duo looked confused, then disbelieving. Then they *both* looked as if they were going to burst into tears.

"I'm sorry . . ." Kevin cocked his head a little, obviously not buying such a wild tale. "I thought you said . . ."

"Kevin, Greg, this is Jeen," she said, and tucked a hand behind J.D.'s scrawny biceps. And fuck all if Solberg didn't look as if *he* was about to cry.

I resisted rolling my eyes.

"I'm sorry . . . I just . . ." Greg glanced at Kevin as if to make certain the world was still round, that the Earth still revolved around the sun, that there was still a God, then he tilted his head a little. "The music . . . it's kind of loud." He flickered his gaze to Solberg, as if to reassess, but nothing about his following demeanor suggested he thought himself out of line. "And I sustained a little hearing damage in Baghdad. I'm pretty sure I didn't hear you right."

"Gentlemen," said the senator. In retrospect, I don't know how he kept a straight face. Had I not been absolutely certain I was about to be dragged from the room by security myself, I would have been on the floor in stitches. "I believe there's been a misunderstanding. But as you can see, Mr. Solberg is, indeed, Ms. Ruocco's invited guest. Her betrothed, in fact."

"Her . . ." Greg began, but couldn't seem to finish the rest of the thought.

"*Sí*," said the senator, and nodded sagely, as if only his calmness in the face of Laney's impending marriage would keep the world from spinning out of control. "Her husband to be."

I think Kevin swore and I'm quite sure Greg crossed himself.

"But thank you for your diligence," Rivera said. "I shall surely keep your constancy in mind should I have security needs of my own in the future."

They both looked a little like somnambulists, hoping to awaken soon. "Thank you," Greg said.

"Very gracious of you, sir," said Kevin, and then they wandered off, surely questioning the hapless humor of the cosmos.

"Well then," said the senator, rubbing his hands together and turning back toward me, "where were we?"

I dragged my attention regretfully in his direction.

"Ahhh, yes, I was inquiring about your origins," the senator said, and lifting an elegant hand, waved me toward a tall, just-vacated table. It was the approximate size of a pansy petal. "Please, let us sit." He smiled. "So that you can tell me every tiny detail of your life."

Oh, dear God. "There is only tiny to tell," I said.

"Don't believe a word of it, Senator," Laney said. "Fani's life could be a novel. Already I feel as if I've known her for years."

"I will listen with rapt attention to every word that falls from her lovely lips," Rivera said, and Laney grinned as she turned away, but Solberg remained as he was, scowling with what looked like painful intensity.

"Don't you have a dress kind of like that, Angel?" he asked.

She laughed like a sadist in a sweatshop. "I missed you," she said, and kissed his cheek.

His eyes immediately assumed that glazed look I had seen Laney invoke in the male species since her fifteenth birthday.

"You're the light of my solar system," he said, and suddenly even being seduced by Rivera's oversexed father seemed more appealing than hanging around the two of them.

I turned toward him. "So you are senator?" I said in broken something or other.

And Laney laughed again.

22

Only a dumb shit brings a water pistol to a gunfight. I ain't no dumb shit.

—Vincent Angler, armed and dangerous

"*F*ani Kolarova?" Vincent said, and grinned across the acre of plush backseat at me.

"I couldn't really run with Jessica Rabbit," I said, and he grinned, his teeth whiter than the buttery leather seats.

"Did you find out what you needed to know?"

"I don't know," I said, and sighed.

"You didn't get no readings on whether one of them is the dude who's sending your friend the mail?"

It had been one hell of a night, but I was almost to Sunland. Almost to bed. "I'm going to have to give it some thought," I said.

He nodded. "And your friend . . . she still ain't got no name?"

"Sorry."

He gave a "That's cool" shrug. "You want me to get rid of the dude that's bothering her?"

"I don't know who he is."

"That's gonna make it harder."

"Story of my life."

The driver pulled the limo up to the curb.

"Well, it's been real, Ms. Kolarova," he said.

"I live to entertain," I said, and he smiled again.

"You let me know if you figure out who the dude is and I'll pop a cap in his ass."

"That might be the most charming offer I've had all month," I said, and he laughed out loud as the driver opened the door for me.

We said our good-nights. I rose to my six-plus height on wobbly heels and made my way to the front door. The light was shining above it just like it was supposed to. I put the key in the lock, let myself in, and disarmed my security system. Harlequin was doing the I-gotta-pee dance done by all mammals. But I took a moment to remove Laney's wig before turning him out. Letting down my squashed hair, I wiggled my fingers against my scalp, then kicked off my killer heels and tripped through the house to the back door. As soon as it opened, Harley nosed his way through, romped into the dust bowl, and squatted. I dropped a half-dozen bobby pins onto the little console near the window and released my long-held breath.

It was then that I heard a noise coming from behind the rosebushes beyond my fence. I glanced toward the house on my right. The Griffins were new to the neighborhood. They'd just moved in a couple of months ago, but it had taken less than a week for me to tire of sixteen-year-old Bryn. If she wasn't playing music loud enough to break capillaries, she was making out with one of her many boyfriends behind the garage. Not that I was jealous or . . .

But in that instant, I realized something was funny. Both Bryn and her current beau were dark-haired. But one of the heads that poked up above the rosebushes seemed to be blond. Or hooded.

Or turbaned!

Shit! The truth dawned on me like the crack of a new day.

That wasn't Bryn. It was Aalia. And she wasn't alone. That much I knew even though she was only visible for a second before she'd disappeared behind the Griffins' garage.

Pawing through my purse, I snatched up my cell and hit 911 with shaky fingers. It was busy. I ended the call and punched in Rivera's number even as I raced back into the house for my Mace.

"Is it too much to ask that this is a late night booty call?" Rivera asked.

"I think he's got Aalia!" I was back outside, gazing through the darkness and shaking like a tambourine.

"What's your location?"

"My place. I saw someone by my neighbors' garage."

"Are you in the house?"

I backed inside, hoping Harley would follow. He did. "Yes," I said, then closed my eyes for a moment and stepped outside again.

"Lock the doors," he said. "I'll be there in a few minutes."

"Hurry," I said, and closing the phone, stuck it in my

bodice. It was a tight squeeze, but I needed it with me and mermaids don't have pockets.

My bare feet were almost silent against my dusty yard. More silent, at least, than my pounding heart. Getting over the fence was neither simple nor pretty, but somehow I managed it. I ducked up against a garage, then taking a shaky breath, peeked around the corner.

Nothing.

Mace in hand, I trotted along the building, stopped at the next corner, and glanced out. And there they were. He wore a turban and a white robe. She seemed to be in jeans. They were almost to Vine Street. Almost to the car that waited there. The engine was running.

Panic spurred through me, and then I was moving. "Hold it!" I yelled, and stepped into the open.

The pair jerked toward me. He was holding her arm. That much I could tell, but little else.

The man spoke, low and guttural, but I couldn't understand the words. They turned away.

"I've got a gun!" I yelled, and pointed the Mace at him.

He glanced over his shoulder at me. Time stood still, and then he smiled. I could see his teeth glow in the darkness.

"No. You do not," he said, and raised his arm. It took me a shattered second to realize he *did* have a gun. That he was raising it. That it was pointed at me. My heart dropped toward my knees as my stomach recoiled in horror. Every instinct told me to dodge for cover, but I was frozen in place.

A bullet *ping*ed in the darkness. I jerked at the impact, stumbling back against the garage, not feeling the pain for a moment. Another moment passed. No agony. I glanced down and found no blood. Jerking my attention back toward the street, I saw that Aalia's abductor was down on one knee and in that moment I realized I hadn't been shot at all.

He had. And suddenly Aalia was racing toward me. I braced myself as she rushed into my arms, then gathered her against me, still holding the Mace, but her abductor was already stumbling to his feet, gun lifted.

I shoved Aalia behind me and raised the protection spray.

It was then that another man stepped into view.

"Put it down, Turk, or I'll fry your ass where you stand." Vincent Angler!

The Yemeni jerked his attention toward Vincent, snarled something as he glared at me and Aalia, then turned and leapt for the car.

Angler snapped off a shot. It *ping*ed against the door, but the vehicle was already speeding away, engine revved as it careened around the corner onto Opus.

Aalia had my left arm in a death grip by the time Vincent loped over to us.

"What the fuck was that?" Even *he* sounded breathless. I was about ready to pass out from asphyxia.

"It's a long story," I said.

"Yeah?" He glanced at Aalia. Even in the darkness she was as pretty as a love sonnet. "Maybe you should tell it in the house, then."

The first wave of adrenaline was starting to dull, leaving me shaken and numb, but I managed a nod. Walking was a little more difficult, what with the shaky knees.

I ushered Aalia through my back door. Vincent accompanied us. She glanced up at him, shy admiration in her eyes.

"This your friend?" he asked, just now loosening his tie.

I knew he was thinking of the weird letter-writer, but there really didn't seem to be a reason to clarify at the moment. "Yes," I said.

He nodded. Aalia pressed a little closer to me.

"You okay?" he asked, and stared down at her. To the uninitiated, it might have looked like a glare. The first time I had met Vincent I had wet myself.

As far as I know, Aalia was more controlled than that. She gave one clipped nod.

"What the hell happened?" he asked, and pulling his tie free, opened the top two buttons of his shirt. A fair amount of firm, black skin showed above the crisp, white V.

Aalia pulled her gaze from his chest, but failed to answer. Her usually olive skin looked pale, her lips almost lavender.

"Was that your husband?" I asked.

She closed her eyes and nodded again.

"Wait a minute . . ." Vincent sharpened his scowl. "You're married to that fucker?"

I felt her wince. Maybe he did, too, because he took a deep breath and shoved the gun out of sight. A black James Bond on steroids.

"That guy was your husband?" he asked.

"Yes." It was the first word she'd spoken since I'd spotted her beside the garage.

"You separated?"

It seemed to take all her courage to raise her eyes to his. "I left him and my homeland some days past."

He glanced at her arm, then reached out and pulled

back the sleeve of her jersey. She remained exactly as she was, eyes as wide as a fawn's. "He do that?" he asked.

She pursed her lips and raised her chin the slightest degree. Pride and guilt all embedded in one confusing cocktail. Human beings—the ultimate mystery. "Yes," she said.

He glanced away. A muscle danced in his jaw. "What's his name?"

"Ahmad Orsorio."

"You gonna go back to him?"

Pride again, less fear, and a smidgen of contempt. "Not so long as there is breath in me."

Vincent stared at her. Something shone in his eyes for a moment, then he gave a short nod. "Then I'd suggest—" he began, but in that moment we heard sirens.

He raised his brows at me. "Another friend?" he asked.

"Probably."

"I'll take off, then," he said.

"Not *your* friends?" I asked.

"Not generally," he said and giving Aalia one more glance, stepped out of the house and into my backyard.

"LAPD," someone yelled, and pounded on my front door.

"Rivera?" I called.

"Open the fucking door or I'll tear the house down," he snarled.

Yup. That was him.

23

Yes, the burka I could wear again. But so could I be
fried in hot oil like the malawah.

—*Aalia Orsorio, spreading
her wings*

I locked my back door, then hurried through the house to
the front door, where I clicked the dead bolt open and
came face-to-face with a Glock. Rivera was behind it,
looking grim.

"Where is he?" His gaze seared past me, sweeping the
bedroom door, the steps, the living room.

This was a new side of Rivera. I mean, he's generally
foreboding, but this was foreboding going on deadly. It
was kind of a turn-on.

"He's gone."

"The house is secure?"

I considered a joke, but decided I didn't particularly
want to get shot. "Yes."

"And the girl?"

"Aalia?"

He still didn't look at me, but swept his weapon sideways, covering every opening. "Is she here?"

"Yes."

He exhaled, then lowered the gun a couple of inches, which was nice.

"Where'd the fucker go?" he asked. Rivera didn't fool around with TV phraseology like "perps" or "bad guys." It almost made me doubt the authenticity of Hollywood.

"North on Opus."

"On foot?"

"Car."

"What make?"

Crimony! Wasn't it enough that I'd saved the girl? "Dark?"

He gave me a peeved look just as Aalia ventured into the living room.

"You okay?" he asked.

"Yes, Lieutenant." She nodded solemnly, cute as a frightened kitten. "I am well and sorry to disrupt your evening."

I raised my brows at her. The woman had almost been abducted by her nut job husband. To my way of thinking the cops should damned well be disrupted.

"Perhaps . . ." She glanced at me. "Perhaps I could make the lieutenant some tea?"

Tea? Sure. Maybe she could whip up a little tiramisu, too, while she was at it. "Of course," I said. "Help yourself to anything in the kitchen."

She hustled away.

"How come *you* didn't offer me tea?" Rivera asked. He

was still gazing at the spot where she had disappeared into the kitchen, but some of the flat-eyed grimness had left his face.

I kept the growl to myself. "Maybe because I was still a little fatigued from saving her ass."

He glanced at me, eyes sparking with humor, and I scowled down my irritation. Everyone was a frickin' comedian.

"What happened?" he asked, and the grin disappeared.

I exhaled noisily, and realized my hands were shaking a little. "When I let Harley out in the backyard I thought I heard something near the garage. I assumed it was just Bryn making out with her latest and greatest, but then I realized something was wrong."

"So you hustled back into the house where it was safe, right?"

I paused for a moment, then, "Maybe not immediately."

He scowled, but continued without pulling out the cat-o'-nine-tails. "What *did* you do immediately?"

It was hard to decide how much to tell him. Sometimes he gets a little miffed when I do things that some might misconstrue as stupid.

"I had my Mace," I said, remembering that little tidbit with pride.

"Your . . ." He swore, then gritted his teeth and held up one hand, as if that little gesture might prevent him from bursting into spontaneous flame. "What else can you tell me about the car besides the fact that it was dark?"

I shook my head, trying to remember, but I don't usually notice cars. Unless it's a Turbo Cabriolet. I'd sell my left boob for a Turbo Cabriolet. What do left boobs go for these days?

"Was it black?"

I thought about that for a second. "Maybe dark blue."

"Full size? Compact?"

"Kind of medium."

"Older model or new?"

"Holy crap, Rivera, I'm a psychologist, not a mechanic."

"Did the bumpers look rounded or was it more boxy?"

"Rounded, I think."

"Was the car running?"

"Yeah. He had a driver."

"Was he armed?"

I squelched a wince. Here's where it got dicey. "The driver or the—"

"Damn it, McMullen! Did someone . . ." He made a circling motion with his hand. ". . . in this vicinity have a weapon."

I paused, then nodded.

He looked mad enough to eat iron. "What kind?"

"What are my options?"

"Semiautomatic? Cannon? Crossbow?"

"I would have noticed arrows."

He wasn't finding me particularly amusing . . . again.

"I think it was a handgun," I said.

I could see a dozen questions boiling up in his eyes, but he skipped over them for a moment as he pulled out his cell phone. Flipping it open, he punched in a number. "What'd you do to your hair?" he asked.

"Nothing special." Actually, I had crushed it under a wig for a few harrowing hours, then loosed it on the world. Apparently, it was now fighting back, because it sprang away from my head as if it were freshly permed.

Someone answered on the other end of the line, but Rivera didn't shift his Dark Man attention from me.

"This is Lieutenant Rivera. I have an armed Yemeni man heading north on Opus in Sunland. He's driving a dark, newer-model sedan.

"Name?" he asked.

I shook my head, but Aalia appeared in the doorway.

"Ahmad," she said. "Ahmad Orsorio."

Rivera shifted his gaze from me to her. "Can you describe him?"

"He is cruel."

Rivera nodded, not mocking.

"How tall is he?" Rivera asked. Apparently, he wasn't one to deal in moods or signs or phases of the moon.

"Perhaps six foots tall by American means," she said.

He ran through a list of questions and she answered dutifully. After a few minutes of relaying that information, he clicked his phone shut. Aalia quietly slipped into the kitchen once again. To me, that portion of the house is simply somewhere to eat junk food while I read trashy novels, and right now there wasn't enough in it to feed a runway model, so she must have other reasons to be there. I wondered vaguely if she had been crying.

Rivera eyed me as he shoved his phone in the front pocket of his blue jeans. I tried not to watch.

"Where were you?" he asked, skimming my copper mermaid form with his hot gaze.

Shit. I hadn't exactly thought of lies to cover this part of the conversation yet, but at least I had lost the wig. "I went to a, ummm . . . party."

"Dressed like that?"

"It was a theme party."

"And you were the little mermaid?" he asked. "All grown up?"

Hilarious. "Yes," I said.

He gave me his patented almost-smile. "You go with Elaine?" he asked, and I stiffened a little, not wanting to divulge too much . . . like the fact that barely a full hour before I had been flirting like a streetwalker with his father. *Kill me now,* I thought, and tried to look confused. Some jobs are harder than others.

"No."

"So you went alone?"

I shrugged, evasive as hell. "She was busy with wedding plans or something." I managed to refrain from that nervous throat-clearing thing I sometimes do.

"So the house was empty when you got home."

"Except for Harlequin," I said.

He nodded and rubbed the dog's ears. Harley closed his eyes and looked as if he might swoon with happiness. Which made me think that if worse came to worse in my so-called love life, which, by the by, it had, I'd settle for an ear rub.

"The house was locked?" he asked.

"Yes."

"Security system on?"

"Yes."

He nodded, satisfied. Maybe I'd get an "Atta girl" if I didn't warrant an ear rub, I thought, but he moved on.

"So you let Harley out. What happened after you'd retrieved your Mace?"

"I went out there just to take a look around. I mean, for

all I knew it was just Bryn but . . ." I shrugged. "It looked like the guy was wearing a turban. So I thought of Aalia. By the time I got to the corner of the garage they were already near the car so I, umm . . ." Here's where it got sticky. "I asked him to let her go."

"Are you serious?"

I bristled immediately. "Of course I'm serious."

"He had a handgun and you have a can of puke juice and you asked him to let her go?"

"I'm a trained psychologist, Rivera. It's not as if I just fell out of the cabbage patch or something. I have some working knowledge of how people's minds—"

"Jesus," he said, and scrubbed his face with one hand. "Why can't I just have a girlfriend who doesn't feel it's necessary to play Wonder Woman every day of her frickin' life?"

"—work. In fact . . ." I blinked. "What did you say?" I asked, but just then my front door burst open.

We jerked toward it in unison, I with my Mace, Rivera with his big-ass phallic symbol.

Ramla gasped and halted in the doorway, eyes wide, mouth open.

There was a blink of silence, then, "My sister," she rasped, attention darting from Rivera to me. "She is gone. I but went to the—"

It was then that Aalia appeared again.

The two women stared at each other for one abbreviated instant, then rushed into each other's arms. A stream of dialogue I couldn't decipher followed. There wasn't much point in interrupting.

"Thank you," Ramla said finally. She was clasping Aalia's hand. "Christina." She nodded solemnly at me, then at Rivera. "Lieutenant, you have my gratitude everlasting."

He was back to his full-body scowl. "I'll have more questions for her later," he warned.

"She will not leave the house. I will make certain of it," Ramla said, and ushered her sister toward the door.

Rivera accompanied them to the Al-Sadrs' house. In his absence, I tried to think. It didn't go particularly well. I needed a couple months to reflect on things. It was less than a minute before he returned.

"You shouldn't have gone outside," he said, approaching rapidly and resuming the conversation where we'd left it.

"Does that mean I'm not your girlfriend?"

He closed his eyes and rolled his head as if his neck hurt. "It means you're a loose cannon, McMullen. Shit! A two-year-old would have known enough to stay inside."

"So I'm not a two-year-old."

"No." His eyes seared me like I was a fine filet. "You're a full-grown woman who constantly insists on getting shot."

"That's just it!" I said, adrenaline rushing through me, jumbling my thoughts. I hadn't been anybody's girlfriend for a long time. "I *didn't* get shot. I thought I had but—"

My own stupidity stopped my words in their proverbial tracks.

The room had gone deadly silent.

"But what?" he asked. He was standing close enough to scatter my brain waves.

"I . . ." I shrugged. "I was wrong."

"He shot at you?" Anger danced a tight jig in his lean-muscled cheek.

"Is it too late to get back to the part about my being your girlfriend?"

"The bastard *shot* at you?" He gritted his teeth as he shifted positions and glared at the back door.

"No. No," I said, shaking my head tentatively. "I just thought . . . Maybe it was someone's car backfiring or something."

"Maybe you should move to a different neighborhood."

"Not just this minute," I said, and taking the one step that separated us, distracted him with a kiss.

24

Guys don't make passes at girls with big asses.

> —Peter McMullen, shortly
> before Chrissy knocked him
> unconscious

Rivera pulled away from the kiss, dark eyes smoking.

"Jesus, McMullen, you sure you went to that party alone?" Perhaps he had somehow sensed my sexual frustration.

"As a matter of fact," I said, "I tried calling *you*. Left you a voice mail." I didn't mention the fact that I was just calling to make sure he was busy and *couldn't* attend the premiere. "You didn't bother returning my call."

Maybe there was a smidgen of guilt in his expression. I pressed my advantage. "I admit I didn't really feel like going alone, but you'd be surprised what I've learned to do solo."

I didn't really plan for the statement to sound suggestive, but the words were out there, along with the vibes. I watched his eyes go sultry. His nostrils flared.

"Lucky for me you made it home without some jackass sniffing at your tail."

"Fortunate," I said, and raised my chin a little as estrogen sluiced through me. Hold on to the gunwale, girls, it's high tide.

"Holy Jesus," he said, and glancing down at the gown's iridescent fabric, cupped my left breast. It made me reconsider selling it. "Is this dress painted on?"

"Yeah." I hoped to sound sassy, but would have been grateful for coherent. "It washes right off."

He drew a deep breath and skimmed his hand over my ribs to my waist. "You must have had your Mace handy at the party, too."

"I kept it around my neck," I said. "Right between my boobs."

He dropped his gaze from my eyes to my body and stopped. "I take it your cell phone was occupied elsewhere at the time?"

I glanced down. I'd totally forgotten I'd shoved it in there. Reaching up, I snagged it from its cozy spot. My breasts sprang back into place like warm bread dough.

By the time I glanced up, his eyes were shooting sparks like fireworks. A muscle jumped in his jaw. "When did we first meet, McMullen?" he asked, and moving a little closer, slipped his palm around my waist and over the slinky fabric barely covering my ass.

I shrugged, trying to look casual, but shit, I could hardly breathe. He expected me to employ my memory?

"August twenty-fourth, 2005," he said.

"Yeah?" I was a little giddy at the fact that he knew the exact date. Or maybe there were other reasons.

"Yeah," he said, and shifted a hard-muscled thigh between my own. "And you still haven't fucked me." His quads contracted against me, but swooning was no longer an option. Taking him down like a oversexed grizzly, however . . .

"The timing's been iffy," I said. "Too many phone calls."

"You know what they say about timing," he said, and kissed the corner of my mouth.

"I don't believe I do." The tone of my voice suggested I didn't know much.

"There's no time like the present."

"That *is* a time-honored sentiment."

"And you're wearing that do-me dress."

Maybe I should have argued with that, but it hardly seemed worth the effort. Besides, when he slid his hand up my derriere I couldn't have argued with anything. His fingers trailed from the slippery fabric onto my bare skin.

Some say near-death experiences heighten the senses. It might be true, because my senses were honed in on him like a bird dog on a chicken wing. I felt his fingers tickle against my back even as the knuckles of his left hand whispered featherlike over my chest, across the swell of my boobs, and onto my neck. His breath smelled of ecstasy in waiting as he kissed the corner of my mouth.

"Do-me earrings," he said as he slipped his fingers beneath my glittery hoops and cupped my neck with his palm.

His lips against my collarbone made my knees go weak. I'll never know exactly how we ended up on the couch, but

228 ~ Lois Greiman

we did. I was leaning up against the armrest like a drunken sailor and he was sitting beneath my knees.

He ran his hands up the arch of my left foot to my ankle.

I'm afraid I didn't quite manage to stifle my moan. He grinned, then propped the pad of my foot against his hip and moved his hands upward, slipping the gown away as he went.

"Do-me legs," he said.

I had never been happier in my life that I had actually shaved. The gown was just past my knees now. I sighed as he massaged my calf. My muscles went lax. My foot slipped forward. It pressed up against his erection.

Our gazes met, fire on lighter fluid. And then he was leaning across the couch, between my legs, eyes dark and intense and—

He stopped, gaze shifting just the slightest degree, body freezing instantly. I felt the drop in temperature immediately.

My mind was scrambling. I turned toward the rear of the house, and then I realized what he was looking at; Vincent had dropped his tie near the back door.

"Who did you say your escort was?" he asked.

I have nothing against lying. In fact, it's generally my first instinct, but it had been a coon's age since I'd seen a guy naked. I wanted to something awful, but history suggested that Rivera wasn't the kind who really appreciated creative fabrications.

I held my breath for an instant, fighting honesty, then, "I can't tell you."

He was frozen above me, one arm braced against the back of the couch, one on the armrest. His biceps stood out in taut relief beneath his dark, touchable skin, and his eyes were screaming lewd suggestions that I dearly wanted to take him up on. "Can't or won't?" His voice was low, gruff, warning me to give the right answer. But Vincent had helped me out long ago when I had needed a friend, and I had no intention of betraying his trust.

"He did me a favor."

His eyes were dark and deadly, but somehow my hormones didn't give a shit that I couldn't tell if he planned to kiss me or kill me.

"Lots of guys would, McMullen," he said. "If given a chance."

I felt anger course through me, but I held it in check. "How sweet of you to say."

He stared at me. A muscle ticked in his jaw.

I swallowed. "It doesn't matter who I was with," I said, and found that with his hard-muscled body pressed against me, I had very little pride. A butt-load of libido, but very little pride. "I didn't do anything with him."

"Except nearly get yourself killed."

"That's not his fault."

"Then why not tell me who he is?"

I scowled. "He's semifamous and doesn't want anyone to know——" I stopped, realizing the flaw in my reasoning. If he didn't want anyone to know we were together he certainly wouldn't have attended a public event with me, but Rivera had already jumped past that point.

"Know what?" he asked. "That he had a gun?"

"What? No. I——"

"He was the one who fired the shot, wasn't he?"

I winced.

"A gun that is probably not registered."

"Listen, Rivera, I didn't know—"

Anger chased frustration across his face. "What?" His voice had risen. His teeth were gritted. He stalked to my easy chair and turned. "That you could have been shot? That you could have been raped and tortured and murdered?"

"Don't get—"

"Dramatic?" he asked, and laughed as he jerked into a seated position. The warmth of his body abandoned me, and in that instant I felt my eyes fill with tears.

He glanced at me, looking angry as hell. "No!" he said. "You are *not* going to cry."

I sniffled a little, feeling like a ninny.

He levered himself to his feet and pointed dramatically toward the back of the house. "You were just accosted by some madman, woman! That's when you should have cried . . . or screamed or swooned or some goddamned thing. But did you? No. You ran out there in a mermaid suit, waving an aerosol can. So don't pretend you're getting all teary-eyed because I raised my voice."

I shook my head, searching for the temper that usually saves me from that particular brand of humiliation. "It's not that. I just . . ." I pressed my knuckles to my nose to stop the flow of snot. "Does this mean you're not going to sleep with me?"

It may have been the dumbest thing I'd ever said, but the words were out there, searing me with their soppy honesty.

For a second every muscle in his body tensed. Then he swore and stormed across the floor. Bending, he scooped me into his arms. His chest felt hard against my boobs, his lips fire-hot against mine as he kissed me.

"You're driving me fucking crazy." He kind of panted the words. My arms had wound themselves around his neck.

"What kind of crazy?" My words came out as a kitten-soft whisper.

He stared at me for a full twenty seconds, then gritting his teeth, he swore out loud, and turned toward the bedroom.

"Mac! Mac!" Laney's voice stormed through the house even before I heard the front door open. Footsteps galloped across the floor and in a moment she was standing there, staring at us with her eyes wide, her face pale.

Rivera stood half-turned toward her, frozen, cradling me in his arms.

She took in the situation like a speed-reader, searching for wounds or blood or dead bodies. "What happened?" she asked.

"I'm okay," I said, but in that moment Solberg gallumped in after her.

"Why's Rivera's car . . ." His voice petered to a stumble. ". . . parked on the sidewalk?" he asked, eyes skittering from Rivera's face to my own. "And why is he carrying a mermaid?"

"Are you hurt?" Laney asked.

I was starting to blush. It's not something I do often. But when I do it's a full-body thing, and I was just now beginning to realize that this looked as if Rivera had made an emergency booty call. Had careened through L.A., jumped the curb, and come charging into the house to service me.

I wiggled uncomfortably in his arms and he released

my legs, letting me slither my slippery tail to the floor. I cleared my throat.

"I'm fine," I said. "Everything's fine. There was just a little bit of trouble with Aalia."

"Her husband?" As usual, Laney had switched tracks with the alacrity of a train engineer.

The excitement of the past hour coursed through me again, firing up cold remnants of adrenaline. "He was pulling her behind the neighbor's garage when I let Harlequin out to pee."

"You stopped him?"

I glanced toward Rivera. "I, ummm, had my Mace."

"Jesus," Solberg said. He looked as white as talcum powder.

"But you called the lieutenant," Laney said.

"First thing."

She turned and gazed at Rivera with that expression that had made lesser men wet their pants. "Thanks for rushing over."

He nodded.

"I know she drives you nuts." I'll never be sure how she managed to sound so sincere. "But she's worth it."

"She's going to get herself killed," Rivera said.

"Don't let that happen."

"Then she'd better quit—"

"I'm right here!" I said. "I can hear you, you know."

"Then quit acting like a harebrained whack job," Rivera said.

"Harebrained . . . Is that what you call saving lives?"

"It is when you're not trained. When you're armed with a damned spray can. When you—"

"Angel," Solberg said, eyes wide in his chimpanzee face.

"That dress!" I was holding my breath. "Wasn't your friend—"

"Jeen," Laney said, and turned toward him, expression as placid as summer as she hugged him. "Thank you for getting me home so quickly."

"But . . . at the party . . . that girl . . ."

"Needs to relax now. Could you run out to the car and get my planner. I have a few details Mac and I need to discuss."

"But . . ."

"I love you," she said, and kissed him on the lips.

True, I was in dire danger of being exposed as the French mermaid at the party—the one who flirted with Rivera's father and subsequently invited a might-be criminal into her house—but I would have rather done thirty days in San Quentin than see my best friend kiss the Geekster on the mouth.

25

And which do you think seems like a better plan?

> —Chrissy McMullen, Ph.D.,
> after Emily Christianson
> said she had weighed her
> options: She could either
> spend her evenings trading
> microbes with a boy who
> had half her IQ, or she
> could become a world-
> famous surgeon

"So everything's going well?" I asked.

It was Monday afternoon and I was back at the office. I had discussed my party conversations with Laney a few days before. Together we'd decided that Morab genuinely liked her and therefore was unlikely to send her threatening mail. Not to mention the fact that he was just too gorgeous to be guilty. There was also the fact that if anything happened to her, everyone associated with *Queen* would suffer.

I had slept on that thought. In fact, I slept through most of the weekend, but I still felt tired. Nevertheless, I had managed to shove myself into a summer suit and strap on a pair of huarache sandals before dashing off to work.

Emily Christianson sat across the coffee table from me. She looked as thin and taut as a guitar string. She was wearing a black pencil skirt and a white button-down blouse. It was very similar to the ensemble she'd worn every time she'd visited my office. Did that mean she just really liked business attire, or did it speak of a deep-seated need to control her environment with an iron fist.

"I aced my calc exam," she said.

"Good for you."

"Well . . ." She sighed. "*I* thought I aced it, but Dad said I could have done better."

"What was your score?"

"Ninety-eight percentile."

I raised my brows in concession to her brainpower. "Did your father say why he was disappointed?"

"There were extra-credit points offered," she said. "I didn't do them. I would have," she said, already defensive, "but I ran out of time."

In retrospect, I thought I'd rather have been called Pork Chop and spent my days fighting off my brother's dead vermin than have to live with such ridiculous expectations. "Parents often set extremely high standards for their children, but it's usually because they want the best for them." On the other hand, it was sometimes because they were assholes. I was dying to know which it was in this case.

"I know I should be grateful that he cares," she said. "I mean, I have friends whose parents are barely present, much less intimately involved in every facet of their lives."

I examined her for a moment. There was something a

little funny about the statement. Something a little off, but I couldn't quite determine what it was. The word "intimately" suggested egregious transgressions, of course, but I didn't get the sense there was anything sexual involved here. "Tell me about your friends," I said. "We haven't spoken about them much."

"My friends?" She shrugged. "They're just, you know . . . kids."

"Who's your *best* friend?"

She almost looked as if she'd like to squirm, but she held herself perfectly still, pinned there by careful control and endless experience.

"I guess it would have to be Colleen. Colleen Anderson."

"Tell me about her."

"She's the president of the debate team. And a member of the math league."

"So you go to the same school?"

For a moment I thought emotion flared in her eyes, but then she laced her fingers in her lap and crossed her legs at the ankle.

"Well, she's going to MIT now."

"But you keep in touch?"

"As much as we can, but we're both extremely busy with school."

"How about extracurricular activities?"

"What?"

"Sports, school dances, that sort of thing. Do you make time for those?"

She pursed her lips. "I'm preparing for college," she said. "I've never felt it was particularly important to learn how to belly dance or French-kiss some guy with an IQ of a cashew."

The conversation went on like that for some time. She told me about her study schedule and her papers due and her appointments with professors from various colleges. By the time her fifty minutes were up I was exhausted. By the time she left my office I wanted to buy her a Popsicle and let her run through the sprinkler like every little girl should. Instead, I once again told her that I'd like to meet with her parents, reminded myself to contact her school about her progress, and accompanied her to the reception area, from which she efficiently escaped into the heat of the day.

To my surprise there was a little woman waiting in one of the chairs. She was small and quiet and as wizened as a raisin. I had seen her face once before. "You're Micky's grandmother, aren't you?"

She nodded. "I'd like to have a word with you, Ms. McMullen." Her voice seemed to scratch against my eardrums.

Dread filled my head. "Is something wrong?"

"Could we talk in private?" Her hands were dark and wrinkled, but looked firm and strong on the ivory curve of her cane. "I can wait if you have other obligations."

"No. This is fine," I said, and ushered her into my office while giving Shirley the "What the hell?" eye over my shoulder. She shrugged in return, but I noticed that she looked a little skittish. There aren't many things short of a full-scale air raid that can make a woman of Shirley's caliber skittish.

So I closed my office door gently behind me and followed the dwarfed little figure into the room. She stood in the exact center, turned, and faced me. "Why haven't you told my grandson to get custody of his boy?"

I managed not to stumble back a pace.

"Won't you have a seat?" I asked.

She thumped her cane on the floor. My carpet, though berber and overpriced, did little to muffle the noise. It dawned on me that there probably was very little that *would* muffle this woman.

"Did you hear me?" she asked.

I thought it was safe to assume that a turnip would have heard her, but I didn't voice that opinion. Back in Schaumburg I had eaten soap for less.

"Please," I said. "Sit so we can discuss it."

"There isn't a thing to discuss. I want you to tell Michael to do right by his son. It's as simple as that."

"Well . . ." I took a seat myself, hoping I would make it look so appealing that she would feel it necessary to follow suit. No go. Instead, I felt as tense as a fiddle string and she had the advantage of height. Not a simple task when you stand five foot naught in your Easy Spirits and weigh in at eighty-two pounds soaked in olive oil. "I'm afraid that's not quite how I do business," I said.

"Business!" She was scowling at me. I had always been of the opinion that Rivera had the corner on the scowling market but this little lady made him look as chipper as a beribboned flower girl. "Is that what you call this?"

"I'm a licensed psychologist, Mrs. Goldenstone. Here to listen to your grandson's problems. To help him work through any—"

"He raped that girl. He tell you that?"

I felt like I had been blindsided. According to Micky, no one knew about the heinous actions of his youth. No one besides himself and his victim.

"My sessions with Micky are confidential."

She stared at me a second, then nodded stiffly. "He tell you about that gal on the subway, too?"

I felt every fiber tighten. "Listen, Mrs. Goldenstone, I'd be happy to schedule an appointment for you and Micky to come in together so that we can have adequate time to discuss—"

"I didn't think so," she said, and jabbed her cane at me. It was the first time since an octogenarian had tried to kill me that I realized what an effective weapon a cane could make. "They were on the midnight train. There was a gal riding alone when three young men come up to her. They were members of the Crips. Michael knew that. He's not naïve. Not with his upbringing. But he protected the girl. She wasn't hurt."

We stared at each other.

"He didn't tell me that," I said.

"He didn't tell anyone. Just told the doctors in the emergency room that he'd gotten in a fight with an old friend. I talked to the girl herself."

"He ended up in the ER?"

"That's what happens when you get shot twice through the rib cage."

I felt myself pale. "When was this?"

"Two months ago."

So I had been seeing him. And I hadn't had a clue.

"I'm sorry he was wounded, but I don't see what this has to do with—"

She raised her chin, scrawny neck stretched. "You know why he did it?"

I struggled with a couple dozen emotions. First of all, I hate to be interrupted and so far I hadn't completed a single sentence since Grams had entered my office. Second,

I felt oddly betrayed that Micky hadn't shared the truth with me. Which was not only unprofessional, but just dumb-ass stupid. Micky was a client, not a boyfriend.

"I would guess it was partly to assuage the guilt he's been carrying around ever since Kaneasha," I said.

She stared at me for a prolonged moment, then, "What else?"

"He didn't want anyone else to suffer as she had?"

"What else?"

"Knowing Micky as I do I would guess he felt some empathy for the young men and didn't want them to have to carry the shame of such a hideous crime."

Her eyes were shining. I didn't know what that meant. But I found, oddly enough, that I hoped it was approval. "And?" she asked, pursing her lips.

"And sometimes he doesn't care if he dies; he believes the world would be a better place without him."

Our gazes held steady and then she nodded slowly.

"There isn't anyone who will care for that boy better than my grandson," she said.

"Micky has some issues to work out."

Her brows lowered. "You know someone who doesn't?"

Good point. Sound reasoning. "Perhaps not," I said. "But now there's the Jackson issue to exacerbate the already existing problems."

"The boy needs a daddy," she said.

"I daresay he does—" I began, but she spoke again.

"But not so much as Michael needs the boy."

Despite my Ph.D., I had never thought of it quite like that. "I'm not sure what you want me to do."

"I want you to quit tiptoeing around the issue and tell him to take the child in."

"It's not that simple. There are laws and—"

"Don't you worry about that. If my Michael believes it's the right thing, he'll do what it takes to make it happen. He's just not convinced he should move forward."

"With cases such as this there is often an overwhelming amount of guilt that makes it difficult for the client—"

She stomped her cane again. "You tell him to quit feeling guilty. You tell him he's got no more time to be selfish."

"Selfish? I don't think it's—"

"What do you call it when you think about yourself more than others?"

"Well . . ."

"He admires you," she said, and narrowed her bird-bright eyes at me. "He likes you."

"Well, I—"

"You tell him to take the boy," she said, and strode toward the door. In a moment she was gone.

I followed her slowly from my office. Shirley was standing behind her desk, eyes rimmed with white by the time I got there.

"You okay?" she asked, turning toward me like a large automaton.

"I'm not sure," I said. "I think so."

"She didn't wrestle you to the floor or nothing?"

"We kept it to verbal combat."

She nodded. "Good thing you can talk. She was Mr. Goldenstone's grams, huh?"

I completely forgot to deny. I didn't even hedge. "Yes."

"She reminds me of my ex's mother."

"Was she made of steel wool, too?"

"Razor wire. She said if I left Harry I'd be haunted till the day I die."

"Are you?"

"Not sure, I ain't dead yet. What you gonna do?"

I stared after Mrs. Goldenstone, blinked once, and tried to bring myself back to normal. "What have you got in that drawer?"

"What you think I got?"

I closed my eyes for a moment and sharpened my olfactory nerves. "Two chocolate chip cookies and some Rice Krispie bars."

"I think you're losing your edge. It's shortbread and brownies," she said.

"I love you more than life," I said.

"Get the milk," she said. "We've got ten minutes till your next appointment and I can see you need fortifying."

By the time I left the office I felt as if I'd been filleted and deep-fried. I had seen seven clients in eleven hours. In between I had taken care of paperwork and made some phone calls. I'd asked Shirley to contact Emily's parents to ask them to come to the office for a meeting, but as it turned out, the phone number was disconnected. So I dashed off another email to Emily's school therapist, telling of my progress and asking for the proper phone number. Then I had sat alone and spent a few minutes reevaluating Laney's letters.

Nothing mind-bending jumped into my head.

It was dark when I reached home. But at least my security light was on, making me feel somewhat . . . secure.

Solberg's Porsche was conspicuously absent. For a moment I was giddy with the thought that I might have Laney to myself, but then I remembered they were spending the night visiting wineries with his parents. She wouldn't be home until the following day, but when I stepped into the foyer the house felt funny. Occupied.

A noise rustled from the back of the house. It almost sounded like a door closing.

"Harley?" I called.

He didn't come wiggling out to greet me.

"Hello?"

No one answered me. The hair was standing up on the nape of my neck. I backed toward the door, and then I heard Harlequin whimper.

26

Cats, you can't train 'em and you can't eat 'em.

—Harlequin

*E*very sensible instinct in me told me to run for my car, to duck and cover, to escape, but the Mace was dangling from my key ring, and damnit, I love that stupid-ass drooly dog.

"Who's there?" My voice warbled a little on the high notes. "I've called the police," I said, and stepped into the living room. It was entirely trashed. All of my worldly possessions were strewn about the space. My hands were shaking in earnest now. I was trying to punch in 911 as I spoke, but it's difficult when you're trembling like a maraca. My index finger skittered off the nine and then something crashed. The phone dropped from my hand as I screamed and jerked toward the right. My Mace was, miraculously, at the ready. But Harley was already scooting back behind the couch, scared by the lamp he'd just broken and my best slasher-film shriek.

I stood frozen for several seconds, felt the emptiness of the house throb around me like a living pulse, and hurried to the couch. One end had been pulled away from the wall, cushions scattered. Harlequin, it seemed, had had the good sense to wedge his big body behind it.

Mace still in hand, I dropped to my knees and crooned his name. He remained as he was, in a full-body shake, and refused to come out. So finally I rose on my own shaky legs and went to the other end of the couch. Pulling it away from the wall, I called to him. He looked up at me with droopy eyes, then crawled forward, belly on the floor, nails spread as he dragged himself forward.

I held my breath as I skimmed him for blood, but there was none that I could see. Creeping forward, he plopped his trembling head onto my knees and closed his eyes with a sigh. I ran my hand along his bony head and down his back. There was a swelling over his ribs. He whimpered when I touched it.

Something banged. I jerked around, and dropped the Mace just as Rivera lurched into the room, Glock ready.

"Get out!" he ordered.

"Harlequin's—"

"Take him with you."

Anger was beginning to overtake the terror in my system, and I considered arguing, but if truth be told, I kind of wanted to get the hell out of Dodge.

Retrieving my Mace, I rose to my feet and called Harley as I headed toward the door. He glanced longingly back at

the space between the couch and the wall but slunk dutifully after me.

We were in the Saturn in a matter of seconds, doors
locked. Harley turned around in the passenger seat, then
draped himself across the emergency brake to lay his head
in my lap. I stroked his ears and stared at the front door of
my house as if it might implode at any given second. A few
minutes had passed when an unmarked cop car pulled up
to the curb. Two men got out carrying bags that looked
like souped-up attaché cases.

I remained where I was, waiting for the tremors to stop.
After a couple of lifetimes, the plainclothes guys exited,
leaving Rivera alone in the doorway. He looked pissed as
hell.

I swallowed my fear, gave Harley a kiss on the snout,
and eased out from under him. He gazed after me for a
moment, then dropped his head back down and closed
his eyes.

Rivera watched me approach as if I were the enemy.
"You okay?" he asked.

Although I dreaded seeing the mess left behind, I was
strangely compelled to do so and stepped past Rivera to
view the chaos.

It was as bad as I remembered.

"It was a burglary, right?" he asked.

I gazed up at him. There may have been a bit of "Are
you kidding?" in my eyes.

"How messy do you think I am?" I asked.

"I just wanted to make sure I didn't make them dust for
prints for no reason. Did you notice anything missing?" he
asked.

"I didn't . . ." I turned in a circle, feeling disoriented. "I haven't . . . I don't . . ." And suddenly the world seemed to be spinning around me.

"Sit down," he said, and lifting a cushion from the floor, pushed me onto the couch. He sat down, too, but didn't touch me. "Breathe."

I nodded. The movement didn't do my equilibrium any good, but in a few seconds I was feeling a little steadier.

"How's Harley?" he asked.

I felt my mouth twitch. "There's a bruise over his ribs, like he's been kicked." I could barely get the words out. I think I heard him swear, but it was hard to be certain. I was already crying.

He pulled me roughly into his arms. "Jesus, woman, you scared the hell out of me." He stroked my hair. "I was on your walkway when I heard you scream, and I thought . . ." He paused, muscles tight against mine.

"I'm okay," I said.

"Are you sure?" He pushed me out to arm's length and searched my face.

I sniffled pitifully, but managed a nod.

He pushed the hair away from my face and stared into my eyes. I stared back. He stroked a tear away with his thumb, smearing it across my cheek. "They were gone when you got here?"

I nodded. "I think so," I said. My voice sounded iffy.

A muscle twitched in his jaw, as if he was fighting a couple dozen conflicting emotions.

"What about your alarm system?"

Guilt swarmed through me immediately. Sometimes I'm a little less cognizant of things than I should be. "What about it?" I asked.

That muscle twitched again. "Did you have it on?"

"I don't . . ." I began, then realized something wonderful. "I wasn't the last one out of the house."

"Solberg?"

I had no way of knowing, of course, but he was so easy to blame. "Probably," I said, and realized suddenly that if circumstances were different Laney could have been here alone. "Oh God," I said. "What if Elaine—"

"Shh," he said, and wiped away another tear. It felt hot against my skin. He kissed its trail. "Everything's fine."

And it did feel fine. I blinked wet lashes at the hot rush of feelings. "Poor Harlequin," I said, and felt another tear swell and flood the breach.

He smeared that one away, too, and followed it with another kiss. "He's tough."

I shook my head. "He just acts tough cuz he doesn't want anyone to know the truth," I said, and felt my mouth tremble. "He's really very sensitive. People just don't understand . . ."

He kissed the corner of my mouth. Feelings raced through me like agitated chipmunks.

"I'm just glad you weren't here," he said.

"But he was all alone. Sometimes he feels like there's no one in the whole world for . . ." I hiccuped once.

He tugged my legs over his, pulling me against his chest. Our faces were inches apart now.

"There's someone," he said, and stared into my eyes.

I stared back, breathless. "Who?"

"Me," he said, and kissed my lips with feathery lightness.

"You care about . . ." I blinked. My lashes felt heavy. My mind soggy. "Harlequin?"

"More than you know," he said, and kissed the point of my chin.

"Yeah?"

"More than I should," he said.

"Why?" I asked.

"You should rest," he said. "Do you mind if I take this off?" he asked, touching my jacket.

I shook my head. "Why shouldn't you like him so well?" I asked.

His fingers made quick work of the buttons. "It's distracting," he said, and lifted his eyes slowly to my face. They looked kind of smoky.

"How so?"

His fingers played up the front of my sleeveless silk blouse. "I'm constantly worrying about him." The tips of his fingers brushed the skin exposed in the V of my shirt.

"Yeah?"

He kissed me there. I tried to stifle a sigh, but I may have failed. "He's got to be more careful," he said.

"Maybe he's got a lot on his mind."

He pushed my collar aside a little and kissed my neck. "What's he thinking about?"

I canted my head to the left. "Laney's wedding. I'm just not . . . *he's* not ready for her to get married."

"You're right. He *is* sensitive."

I considered nodding, but didn't want to interfere with the magic he was working on my neck.

"She's Brainy Laney Butterfield with a big-ass wedding at the Pavilion, which is all wrong for her, by the way. And she's marrying the Geekster. The Geekster! If he's the best *she* can find . . ." I let my voice trail off.

He pulled away a couple of inches and found my eyes with his. "Then what hope is there for you?"

"For Harlequin," I corrected, and he grinned.

The expression tweaked something in my gut. Maybe that's why I didn't immediately notice that he had loosed the top button of my blouse. But when he tipped his head and kissed the tight valley between my boobs, I was pretty much aware.

In fact, I may have gasped.

"I think there are good things in store," he said.

I seemed to be gripping the hair at the back of his head with my right hand. Not sure how that had happened. "Yeah?" I rasped.

His eyes were steaming. Swear to God. "Yeah," he said.

"When?"

"How about now?" he asked.

I felt every hormone in my body do the rain dance. They would have done the fertility dance, but they couldn't remember the steps.

He was rising to his feet, me in his arms.

"Do you hear a phone?" I asked.

"No."

"Do you have yours with you?"

"You want me to call Harlequin?"

"I want you to flush it down the toilet," I said.

He chuckled. The sound sent a little thrill of excitement screaming from my ears to my belly button.

"Maybe we could just ignore it."

"Hasn't happened in the past."

"You weren't crying in the past," he said, and stepped toward the bedroom.

"Seriously?" I said. "That's all it would have taken? A few tears?"

"What can I say? I'm a sucker for drippy women."

The path to my bedroom had never been so long. I could feel every breath that left my body.

"Had I known that, I could have faked a flood."

He set me on the bed. It creaked a little beneath my weight, but only sighed at his. "You're not going to have to fake anything," he said, and kissed me.

27

A man's world? Are you shitting me? It hasn't been a man's world since Eve showed up naked.

—Jack Rivera, post-coital

The world spun to a slow halt while Rivera and I kissed.

"You sure you don't hear a phone?" I asked when he pulled away. There must be a phone. There was always a phone.

"Not ringing," he said, and pulling his cell from his pocket, held it up for inspection. "Where's yours?"

"I think I dropped it when the lamp broke."

"I'll take care of them," he said, and headed into the living room. In a moment he was back, sans phones.

"They're gone?"

"Under the sofa cushions."

"I must be either dead or dreaming," I said.

"You're not dead," he said, approaching the bed, then slowly kissed me again.

I reached up and undid his shirt. His chest was smooth and hard and pretty.

"Maybe I'm in heaven," I said, gazing up at it.

"The rest of me is even better," he said.

"Really?"

"Want to see?"

"More than anything," I said, and he stood up and undid his jeans. In a minute he was naked.

I sat there staring and hoping I wouldn't burst into tears again.

"You okay?" he asked. He looked ungodly comfortable in all his naked glory.

"I love life," I said.

"You were just burglarized."

"Don't ruin the dream," I said.

He chuckled, then reached for my hand and pulled me to my feet. "You can't sleep fully clothed."

I shook my head. "That would be wrong."

His fingers made quick work of my buttons. Clever fingers. In a moment I was standing in nothing but my underwear and huaraches.

I moved to kick off the shoes, but he stopped me. "My job," he said, and kissed my left breast.

My heart did a funky little jungle beat in my chest. "You want to take my shoes off?"

"Eventually," he said, and kissed the other breast.

I grabbed the bedpost to keep the world from spinning into outer space, but then he cupped my boobs together in both hands. I made a little sound in my throat that even *I* didn't recognize, but he seemed too busy to acknowledge the feelings behind it. In fact, he was working his way down my midline.

I tightened my grip on the bed knob. He kissed my belly button, then dipped his tongue inside. I screamed like a virgin and he snagged my panties with his index finger, dragging them down a half an inch.

"Jesus, woman," he breathed. "What are you going to be like when we get to the good stuff?"

"There's more?" I rasped.

"I'll think of something," he said, and chuckled as he lowered himself farther. I spread my legs, teetering on my heels and dropping my head back.

"Think fast," I rasped, and he kissed me where I was wet and hot and achy.

Every muscle in my body spasmed and suddenly I tilted sideways. It took me a moment to realize the bed knob had come loose in my hand. Another to realize he was holding me upright, hands on my waist, body hard as marble against mine.

"You okay?"

I was breathing hard. "I think so."

"You keep making so much noise you're going to wake yourself up."

"There's duct tape in the kitchen."

He chuckled and wrapped his hand around mine, which was still wrapped around the bed knob. Kissing my wrist, he eased my fingers open and relieved me of the metal sphere. Then he sucked my pinky into his mouth.

My body quaked. He kissed the palm of my hand. I groaned.

"Chrissy."

I could barely open my eyes.

"Don't you dare come without me," he said.

"If I were you I wouldn't dillydally." My voice was a little throaty. A little raspy. Kind of gritty.

He pressed up against me. He was throbbing. Truly, there is nothing in the world I like more than throbbing. He slipped his hands into my panties, squeezing my buttocks. "I thought women liked it slow," he said.

"Don't be stupid," I said. I felt as if I were having an out-of-body experience, which, come to think of it, would have made me bitchin' mad. I mean, if there was ever a time I wanted to be in my body, this was it.

"Trying not to be," he said. "Take this."

It took me a moment to realize he was holding a condom. I have no idea where he'd been keeping it.

"Don't dally," he reminded me.

I tore the foil away with my teeth. There was a moment of panic on my part when I feared I had forgotten how to apply the thing, but finally he was sheathed and raring to go.

"Ready?" he said.

"If I were any more ready you'd be superfluous."

"Never," he said.

"Don't be so sure. François is one sweet-talking—" I began, but suddenly he lifted me up and pushed into me in one smooth glide.

The earth moved. I shrieked. He groaned. In approximately thirty-two seconds, it was over. I was panting like a bulldog, sweaty as hell, and happy as a songbird.

It took several minutes before either of us could talk, and when he did his voice was gruff. "Sorry," he said.

I still couldn't think straight, but I was cognizant

enough to realize I was one lucky little nuthatch. "For being as big as a frickin' train?" I asked.

"I'm usually . . . I didn't mean to go so fast. You're just so . . ." He paused to breathe.

"Just so what?"

He stared into my eyes. "Just so fucking sexy you make me crazy."

"You already got my clothes off, Rivera. No need for sweet talk."

He stared at me, eyes like lasers. "You don't think this is over, do you?"

He was looking at me like I was a mocha turtle sundae. The desire in his eyes made my caramel simmer.

I skimmed my gaze down his body, and just past his navel saw that this was definitely not over.

"I hope you've rested up," he said, and kissed me again.

By midnight we had moved to the floor. By 1:17 we had found the bed.

Dehydration pushed us into the kitchen. At 5:05, I realized I had been entirely wrong about there being enough room on the counter for two.

Panting, Rivera rolled onto his back. I pulled a bag of grapes out from under his left shoulder, considered taking some nutrition, and decided I didn't have the strength.

"I've got to get home," he said.

"Now?"

"Five hours ago," he said, and sitting up, swung his feet to the floor. The scenery from behind was almost as stimulating as the frontal view.

I found the strength to run my hand down his back. He looked over his shoulder, eyes smoldering. "Don't get me started."

"You haven't even started yet?" I asked, and sat on the edge of the counter. My clothes were long gone. All that remained was one shoe. I have no idea how that had survived.

He kissed me, then pulled away and growled. "I have to be at work in three hours."

"You could sleep here."

"Maybe if you were dressed in full armor and put a padlock on your chastity belt."

"Would a bike chain work?" I asked, but he was already headed for the bedroom and his long-lost clothes. His buttocks bunched and gathered on every step. I slipped off the lone sandal and followed

By the time I reached the bedroom, he was pulling his jeans over bare skin. The sight did something lascivious to my nether regions.

"Don't look at me like that."

"Like what?"

"Like you could do it again."

"Do what?" I asked, and dangled the huarache from two fingers.

He stood there staring at me, body tense. Then he swore and kissed me with enough heat to bake a vase. "Come with me," he said.

"To your house?" I'm not sure why I was surprised. It wasn't as if I hadn't been there before, but I had never stayed the night . . . or the morning . . . as the situation happened to be.

"You can't stay here alone."

I glanced around. As it turns out, I had almost forgotten the burglary. "I have to get this cleaned up."

He kissed me again. "Tomorrow."

"It *is* tomorrow," I said.

"Don't be stubborn, McMullen . . ." he began. The edgy, bossy tone was already sneaking back into his voice, and for a moment I felt my hackles rise, but then I remembered that he was buck naked under his jeans and somehow that made everything better.

"I'll lock the door and arm the system the second you leave," I promised.

"You think I'm nuts? I can't leave you here alone."

"So you're staying?" I asked. "Great," I said, and turning, sauntered away. I could feel his gaze sear my backside. "I'll get some clean sheets. I'm sure you'll get plenty of sleep before you have to give one hundred percent to the LAPD."

He answered with a growl. I turned, all innocence, shoe still dangling from my fingertips. His brows were lowered, and I think I saw his jeans shift a little at the crotch. I raised my gaze slowly to his. A muscle danced in his jaw. I believe he may have been realizing we had just had sex about forty-two times and that forty-three might kill him.

"You'll lock your door?" he asked.

"Of course."

"And arm your system."

"I'm not stupid."

"If something happens to you I'll never forgive you."

I laughed. The world looked surprisingly rosy on zilch sleep and eight hours of mind-blowing sex. "I'll keep that in mind. Go home."

"You'll keep your phone on?"

"The landline and the cell."

"Is it fully charged?"

"Absolutely."

"You don't know that."

I laughed. Rosy? The world looked absolutely giddy. "I'll be fine, Rivera. I promise."

He blew out a hard breath. "Keep Harley—" he began, then glanced around. "Where *is* Harley?"

The truth hit me in a rush. "Oh shit! I—"

"We forgot him in the car," he said, but I was already heading toward the door, flooded with guilt.

"You go out like that, McMullen, and I'll never be able to sleep again."

I turned, embarrassed for the first time by my lack of clothing. I had honestly forgotten.

"I'll do a perimeter check around your house," he said. "Then I'll bring him in."

"I can—"

"You get some clothes on before my hard-on becomes permanent."

"That's not physically possible," I said, and glancing to the left, spied a grape that had gone AWOL sometime before midnight. Turning, I bent to retrieve it. I could feel his gaze follow me like a spotlight.

"Jesus," he said, and turned away. In a moment I was alone.

I managed to stifle my laughter, but my mood was positively euphoric. By the time he returned I had found a robe. I dropped to my knees as Harlequin loped up to me, all wiggles and squirms.

I crooned at him a little, engaging in the kind of baby

talk that makes me sick when other people do it. He sat down on my bare foot and licked my sleeve.

"I guess he doesn't hold it against us," I said.

"He was asleep in the backseat," Rivera said. "Twitching like a Taser victim and drooling on his paws."

"Well . . ." I rose to my feet, feeling strangely uncomfortable suddenly. I cleared my throat. "Thanks for . . ." I shrugged. "Everything."

"Anytime."

"Really?" My face felt warm. His eyes looked hot.

"I might need a few hours to hydrate," he said.

"I'm sorry it got so late."

His eyes said something I couldn't quite read. "I'll call you when I get to work," he said.

"I'll be fine," I said, and then he kissed me.

"You're a hell of a lot better than fine," he said, and turned away.

I planned to go to bed immediately, but Harley looked hungry, so I fed him a half a bag of dog food, then rummaged in the fridge for something for myself. There were two onions trying to grow their way to freedom, leftovers from ten days ago, three eggs, and a half a carton of soy milk.

It seemed like a sign from God. I mean, my chocolate chip cookie recipe called for three eggs. In five minutes I was adding the chips to the batter and humming.

It was then that I heard a sound at the front door. For a moment my breath caught in my throat, but then Laney spoke. Her footsteps rushed down the hall.

"Mac! Mac!"

"In here."

She appeared in the doorway of the kitchen like a frantic doe. "What happened?"

I felt the blush rise to my cheeks. "Nothing. Why?"

"Nothing! I've been trying to call you since nine o'clock last night."

"Oh! I'm sorry. I must have put my phone . . ." I didn't let my gaze skim to the pile of cushions under which Rivera had hidden it. ". . . on vibrate. Where's Solberg?"

"I left him at the inn with his parents. You—" She stopped, scowled. "Are you baking cookies?"

"Yeah. Well, making dough." My cookies rarely see the inside of an oven. Why waste the electricity when dough is the ambrosia of the gods? I gave the ambrosia a good stir. "I—"

"Are you making cookies at six in the morning after you've been burglarized?"

"Oh." Maybe it was a little surprising that I had forgotten that little tidbit of information. "I just . . . I was kind of . . ."

She gave me a narrow, assessing glance. "When did Rivera leave?"

"What?"

"Rivera." It was the only word she repeated.

The blush had moved down to my clavicle. "What makes you think—"

"You're humming."

"Am not."

" 'Feliz Navidad.' "

"I am not."

She stared at me a minute longer. "He got naked!" she said.

I stirred the dough again. "Did not," I said, but she had seated herself by the table. I could feel her staring at me.

"Tell me about it."

"Listen, Laney, I don't know what you think happened, but—"

"Was he worth the irritation?"

I opened my mouth to deny everything, but I was dying to tell her. "Holy cow!" I said, and launched into the tale.

28

Sex is all right, but it's damned hard to compete with a fresh-brewed cup of coffee.

> —Grandma Brady, whose
> memory might be slipping
> a little

I saw two clients the next morning, an unhappy sex addict and a happy asexual guy who was sure he should be miserable.

Rivera called that afternoon. I knew I should have been tired, but it was holiday heaven in my head. I was humming "Welcome Christmas" by the Whoville Whos when Shirley buzzed to say Rivera was on line one.

"How you doing?" he asked, voice all low and rumbly in that way that makes my brain cells go limp.

"Quite well," I said, and smiled as I settled back in my chair. "How about you?"

"I can't get you out of my mind."

"The city of Los Angeles deserves your full attention."

"Then you shouldn't sit on the counter wearing nothing but a shoe."

I laughed. The sound was funny. Like a sex machine running on all cylinders. We bantered a little, then said our good-byes.

By the time I pulled up to my curb that evening, the high had worn off a little. When I saw the interior of my house I stopped and blinked. It was clean like it had never been clean before. As I stepped into the living room, I realized that even the air sparkled.

"Laney?" I said.

She stepped out of the kitchen wearing an apron over her cutoffs and looking like June Cleaver with good hair.

"You're home early," she said.

"Last client didn't show. I thought you had meetings all day."

"I canceled them. Did you know you have two vacuum cleaners?"

"Weren't you supposed to meet with . . ." I searched my memory banks for the name she had given me but it was gone. "God or somebody?"

"My director. I told her the house was messy and I couldn't make it."

"Are you crazy?"

"Your upstairs carpet is blue."

"You blew off your director to clean my—" I paused. "Blue?"

"Who knew, huh?"

"It's always been brown."

"I rented a steam cleaner."

"Laney," I said, shielding my eyes from the glare of the counter and dropping my purse onto a chair. "You didn't have to clean all this."

"I know, but the Department of Health can be so nasty if they get involved."

I made a face.

She laughed. "My natural-health recipe box is missing."

"Are you serious? The rosewood one that Foxy made for you?"

"Yup."

"With the Green Goo recipe?"

"Yes."

"And the Brain Brightener recipe?"

"Maybe they realized they've been killing themselves with their high-sucrose diet and decided to make a change."

"A health-conscious burglar?"

She shrugged, letting that unlikely delusion shatter. "Or maybe they were hoping for electronics and settled for an etched wood box."

"You think they wanted my computer?"

"Apparently not after they saw it," she said. "Because it's still here."

"Well, at least we know the guy was value-conscious." I plopped down in the nearest chair. "Are you okay?"

"Sure. I'm so sorry we forgot to arm your security system."

I shrugged. "I'm sorry about your recipes."

"Really?"

"No," I said, and suppressed a shudder at the memory of green potable slop. "But I'm sorry I'm not sorry."

She sighed. "I think I remember most of the recipes. I'll miss my jean jacket more."

"They took your jacket, too?"

"It's gone."

"Maybe you forgot it somewhere."

She shook her head. "I shoved it into my bag on the way home from the flower shop the other night. It's not there."

"Weird," I said.

Our gazes met. Hers was atypically solemn. "I'm sorry I got you into this, Mac."

I shook my head. "There's no reason to assume this has anything to do with you."

"They only took two items," she said. "They're both mine."

"You have better stuff than I do. Besides, we don't know they didn't take more. It could take weeks before we realize what's missing."

"Besides the bushel of dirt that had been ground into your carpet."

"And the mushrooms that were growing beside the toilet. You didn't get rid of those, did you?"

She smiled, but the expression was tight.

"You think this has something to do with the letters," I said.

She shrugged. Her brows dipped toward her evergreen eyes. "How many crazies can be out there?"

"This *is* L.A. Even you can't count that high."

"I should move out."

"You planning to bail on me when things get dicey?"

She caught my eye. "I'm serious."

"I am, too. Do you have any idea how many houses are randomly burglarized in L.A. each year?"

"I can't count that high?"

"That's right," I said. "And you hardly live in any of them."

"They didn't take your stereo."

"Maybe they didn't need a twenty-year-old turntable."

"You said they dusted for prints?"

"So I'm told."

"Did they find anything?"

"I don't know yet."

She nodded, then silently scrunched up her face and covered it with her palm.

"Laney?" I said, moving toward her.

She wiped her nose with the back of her hand and waved me away. "I know. I think I'm losing my mind."

"What's wrong?"

"Nothing. Everything. I don't know." She gave me a watery glance. "I just . . . there's so much. I should be running lines for the Gabriel movie. And that's on top of the wedding. Flowers, music, seating. Did I tell you the swans are molting?"

Swans? I gave her a look. "Why are you worried about fowl?"

"Jeen's mom thought we should have swans."

"Are you marrying his mom, too?"

"I don't know. I can't remember. I just . . . I just want to be married."

I stifled my wince and didn't mention the fact that evidence *was*, in fact, quite good that she may have lost her mind if that was the case. "To Solberg, right?"

She gave me a look.

"Right," I said. "Of course."

"But I want to make Jeen happy."

"Happy!" I said, and swallowed a chuckle. "You're the Amazon Queen. You can't help but make him happy."

"That's just the thing. I'm *not* the Amazon Queen, Mac. I'm not any of the things people think I am."

"Solberg's not people," I said. She gave me a scowl, so I hurried on. "Of course you're not some half-naked jungle girl, Elaine. You're better than that. You're Brainy Laney Butterfield, the smartest, sweetest, most beautiful woman in the world. I'm sure Solberg would be tickled pink if you stood up in front of a justice of the peace wearing a gunnysack and eating a radish."

"I don't like radishes," she said, and pressed her knuckles against her mouth.

"Laney!" I said, and took her hand. "What is it?"

"My life's a mess. And now I've made your life a mess, too."

"What are you talking about? My life has always been a mess."

"No, it—"

"Oh, don't even lie!" I said. "My upstairs carpet is *blue. Blue!*"

She laughed a little and I smiled, feeling better. "You're getting married soon," I said. "For better or worse. Swans or no swans."

She nodded, then winced a little. "But what about you?"

I looked at her askance. "What about me what?"

"We've been a pair for so long. And I always thought you'd get married first."

"Seriously?"

"Yeah. I mean, I thought you'd find the right guy and

live happily ever after so I wouldn't have to worry about you."

"Happily ever—"

"Well, you know, grouchily ever after, or whatever. I just thought you'd be . . . settled."

"Settled."

"And now not only are you unsettled, you've got some nut job breaking into your cute little house."

I glanced around. "It is kind of cute, isn't it? When you can see the floor. Blue," I mused.

"Get over it."

I shook my head. "Are you saying you're worried about me?"

"Of course I'm worried about you." Tears welled in her eyes again. "You're the best person I know."

I stared at her an instant, then glanced over my shoulder before turning back to her. "Me?"

"You know it's true."

"Are you drunk?"

"No. I . . . Oh crap," she said, and rubbed her eyes with her right hand. It was the harshest language I had heard exit Laney's mouth in years. "And now I can't even tell when you're kidding."

"You're just tired. Lots of people don't think I'm funny when they're tired."

"Or any other time.

"I've hired you a bodyguard."

It took a moment for me to realize what she said, at which time I canted my head and asked for clarification.

"I can't stand knowing you're in danger, Mac. I can't. I mean, I have a thousand things going on in my head and I can't—"

"You hired a bodyguard?"

She took a deep, calming breath. "Yes."

"For me."

"Yes."

"When you're the star."

"I'm not a star, Mac. I'm just a . . . Just a woman on my fourteenth minute of fame."

"Laney, you're one in a million. You've been a star since the day you were born. Since the second you were conceived. Since—"

"Please accept a bodyguard."

I stood there staring at her, mouth open. "I had sex for the first time in years," I said.

"I realize—"

I held up my hand. "In fact, I had sex for the first, second, third, fourth, and fifth time in years. You think I want that to stop now?"

"He doesn't have to accompany you into the bedroom."

"Did I say we did it in the bedroom?"

She stared at me for a minute, then, "Ick?" she said.

"I hope you used some heavy-duty cleaner on the kitchen counter."

"Baking soda," she said. "It's environmentally friendly."

"You might want to dine in your room from now on, then," I said, and she laughed. I squeezed her hand. "I don't want a bodyguard, Laney."

"I ordered a really cute one."

"Is that the word you used when you called the agency?"

"Yes. I said I wanted a cute buff one."

"Seriously?"

"I really am losing my mind, aren't I?"

"It's possible."

She blew out her breath. "That's unfortunate. I'm kind of famous, you know."

"So I've heard."

She sighed. "What are we going to do?"

I stared at her. "We're going to figure out who broke into my cute little house."

"Any ideas how?"

"We're going to use our brains."

"Wow," she said.

29

Love your enemies. In case your friends turn out to be
dumb shits.

—*Donald Archer, whose*
friends are kind of . . .

We went through every piece of mail she had, evaluated
every word, considered every comma. By four in the
morning I felt as if my eyes had been sandblasted and my
mind fried in extra-virgin olive oil.

I flopped back onto Laney's bed and covered my face
with my hand. "I hate people. I literally cannot tell you
how much I hate people."

"How quickly the bliss of sex fades."

"Not like chocolate," I said.

"That stuff'll stay on your hips forever. Unless you
drink enough of my Cellulite Chaser."

"Oh, dear God," I said, and covered my head with
a pillow. "Please, please, please don't make me think

about your all-natural, made-from-clay-and-nothing-else recipes that . . ." I paused, removed the pillow, stared at her.

"What?" Her expression had gone serious, expectant.

"The letters . . ." I picked up the first one, skimmed it rapidly. " 'Natural,' " I said and retrieved the next. " 'God given.' " The next. " 'Earthy. True.' "

"He's not religious," she said, glancing down at the nearest missive. "He's a naturalist."

"And now your Green Goo recipe has disappeared."

She was frowning.

"Who knew about it?"

"No one," she said. "Foxy swore me to secrecy when she gave it to me years ago."

"So only your hairdresser knows."

"Not Nadine," she said. "She's producing her own products. Hopes to start a natural—" Her words stumbled to a halt.

After my meeting with Morab the sex slave, and Senator Rivera the sex *addict*, I had almost forgotten that I'd met Nadine. "Has she asked for your recipe?"

"Not outright."

"But you think she'd like to?"

Laney looked unhappy. "She's a good person. Started the condors program."

"Which you've donated to," I guessed.

She shrugged, noncommittal. "But I still get the idea she thinks I should . . ." Her words trailed off again. "I mean, I thought we were friends."

The room went silent.

"Is it her?" I asked into the quiet.

She said nothing for several seconds, then glanced away. "Maybe."

I took a deep breath, feeling down to my soul that we'd found our culprit. "This isn't something you should feel guilty about," I said.

"I know," she said.

"But you do."

"It's just that I've . . ." She paused and shrugged.

"Been so lucky."

"Blessed, really."

"It's not your fault that Nadine didn't make it big."

She stared at nothing, seeming to search for some way to believe she was wrong. But finally she closed her eyes and gave up. "What do we do now?"

"I suppose we should ask the police to question her," I said. "Or I could—"

She jerked toward me. "You're going to stay out of this, Mac."

"I know. I was just wondering who to call. I don't know whose jurisdiction it would be. It might turn into a pissing contest."

"Pissing contest or not, this is their job. Not yours."

"I know."

She stared at me a moment, then nodded. "Maybe we call Rivera and let him figure it out."

"At four in the morning?"

"Probably not."

"First thing when I wake up."

"You promise?"

"Of course I promise."

She narrowed her eyes.

"What do you think? That I *want* to get involved with another crazed lunatic?"

She paused. "Sometimes I wonder."

"Are you kidding? In the past few years I've been attacked by a tight end, a psychiatrist, an investor, my brother's *friend,* an octogenarian, and a cuckolded father. You think I want more of that?"

She was still staring at me. "Exciting, isn't it?"

"Listen, Brainy Laney Butterfield, my life may not be as wildly stimulating as yours but that doesn't mean I feel a burning need to stick my nose into situations that are likely to get me . . ." I paused, thinking. "Holy shit," I said, realizing the truth. "I feel a burning need to stick my nose into situations that are likely to get me killed."

"I know."

"Why?"

She shrugged. "You're the shrink."

"Maybe we can blame it on potty training."

"Okay."

"Maybe it's . . . It's probably my mother. Did you know she—"

"Yes."

"What?"

"I know everything about her. But I don't care what it is."

I looked at her, alarmed by the tone of her voice. And sure enough, she had tears in her eyes again.

"I just want to make it stop," she said. "Put it in the hands of the police."

Something in me resisted the idea. But I fought it down. "Okay," I said, shaken by the realization of my own neuroses. I was pretty damned sure licensed psychologists were not supposed to be neurotic.

She stared at me, then nodded. "I love you, Mac."

"I know. It's one of the great wonders of the world."

"It's a wonder you put up with me."

"You're joking, right?" Through the years Laney had saved my ass in more situations than I can count. I owed her everything, including my ass.

"Not so much," she said.

"You need sleep more than I do," I said, and reached for her hand. She gave it. I hoisted all twelve pounds of her to her feet. "Go to bed," I said, and she wobbled off to brush her teeth.

$\mathcal{M}$y brain was as fuzzy as a Georgia peach when I called Rivera first thing in the morning. He contacted the necessary people, and despite the fact that I stayed out of the way entirely (or perhaps *because of*) things happened quickly after that.

I was in a session with a narcissistic who had no apparent reason for his condition when the phone rang. Shirley answered it and subsequently informed me that I should call Rivera. The lieutenant informed me that the cops had gone to Nadine Gruber's house. When they had informed *her* of their suspicions about the letters, she had immediately broken into lovely, self-controlled tears and admitted her crimes. After some probing, she had even confessed to breaking into my house to obtain the lauded Green Goo recipe. There might be a sound bite on Channel 9. Apparently attractive but crazy hairstylists made good press.

Later that night I spoke to him again.

"So that's it, then," I said.

"Disappointed?" he asked.

"What are you talking about?"

"Anticlimactic," he said. "Boring."

"I like boring."

"No you don't."

"Dull is an aphrodisiac."

"I'd be insulted if I believed you."

"Believe me. If you were any more boring I'd be sleeping right now."

He chuckled, drew a deep breath. "How are you doing?"

"Hush, I'm sleeping."

The line went quiet for a moment, then, "You did good work on this."

I blinked, glanced at the receiver, then scowled. "I must be more tired than I realized. I thought you said—"

"We had a half a dozen people on this case. No one else caught the hair connection."

"Maybe *you're* more tired than I realized."

"Why can't you just take a compliment?"

I smiled. "Lack of experience."

"What are you doing tomorrow night?" His voice was all rumbly again. I considered telling him that I hoped I'd be screwing him, but that seemed to lack a certain amount of panache. "Buying groceries," I said instead.

"Didn't you do that just last month?"

"You are a funny man, aren't you?"

"That's probably why you love me."

"I suppose," I said.

I think it took us both a minute to realize what I'd just said. Another minute to assimilate the words. But I didn't try to retract them. Perhaps that makes me masochistic as well as neurotic. But there it was.

"Get some sleep," he said, and there was extra warmth in his voice now. Something that made me tingly and warm and hopeful. "I'll talk to you in the morning."

I slept like the dead that night . . . until two a.m., when something disturbed me. I awoke, heart pounding, utterly alert. Not like me at all. I glanced sideways, breath tight in my throat, but the doorway was blessedly empty. One stifled glance around the room assured me that all was well. But something had awakened me.

Stiff with fear, I pulled the blankets back and reached over Harlequin for my Mace. It felt cool and solid in my hand. I rose to my feet. Flipping on the light was harder than hell, because truth to tell, I didn't want to see what was inside my house. But the glare of the overhead bulb showed nothing out of the ordinary. Still, something was wrong. I felt it in the arch of my left foot.

It wasn't until that moment that I remembered Laney. Even though she had told Solberg that the letter-writer had been apprehended, he'd refused to return to his house in La Canada. Instead, he had bedded down on the carpet upstairs, just outside Elaine's bedroom door.

I found him there, undisturbed, but he awoke when I approached.

"Laney?" he croaked.

I glanced through the open doorway and saw her lying there, eyes closed, face serene in the diffused moonlight.

"She's fine," I said, and doing a rudimentary check of the other rooms on that level, ventured downstairs.

I had just reached the bottom when something lunged at me.

I squawked and stumbled backward, struggling with the Mace. But in that instant, my attacker turned tail and ran. Literally. It took me several heart-racing seconds to realize I'd just scared Harlequin out of his wits. And myself out of mine.

"Harley," I called. He turned, looking sheepish and tired, muzzle still wet from its sojourn in the toilet. "I'm sorry. Come here, handsome." He ambled over, head bowed. I scratched his ears and realized my mistake; he'd been fast asleep beside me when I'd awakened, which meant there was no intruder. Harley had been as jumpy as a crack addict since the break-in, and he had ears like parasails. He wasn't about to miss an opportunity to worry about some nocturnal noise.

Kissing his snout, I straightened and headed toward the bathroom. It was then that I saw a light flicker in the Al-Sadrs' yard.

30

The Irish don't really like anything they can't punch or drink.

—Pete McMullen, Irishman

*F*or a second I was sure I was imagining things, but then I saw two bodies moving around the corner of the house. Their clothes were dark except for the man's white turban.

Ahmad had come back for Aalia!

Anger fumed through me. I was out the door without a second's thought and yelled something inarticulate. The bodies jerked. I heard a muffled grunt, and then Aalia fell. I saw her hit the ground. Saw Ahmad straighten and glance toward me, and in that instant a thousand emotions exploded inside me. But the first and foremost was rage. He turned and jogged toward the alley, and it was then that I entirely lost my mind, because in a fraction of a second I deduced that I could beat him to his car. I was sprinting before my brain sent an impulse to my good sense, and now he was running, too. But I was fueled by rage and insanity.

My legs were pumping like sparking pistons. All I could think of were the scores of men in my past. The ones who had lied and bullied and belittled me.

I hit Ahmad five feet before he reached his car. Bowled over, he rolled toward his back tire, then scrambled to his feet. But I wasn't about to let him get away. Not this time. From my knees, I raised my right hand and sprayed him directly in the face, but he kept coming. I shrieked and skittered away, but there was nowhere to go. Somehow I had gotten turned around. His car was behind me. I jerked upright as he lunged toward me. With a squeal of terror, I reached behind me, yanked his car door open, and tumbled inside.

He made a grab for the handle. It was nothing short of a miracle that his vehicle was unoccupied and I was able to hit the LOCK button.

From the interior I saw him stagger to a halt. He stumbled, then fell to his knees. He'd just started retching when I hit the horn. It blared in the dark silence like an air raid alarm.

Taabish Al-Sadr was the first to pop out of his door. He stared in my direction. From where I was sitting I couldn't see Aalia's prone form and wondered desperately if she was all right. I tried to open the window to tell her brother-in-law to save her, but the window wouldn't budge without a key. With one more terrified glance at the hacking Yemeni, I scrambled over the parking brake and pushed open the passenger door.

"Call 911!" I shrieked.

Al-Sadr stared at me, frozen in place.

I could no longer see Ahmad and prayed he was still coughing up his liver instead of scrambling around the bumper to yank me out of his car by my hair.

"Aalia's hurt!" I screamed. "She may be dy—" I began, but in that instant I saw two women huddled in the light of the doorway behind Taabish. Adrenaline was flowing at a pretty good clip and blood was pounding in my ears like a tidal wave gone mad, but I was lucid enough to recognize that one of the women was Aalia.

"Ms. McMullen?" Taabish called, advancing toward me across the lawn.

I slammed the door shut, hit the locks, then shimmied back across the brake to stare through the driver's window. Ahmad was still on all fours. Still retching. But his head didn't really look as if it was covered with a turban anymore. It almost looked like he was blond.

I glanced at what I had thought was Aalia's body. It didn't appear as human as it had earlier. In fact, it looked a little like a felled tree, heavy on the top and skinny in the middle with one big lump of something at the end nearest me.

"Christina, what happens here?" Aalia called from the door. She took a few steps toward me.

"Go inside," Taabish warned, waving her back. "The police will soon arrive."

So he'd called 911. Good, I thought, but just then Ahmad lifted his head above his shoulders and for the first time I noticed that his face was as pale as mine.

Gathering his strength, he stumbled to his feet, raised

his hands shoulder height, and wobbled sideways a little, still coughing. "I'm sorry." His words were as slurred as a sailor's on shore leave. "I just . . ." He took a moment to shake his head and lean against his bumper. "I was worried about Aalia."

Taabish took a step closer. "Who is this man?"

"Skip . . ." He paused, steadied himself, bent double and coughed some more. "Stephen," he corrected. "Stephen Vance, sir." His trachea rattled on an inhalation. He wiped his nose with the back of his hand. "I met Aalia at Starbucks last weekend."

"Skip?" Aalia asked, and disengaged from the doorway.

"What do you do here in the dark of the night?" Taabish's voice hadn't softened any. And I saw now that he held a baseball bat in both hands.

"Aalia said . . ." Skip staggered again, wiped his eyes, and ricocheted off his left headlight. Mace is hell on eyesight. "She said she missed Al Mahwit so I brought her a coffee tree." A garbled rasp rattled up his throat. "So she would feel more at home."

Oh crap. I felt a little sick to my stomach as we all glanced at the tree that apparently was *not* bleeding to death on the lawn.

Taabish was the first to turn back toward Skip. "My sister by law, she is yet married in the eyes of Allah," he said.

"I know that. I realize that, sir." Skip coughed, wiped his mouth, and generally looked as if he were going to die. "I just thought she could use a friend. I wanted to surprise her."

Aalia had advanced a few feet, and because I had a front-row seat, I saw that the look he shot in her general direction had very little to do with friendship and a hell of a lot to do with adoration.

I couldn't decide if I should feel hopeful or jealous. I had always kind of wanted my own stalker, but Taabish didn't seem to see the beauty of the situation.

"My sister by law does not need a friend in the dark hours of the night," he said.

"I'm sorry, sir. I just . . . I know she's been scared and I couldn't sleep, so I . . ." He glanced through the window at me as though he kind of wished he was inside the car and maybe driving peacefully through some remote area of Nebraska. "I just thought I'd come by to make sure she was okay."

"She *was* okay until you invaded our privacy in the small of the night."

"I didn't mean to—" he began, but then he started hacking again. It took him a while to straighten enough to stare through the window at me. "Holy cow," he rasped. "What was that stuff?"

I tried not to wince. "Mace," I said, raising my voice to make myself heard through the window. "It's the first time I've tried it."

"Pretty effective," he said, and made a strange gargling noise. It almost sounded like a painful chuckle. "I'll have to get Aalia some in case—"

"You will get my sister nothing," Ramla said, and hustling to Aalia, pulled her toward the house. Taabish had drawn the bat back behind his body, and though I didn't think they had a plethora of budding softball leagues in Yemen, he looked as if he had the general idea of how to hit a ball into the outfield. "She is a good follower of Allah."

"I'm sorry—" Skip began again, but his apology was interrupted by the sound of sirens.

The police arrived moments later yelling for everyone to remain where we were.

We did. Me, still huddled inside the car; Al-Sadr with his bat still drawn back; the sisters frozen on the front lawn. And Skip, looking lost and ridiculously young, gazing at Aalia blindly, with his hands raised well above his head.

In the end, the officer first on the scene handcuffed Skip and eased him toward his squad car.

Once there, they stood for an instant as pertinent information was jotted down. I had a few minutes to speak to him before they hauled him off.

"I'm sorry," I said. "I thought—"

"No." He shook his head, glanced longingly toward the Al-Sadrs' house, even though Aalia had long since been shooed inside, and turned bravely back to me. "Don't be sorry. I'm just glad to know she has a friend like you to look after her."

"*H*e really said that?" Laney had awakened at the first sound of the siren and hustled the police toward the backyard. We were sitting on the couch, pondering the intricacies of life. Well, she was pondering. I was eating the remainder of the Crazy Chrissy's Caramel straight out of the jar. I have a strong conviction that calories consumed after a major trauma are not accounted for in the metabolic process. This theory has yet to be proven by the scientific community, research groups being what they are.

"Yup," I said.

"While he was handcuffed?"

I peeled off another spoonful of midnight delight. "Yup."

She glanced at Solberg. He was sitting close enough to be a pimple on her ass. If a pimple would dare grow on her ass.

"I'm sorry," he said.

She smiled and touched his hand. "Don't worry about it."

I glanced from one to the other and licked the spoon. "Sorry for what?" For being a cowardly dweeb who wasn't good enough to spit shine Laney's Manolos?

"Jeen didn't want me to leave the house," she said.

"Sorry," he said again, and managed to tear his gaze from her face long enough to give me a guilty glance. "I didn't know you were out there."

"You didn't hear the commotion?"

"Well . . ." He swallowed. "I didn't know you were involved. And I thought . . . you know, someone was after Laney."

"The letters have made us all jumpy," she said.

"I'm usually more stoic in a crisis," he said.

"Yeah," I said, "he hardly ever cries like a baby just because you're trying to leave the house."

They both shifted their gazes to me, making me almost choke on my next spoonful. "You *didn't*!" I said.

"I wasn't *crying*!" he said. "I was just . . . faking it. Trying to convince Laney to remain inside . . . where she's safe."

"You *cried*?" I couldn't believe it. I could hardly wait to tell Rivera, I realized, and wondered with a grin when that had started. "Like . . . real tears?"

"I was faking it!" he insisted, but his face was red.

I considered needling him some more, but the truth is, if Laney insisted on putting herself in harm's way, I'd probably tear up a little myself.

"Well . . ." I ate more ice cream. "I'm *happy* you kept her inside."

"I didn't know who was out there," he repeated.

I shook my head, amazed at the whimsical ways of the world. "Turns out it was just some lovesick boy mooning over Aalia."

"How can you be sure he wasn't sent by her husband?" Solberg asked.

"He was bearing a coffee tree."

"Maybe it's a ploy," he said.

Leave it to Solberg to see boogeymen in gift trees. "The police searched his car, all he had was a college textbook and a Snickers bar, and that's only dangerous to his glycogen level."

We talked a little longer. Finally Solberg nodded off, slumped against the corner of the couch. He looked a little like an overgrown Yoda propped up against the cushions as he was. If I didn't hate him so much I would have admitted he was almost cute in that so-ugly kind of way that lizards and newborns share.

"Did he really cry?" I asked.

Laney sighed. "He hasn't been getting enough sleep."

"Some people don't burst into tears when they're tired," I said. "They just get grouchy."

"You would know," she said.

I had finished off the ice cream a while ago and wished I hadn't. After all, I was still holding the spoon and it seemed like a terrible waste of energy.

"Even after I realized the kid had come bearing gifts, I still thought he might be trouble," I admitted. "But now I think he's just a nice guy. Worried about little Aalia. It's kind of cute in a creepy, stalkerish sort of way."

"I'm afraid they've got a lot against them."

"How do you mean?"

"Aalia and Stephen. Religion can be as divisive as it can be enlightening. Could be Mr. Al-Sadr would be more comfortable with an abusive Muslim husband than a doting American boyfriend. The fact that Aalia is wearing blue jeans and spending her Saturdays at Starbucks is probably driving him crazy."

I shrugged, willing to let them work that out for themselves as I glanced at Yoda once again. "What'd he do? Block the door with his meager body when you tried to leave?" I asked.

"He ordered me to remain inside."

I felt my eyebrows make a dash for my hairline. "He *ordered* you?"

"It was kind of sweet."

I glanced toward him. Turns out little Yoda had more balls than I'd given him credit for. Laney had been practicing yoga and kickboxing for more than a decade. She could have tied him in knots without turning a hair. "What'd you do?"

"I think I may have sworn at him."

"Seriously?"

"I kind of like you, Mac. Even when you're grouchy."

"You *swore* at him?"

"Maybe."

"Is that when he started to cry?"

"Right about then."

"Said he'd die if anything happened to you?"

"Something like that."

I nodded, ruminating and licking the dry spoon. "You know what bothers me the most?"

"That you kind of want a stalker of your very own."

"Yeah," I said, and sighed.

31

I truly believe it is emotionally damaging to be amicable for long periods of time.

—*Christina McMullen, Ph.D.*

I slept like a chilled reptile for the rest of the night. But by morning my mind still felt nubby. Sometimes running acts like a brain defuzzer, so I trundled up Chestnut Hill with Harley at my side in an attempt to wake up my cerebellum, but when I reached home I felt sweaty *and* nubby.

I reached the office at 7:50. At 8:10 Shirley buzzed to tell me Rivera was on the line. I took a fortifying breath and picked up the receiver.

"I swear to God I'm not trying to get myself killed," I said. "I just . . . I was really tired, and I saw someone in the Al-Sadrs' yard and I thought—"

"They picked up Ahmad Orsorio last night."

My mouth was still open, trying to yammer out a defense. "What?"

"He'd checked himself into Glendale Memorial. Guess the bullet in his leg was giving him some trouble."

"They got him?"

"The bastard's femur was broken."

"So what happens now?"

"Now he has an armed guard at his bedside till he goes to trial or gets shipped back to Yemen in disgrace."

I sighed. "I *love* happy endings."

Rivera chuckled. "So your bad-ass friend that shot him . . . what's his name? I'd like to thank him."

"I'll make sure to relay your gratitude."

"I'd rather do it in person."

"I bet you would," I said, and hung up a few seconds later.

One would think with all these ugly loose ends being tied up, I would have been as cheery as a picnic basket that weekend, but something was gnawing at me and I wasn't sure what it was.

By Friday I had eye bags the size of feed sacks, which made Laney's chipper countenance that much more irritating.

"Good morning."

"Really?" I said, and gave her a malevolent stare through one sandbagged eye. I was just pouring myself a bowlful of Cap'n Crunch. Diabetes in a bowl.

"I've made a decision about the wedding," Laney said.

"You're calling it off?" I asked, and added milk to the Crunch.

"I'm leaving all the details to Jeen."

"Aren't the details pretty well set?"

"He said he's sorry I've gotten so stressed. He's going to make some changes."

"Like what?"

"I don't know. He's going to find a place where the paparazzi won't figure out the location of the ceremony, for one thing."

"He's going to change the venue?"

"Not sure," she said. She was busy pouring Green Goo into a Klean Kanteen. Apparently, she'd learned to make do without her recipe.

"Didn't you pay an arm and a couple vital organs as a deposit for the Pavilion?" I asked.

"Something like that."

"Can you get it back?"

"Maybe a gallbladder." She was already making a beeline for the front door, but stopped halfway there and turned with a scowl. "Shoot! Do you think the cops can convince Nadine to give my jacket back?"

"She probably sold it on eBay for an arm and a spleen."

She gave me a look. "Any chance that joke's going to get old anytime soon?"

"Doubtful," I said, munching a mouthful of the captain's finest.

She sighed. "Can I use your jean jacket?"

"It's nine hundred degrees out there."

"But it'll only be eight seventy-five this evening."

"If you'd gain a couple ounces of fat maybe your body could regulate its own temperature instead—"

"Mac—"

"Sorry." For one shuddering second I contemplated the idea that I was beginning to sound like my mother. But I would not consider suicide. Not until I started scrubbing my counters with Hi-lex. "It's in the closet."

"Thanks," she said, and pacing over, snapped the jacket from its hanger before striding, long-legged and cool, toward the door. "Oh, Mac?"

"Yeah?"

"You're nothing like your mother," she said, and disappeared.

$\mathcal{M}$y workday went pretty smoothly until three o'clock when Shirley buzzed me, saying I had a call from a Courtney Paxton. I picked it up in a moment.

"Christina McMullen," I said. I sounded confident and intelligent. Role-playing—highly recommend by leading psychologists and certified nut cases.

"Yes, Ms. McMullen, I'm the therapist at Northmont High School. I had a message to call you regarding Emily Christianson."

My mind clicked into gear with little more than an audible groan. "Oh, yes. Thanks for returning my call. I was hoping to get a little more information about Ms. Christianson."

"Such as?" She sounded a little wary.

"Any pertinent findings regarding her emotional and physical health."

"As you probably know, she's an excellent student." She paused a second. "We had no warning that she was troubled until she was found bleeding on the tile in the girls' restroom."

"So you had no prior sessions with her?"

"There was no reason to," she said. Did I sense a shadow of guilt in her voice? "She exhibited no prior behavior that would suggest self-destructive tendencies, and when I *did* speak to her, she said her parents were insisting that she see someone . . ." She paused as if checking her notes. ". . . more qualified to handle her specific issues."

And they had chosen me? How? Why? "Well, I guess it doesn't matter who she's seeing. The important thing is that she's getting help. I'll continue sending you updates to keep you apprised."

"Updates?"

"The emails," I said. "Regarding her progress."

"I haven't received any updates from you."

I frowned and read off her cyber address to make sure I'd sent my missives to the right location.

"That's right, but I didn't get them."

"That's funny." My brain was clicking along a little faster now. Apparently, my churning system had realized it wasn't going to get its mid-afternoon nap and had decided to function anyway. "I can't seem to contact her parents either."

"Her mother is a celebrated cellist for the L.A. Philharmonic."

"So I'm told. Ioan Banica."

"She's never come to a parent/teacher conference."

"Have you called her to find out why?"

"We have three thousand and forty-three students in a facility built to house half that many, Ms. McMullen."

I kind of thought that might be a no.

"And I believe Ms. Banica is currently on tour with an elite string quartet."

"Do you know the name of the group?"

"I work at three different schools every week and review a dozen cases every day."

I stifled a sigh, thanked her, and didn't voice the opinion that she had been little more than catatonic. After hanging up, I immediately began Googling Ioan Banica.

$\mathcal{B}$y the time Emily arrived on Monday morning, I had gathered an arsenal of knowledge. But my smugness dehydrated a little when I saw her eyes. They looked sharp-edged and jaded beyond her years. But her motions were as prim and cautious as usual.

We spared less than two minutes on salutations. Emily wasn't a small talk kind of girl.

"I was wondering if you had a chance to speak to your parents about accompanying you here," I said.

She pursed her lips and adjusted a fold in her skirt. "I'm afraid it's a busy time for them. Mother is on tour, and Dad's picked up a second shift."

"Oh, where is your mom now?"

"Helsinki, I believe."

"Really? Because I thought I heard she was performing in New York," I said, and watched her like a hawk on a field mouse, but her expression didn't even flicker.

"Did you find that on the Internet?"

"Yes."

She shook her head. "Misinformation. It's becoming increasingly problematic."

"It was on the quartet's official website."

"I'll have to inform Mother of the error."

Her prim certainty made me falter for a second, but I regrouped. "I saw a picture of your mother."

If she was increasingly tense, I couldn't tell. But then, one could say the same thing about pressed steel. "Some people think I look like her. But I don't see it."

"Romanian, isn't she?"

"Yes. Born in Craiova. They have a very strong work ethic there."

I nodded. "She's quite beautiful."

"I'll tell her you said so."

"I tried to call her."

"I told you she wasn't home much."

"There was no answer."

"She won't have a cell phone. Thinks they're invasive to the creative . . ."

"So I went to your house."

I literally watched her face pale. Heard her catch her breath. Felt the tension tighten. "What?" Her voice was small, as if she were very young.

I let the seconds tick away, not because of any sort of ploy, but because for a moment I couldn't bear to shatter the scenario she had so carefully crafted. But there was no skirting the issue. Not if there was any hope for her.

"Lots of people are ashamed of their families, Emily."

It took her an instant to respond, but finally she breathed a laugh. "I don't know what you're talking about. I'm not ashamed of my family. My parents may be strict, but only because they want what's best for me."

I ignored her lies. "My mother wouldn't allow me to shave my legs until I was fifteen."

"They insist that I make something of my life."

"I was as hairy as a gorilla at my freshman dance."

"When Mother was my age, she had already played for Gorbachev."

"Dad told my first boyfriend he'd cut off his wiener if he touched my tits. Those are the exact words he used. In front of me. I thought I was going to die."

"Dad's ancestors were slaves. It's documented. Some plantation in West Virginia. I believe that's why he's so determined to see his progeny succeed. Were you aware that slaves were forced to marry against their will so that the owner would have new blood?"

"I was fifty pounds overweight. With acne. I played the tuba, which I could barely fit into. My father called me Pork Chop. I'm not sure—"

"Pork Chop!" She was on her feet suddenly, fists clenched, face florid. "And you're angry? Because of some pet name your father called you? My father gave me this!" Ripping the binder from her ponytail, she turned, clawing at her scalp. Against her dark hair I could see a jagged scar. "He dropped me . . . when I was six months old. Dropped me down the stairs! It might have been an accident. But we'll never know. He was killed in San Quentin three years ago. They think it was a drug deal gone . . ."

Her voice paled to nothing. She was breathing hard.

"Your mother's an alcoholic." I dropped the words softly into the quiet.

She pursed her lips and glanced toward the window.

"You're working two jobs to pay the rent," I added.

"My mother is performing in Helsinki," she said, but a tear had collected in the corner of her right eye and rolled with soulful sadness down her hollow cheek.

"You're getting home at midnight, then staying up till

four so you can ace your tests and keep up the charade."
Some of this I had learned through phone calls and research. Some I had surmised. Her mother had been all but
comatose when I'd spoken to her. "It's got to be hard to
keep track of all the lies."

"She's a consummate artist," Emily whispered. "The
critics say her music makes the nightingales hang their
heads in shame."

"You don't want to be like them," I said. "That's why
you came to see me."

Another tear fell softly after its mate, swelling along the
same course. "I'd be lucky to be half so talented—"

"You *won't* be like them," I said. "Unless you're unable
to face reality."

She looked at me suddenly, eyes blazing with anger and
frustration and a world full of fear. "You don't want to
hear the reality."

I took a deep breath and steadied myself. "I think you're
right," I said. "But try me anyway."

32

I'd rather be schizophrenic than alone during school lunches.

—*Emily Christianson,*
Chrissy's favorite psychotic

$\mathcal{A}$s it turned out, Emily Christianson was right. I didn't want to hear her reality. Because it made it almost impossible to feel sorry for myself. I considered that as I stood in my kitchen making an abbreviated chef's salad and trying to talk myself out of drinking the French dressing as an appetizer.

True, my parents may have had the instincts of killer bees, but at least they hadn't abandoned me to the world at the ripe old age of thirteen. Well, actually, her father who had vacillated between neglectful and horrifying, had left her long before that. By comparison her mother was a virtual saint, but her weaknesses had finally destroyed any hope of the two of them forging a meaningful family unit.

In fact, Emily, whose real name wasn't Emily at all, had, over the course of the past three years, created an entirely fictional universe for herself. Her ability with computers had enabled her to make that fiction seem real to nearly everyone she met. Not to mention allowing her to deflect the emails I had sent to her school therapist. Two years ago she had gone through a great deal of trouble to change her identity and she had no intention of allowing me to ruin things.

Her ploy had worked shockingly well, until the stress of an unlivable life had become too much to bear. It all left me baffled and melancholy. In the end I had promised to tell no one of her duplicity if she began seeing me twice a week, at least until I could figure out what to do.

The entire situation had me feeling out of sync. I had always believed that people were basically who they were. They could change their situations, their surroundings, and their actions. But eventually their true colors would show through. For instance, Nadine Gruber seemed as though she had her shit together, like she was content with her circumstances, but in the end, she had acted on her frustrations. In fact, she had gone so far as to trash my house just to score the Green Goo recipe and Laney's jean jacket.

Which seemed strange, because the Goo tasted like the devil's nectar and jean jackets are a dime a dozen. Of course, that had nothing to do with a neurotic's reasoning. Then again, the letters Nadine had sent didn't exactly seem like the work of a whack job. They were too well composed, too neat. Too—

My front door opened just as I was ruminating. I jerked toward it, still jumpy even though my troubles were behind me. But it turned out my problems were bigger than I'd expected; Solberg still had a key to my house.

"Hey, Angel." His voice scraped down the hallway, followed by his footsteps. "You ready?" He appeared in the doorway of the kitchen like a grinning nightmare. "Where's Laney?"

I scowled. Something had soured in my stomach. "I thought she was with you."

"No-kay doke," he said. "I was arranging a little surprise for her, but I told her I'd pick her up at seven. We're meeting my parents in less than an hour."

"Your parents?" If I had been informed of this eventuality, I had forgotten about it entirely, but regardless, Laney would dress up for a rendezvous with Solberg's family. So why hadn't she returned home?

It was in that moment, that tiny flicker of time, that a number of thoughts collided in my mind: The disarray of my house after the break-in juxtaposed against Nadine's perfectly formed letters. The memory of Laney's stolen jacket . . . so like mine. The jacket I hadn't worn since pulling it over my pj's and careening to Glendale following Micky's call for help. Lavonn's dilated eyes. Jackson's dreamy, drawled warning. Blood dripping on rosewood. Missing recipes. Clean toxicology reports. Intensity!

I was scrambling for my phone in a matter of seconds, but Solberg's cell rang before I ever touched mine. It jangled out the wedding march as I straightened, breath held, premonition skittering along the arches of my feet.

"Probably someone regarding the new venue," he said, grinning as he answered. " 'Ello."

"Hello. . . . Solberg?" I could only hear a few of the caller's words.

Solberg was still grinning at me. "That's right. The future Mr. Butterfield."

There was a pause from the caller. I was holding my breath.

"I hate to . . . but I'm afraid your fiancée has fallen . . . bad luck."

Watching Solberg's face, it was as if the world had suddenly ended. His expression went from unfettered glee to blank nothingness in a shattered heartbeat of time. His lips parted, but for a moment no sound came out.

"Who is it?" My own voice sounded raspy over the harsh beat of my heart.

Solberg shook his head, trembling and pale.

"Who is it?" I asked again, but he didn't respond. I snatched the phone from him.

"What have you done to her?" My tone sounded abrasive now, high-pitched with terror and dread.

"Ms. McMullen, I presume?" The man on the other end of the line sounded amused.

My stomach twisted into a hard knot of dread. "What do you want?"

"Me?" He laughed. The voice sounded vaguely familiar. "I simply wanted what was mine, Ms. McMullen. But now I'm thinking I might want what was Mr. Solberg's, too."

There was something in his tone that made me want to curl into a fetal ball, but I kept myself upright, barely breathing. "If you hurt her you won't get anything."

"Hurt her? Why would I do something so vile?"

"I'll give him whatever he wants." Solberg's voice was little more than a croak. Two patches of red flamed in his cheeks, and his eyes looked manic.

"How much do you want?" I asked and the kidnapper chuckled.

"That's the spirit."

"How much?" I asked, again.

"Twenty million."

I felt the air rush from my lungs. Felt the floor give way beneath me. "Are you out—"

"I can do that." Solberg's voice was clear now. He straightened slightly. "I'll just need a little time."

I turned my attention back to the phone, repeated his words.

The line went quiet for a moment, then, "If you go to the cops there will be retribution."

Retribution! The word rang like a death knell.

"No cops," I said. "But I want to talk to Elaine."

"Perhaps you're not aware, Ms. McMullen, but we don't always get what we want."

I felt calmer now, almost numb. "So I've heard," I said. "But *you'll* get twenty million. Guaranteed. If she's safe."

"You're so distrustful." He sighed. "I'm afraid I have no desire to allow you to speak—"

"There'll be an extra million if you put her on the phone," I said.

There was a moment of breathless anticipation, then a huffed laugh. "Ahh, capitalism at it's finest," he said, then paused for a moment. "You get one second for every million I'm to receive," he said, then aside, "I must warn you, Ms. Butterfield, people have been underestimating me since my conception. I hope you will not be so foolish."

In a moment she was on the phone.

"Mac?" Her voice was soft but steady.

"Laney!" Relief sluiced through me, but I funneled it

away, focusing on her words, her inflections. We had twenty-one seconds. I concentrated on using every one of them, on keeping my voice low. "Where are you?"

"I'm worried about my cat." Her voice sounded strange. Dreamy. Shocky.

My mind was racing. Laney didn't have a cat. Never had. "What's going on? Are you drugged?"

"She's so old."

My mind clicked into gear. I scrambled for a pencil. Drugged or not, Laney wouldn't waste this time. "How old?"

"The same age as Jeen."

No pen. No pencil. Not even a chunk of charcoal. Desperate, I stuck my finger in the French dressing and wrote Solberg's age on a nearby piece of junk mail.

"You know Muffy," she added.

I scribbled down the name, barely legible.

"Who is he?" I was all but whispering.

"Take care of Trivette, too."

I wrote it down, though it made no sense at all. My hand was shaking. "Laney . . ." My voice trembled. "I don't understand."

"He had that hairless sphinx. Weird. We should have given it a sweater. But he wouldn't have used it. People don't change."

"What do you mean? Who's—" I began, but the phone was taken away and her kidnapper was back on the line.

"So Hollywood," he said, "worrying about a cat when the world is on fire."

"Don't hurt her," I said.

"I've no desire to. But regrettably I may be unable to

prevent it if my demands are not followed to the letter," he said, then, "Tell Mr. Solberg to collect the necessary funds. I'll call him soon to let him know where to wire the money."

"Wait!" I felt frantic, terrified, but the phone had already gone dead.

33

If it wasn't for vinyl I'd be naked all the time.

—*Teddy Bactrin, one of*
Chrissy's too honest beaus

Solberg and I stared at each other, lost and horrified. He turned like an automaton, and I blinked, coming back to myself.

"Where are you going?"

"To get the money ready."

I nodded, broken, crushed, but when my gaze swept across my scribbled notes I spoke again. "How old are you?"

"What difference—"

"Your age!" I was trying to rally. "How old?"

"Thirty-seven. Why?"

"Because Laney doesn't waste time." My brain was beginning to click a little. "Did you ever have a cat?"

"A cat? No. Wh—"

"Who's Muffy?"

"Are you crazy? I don't have time—"

But I grabbed his shoulders, shaking him. "Who's Muffy?"

"I don't know. I—Wait." He blinked. "I used to date a girl called Muffy."

For a moment all sensible thoughts fled. Muffy? Really? I shook my head. "Get on your computer."

"What?"

"Your computer. You have it with you, don't you?"

"It's in my—"

"Get it!"

He paused a moment, but finally he scrambled away. I grabbed a pen from the drawer and wrote down the twenty-one-second conversation as closely as I could remember. I had asked where she was. She'd begged me to take care of her cat, who was thirty-seven years . . .

"What do you want?" Solberg was panting when he ran back in. He was carrying something that looked like a beefed-up coffee can. But there was no time to dwell.

"Find Thirty-seventh Avenue," I said.

"In L.A.?"

"For now," I muttered, then closed my eyes, trying to think, to wish away the panic. What was the cross street? Not Muffy. That would have been too obvious, too dangerous. "What was Muffy's last name?"

"Muffy?" He glanced up. A little color had returned to his lips. "Newton."

"Find Thirty-seventh and Newton."

He typed madly. The keyboard was in the shape of a cylinder. "There is none."

I wanted to ask if he was positive, but there was no point, so I paced, then spun toward him. "What was her real name?"

"Muffy *is* her real name."

"Seriously?"

"But her cousins called her Marigold."

Our eyes met.

"Thirty-seventh and Marigold!" He was already typing.

I'd asked who had abducted her. "Do you know anyone named Trivette?"

He shook his head, distracted, then yanked his attention toward me. "East L.A. Looks like residential slums." He was already on his feet.

"Where are you going?"

He paused, cheeks bright, fists clenched. "To kill him," he said.

For a moment I was too shocked to take him seriously, but when he turned away I grabbed his arm. "How? Solberg, think. We don't know who he is. We don't know *where* he is. Not specifically."

"I'll find him." His voice was gruff, unrecognizable. "I'll find *her*."

"He's probably armed."

"It doesn't matter," he said, and tried to pull away, but I tightened my grip.

"It matters if he hurts Laney."

Every molecule of color drained from his face. His arm went limp in my hand. "What do we do?"

"I don't know, I—" A thought flashed through my mind, so quick I could hardly catch it. "Texas Rangers!" I hissed the words.

He stared at me, almost hopeful, waiting.

"I told her Jackson looked like Jimmy Trivette, from *Walker, Texas Ranger.*"

"Who's Jackson?" he asked, but I was already dialing the phone.

Micky Goldenstone answered on the second ring. My voice sounded odd, cranked tight.

"Where's Jackson."

There was a pause. "Who is this?"

"Christina McMullen. Micky, is Jackson still in the hospital?"

"No."

"Is he in custody?"

"His handgun was registered. He had no priors. They released him until the trial. Why?"

I felt my stomach twist. "Is he with Lavonn?"

"I don't—"

"I need you to find out."

"Are—"

"Do you think he's capable of kidnapping? Do you know—"

"What the fuck's going on?" His voice was a snarl.

"I think he's producing a drug called Intensity. I think Lavonn hid it in my jacket. Laney was wearing it today and she's been kidnapped."

There was a second's pause. "I'm on my way to Glendale." I heard a door slam.

"Micky . . ."

"Yeah?" His tone was terse, taut as a stretched wire.

"His old girlfriend, the one he made serve him . . ."

"Becca."

"Yeah." Laney had mentioned sphinx cats and the only

reason I could think of was because they were a virtually naked breed. "If Becca didn't do what he wanted, what happened?"

"I don't know," he said, and let silence fill the miles between us like a swirling tornado. "I can't find her."

*I*t took Micky forty-two minutes to reach Jackson's home in Glendale, but he wasn't there.

It took Solberg an hour to realize it could take days to secure twenty-one million dollars.

Long before then he found a live online image of Thirty-seventh and Marigold. I had no idea how he'd tapped into it or if it was legal. Nor did I care. From the picture on the screen we could see that most of the buildings were boarded up. Anemic-looking weeds were scattered about dusty yards and stray furniture adorned broken sidewalks.

Solberg's phone rang as we were gazing at the screen. We turned toward each other, breathless, terrified. He answered, knobby hand visibly shaking.

"I need more time to get your money."

"I'm afraid that's not possible, Mr. Solberg."

"I want to talk to Laney."

"She's indisposed just now."

"If you hurt her, I swear to you . . ." He ran out of words, out of hope.

"What do you swear, Mr. Solberg?"

"Give me one minute with her and I'll give you ten thousand dollars in cash."

"But cash is so trackable. You're not trying to trick me, are you, Mr. Solberg?"

"I don't care what happens to you." His expression was grim, his tone the same. "I just want Laney back."

"Very romantic. I'm touched. And I had almost given up on the power of love. Tell you what, give me an even twenty-five million and I'll let you talk to her."

His hand tightened on the phone. His Adam's apple bobbed. "I don't know if I can get that much."

"That's interesting, because I don't know if she'll ever be able to talk again if you don't cooperate. In fact, maybe the whole arrangement is off if you can't find it in your heart—"

"I'll get it!" Solberg said.

"Ahhh, love will find a way. You are single-handedly restoring my faith in mankind, Mr. Solberg. And for that, you'll get a few more seconds to talk with your beloved. But I think I'll put you on speakerphone this time. I'm wondering if your amoretto isn't a bit brighter than her gorgeous body suggests."

She was on the phone in a minute.

"Jeen?"

"I want to hear." I only mouthed the words, but he understood. His hands shook as he bumped the button for speakerphone.

"Angel." He sounded faint with relief.

"Is Muffy okay?"

"She's fine," I said. "I brought her to my house. She's watching TV in the other room. *Starsky and Hutch.*"

There was almost a sigh in her voice. "I used to love that show."

"It's the one where Hutch pretended to be Emma."

She paused for a moment. I held my breath, praying she was coherent enough to remember the hours we had spent watching every episode. Praying she understood my meaning.

"That was a good one," she said finally. "I want to watch it when I get home. I want to watch three stories in a row. And I want to come home soon. Please, Jeen, bring me home."

His knuckles looked white against the gold metal of his cell. "I will, baby. I promise."

"Before I see the sun set. Please. I'm cold. I'm scared. Get me home," she said, and began to cry noisily.

"Secure the funds," the kidnapper said, and hung up.

Solberg dropped to his knees. He was rocking back and forth, face crunched in agony. "What has he done? What has he done to her?"

"Not much," I said, but my throat felt tight with terror and anger. "Not yet."

"What are you talking about? She's crying!" Solberg screamed the words at me, but his anguish did nothing but galvanize me.

"No she's not," I said.

"I heard her. She's—"

"Faking it," I said. "Now get up. We're leaving."

"She's crying," he whispered, ashen, but I was already hurrying into my bedroom. "She doesn't make any noise when she cries, Solberg. Unless she's acting," I said, and stepped back into the living room carrying a wig, a baseball bat, and a robe.

He wobbled to his feet. "What are you doing?"

"I'm bringing her home," I said. "You coming?"

He nodded jerkily and staggered to his feet.

"You're going to need this," I said, and handed him the bat.

He took it in two fingers.

"But you're going to have to bring your own balls," I added, and stared at him. "You got 'em?"

He swallowed and straightened his back.

"Good. You drive. We'll take my car. It'll cause less—" I began, but at that moment the doorbell rang. My heart stopped. I glanced at Solberg, but he was too stunned to react. My knees felt stiff as I made my way toward the door.

Aalia stood on the far side. Her gorgeous face was sober, her dark eyes wide and earnest. "I wished to thank you for your help," she said, "before I must go."

I realized finally that she was dressed in the same clothes I had first seen her in at the airport. Low-slung jeans and a long-sleeved jersey. Only the sideways cap was missing. A warning bell clanged in my head, but the din was already so loud I could barely distinguish the noise.

"Listen, Aalia, don't do anything rash. I have to go now, but we'll talk when I get back."

She shook her head. "I cannot stay with my beloved sister and her husband. I have come all this long way to be free. To make my own decisions and my own friends but they . . ." She paused again. Her expressive eyes narrowed. "What happens here?"

I tightened my grip on the wig. "Nothing. I just have to go out for a while."

"Something . . ." She paused. "It is wrong."

"Please . . ." Panic was beginning to boil in my gut. "Just go home before—"

"Something has happened bad."

"I don't—"

"I will help," she said, and pursed her lips.

"Listen—"

"Where you go, I go," she said, and there was no time to argue.

In a matter of moments the three of us were striding toward the Saturn. A baseball cap was now on Aalia's head. Solberg carried the keys. He popped the locks and got behind the wheel. I chose the backseat.

We pulled away from the curb at Mach speed as he glanced at me in the mirror. The sun was just setting.

"Where are we going, Chrissy?"

"To an apartment building on Thirty-seventh and Marigold."

He nodded, pale but determined. "Which side is she on?"

"She can watch the sun set," I said. Everything seemed sharply defined now, finely etched and crystal clear.

"West side," he said.

"Third floor."

"How . . . Three stories," he breathed.

"Yeah." I nodded grimly. "And Solberg . . ."

I could feel him watching me in the mirror.

"She's naked."

He blanched, but kept driving, narrow lips pursed tight. "How do you know?"

"She said she's cold. She said people don't change. She doesn't believe that. Never has. But Jackson has traumatized women like this before."

He nodded once and when he spoke, his tone was deadly even. "I'm not a violent man by nature." He glanced toward me, eyes steady in the Saturn's narrow mirror. "I want you to remind Angel of that later."

"She knows."

There were tears in his eyes. "I don't want her to forget." One tear dripped silently down his thin cheek.

"I won't let her," I said.

He nodded, then tightened his hands on the steering wheel. "What now?"

I sketched out the plan as he drove, then took a deep breath and dialed Rivera.

"What are you wearing?" he asked.

I glanced down. I had undressed in the car and now wore nothing but a robe and a wig, but I put those embarrassing truths out of my mind.

"I need your help," I said.

"Should I rest up?"

I looked toward the front seat, hoping they couldn't hear the conversation.

"Laney's been kidnapped."

There was a momentary pause filled with tension and angst, then, "Listen to me, McMullen. I want you to stop whatever you're doing. I want you to go home and lock your doors."

I nodded. "I'll do that," I said, "when she can go home with me."

"McMullen, this is police business. If you interfere—"

"You'll have to threaten me later. Right now I'm in a hurry. I think she's been abducted by Jackson Andrews. She's in an apartment building on Thirty-seventh and Marigold. If we're not out of there in ten minutes we're going to need an ambulance and backup."

"Backup! Are you nuts?" His voice was rising with every word. "You're not a cop, McMullen. Get your ass—"

"Rivera."

There was a pause. The tension had amped up a thousand percent. "What?"

"I think I love you," I said, and hung up just as we pulled over to the curb on Thirty-sixth Street.

I switched my phone to vibrate and dropped it into the pocket of my terry-cloth robe. It was almost dark. I glanced at my cohorts, feeling chilled to the bone and scared enough to pee in my pants. If I had any on. Which I didn't.

"Are we ready?" My voice sounded funny—distant and vague.

My companions nodded in unison.

I took a deep breath. "Call me when you're in position," I said, and, reaching over the parking brake, pulled the keys from the ignition. I wrestled off my Mace and handed it to Aalia. "A brand-new can of protective spray," I said. "Flip the red trigger, then point and spray."

She stared at it. "What of you?"

"Don't worry about me. I'm going to be running like a raped ape," I said. Secretariat wouldn't be able to catch me.

Solberg tightened his grip on the bat and stepped from the car. They headed south on Thirty-sixth together, but would split up before they could be seen from the third floor of Terrace Garden Apartments. I held my keys in a death grip and headed north.

Half a block up, a multicolor cluster of boys whistled catcalls. But I was too occupied to either appreciate their sense of humor or be offended. Upon reaching Sandcrane Street, I turned left. My bellowing breath sounded like a freight train. By the time I reached the cross street I felt as if I was going to pass out. There was only one streetlamp working. But maybe that was just as well. Anyone who would mistake me for Laney would have to either be blind or high. I said a quick prayer that Jackson was both.

Staring at Terrace Garden Apartments, I hurried across the street and took a breather behind a battered jade plant. I counted three stories up and ran my gaze across the row of windows. All of them were dark. Several looked broken. But the second-most southerly one seemed darker than the others. As if a blanket had been strung across the opening.

My phone buzzed just as I slipped between two vehicles. The pickup truck was up on blocks, the little Geo seemed to be short an engine. They wouldn't be leaving anytime soon. Hunkering down between the two bumpers, I recognized Solberg's number and flipped open my cell.

"Are you in?" My voice sounded hollow and empty.

Solberg's was similar. "We found an open door."

I closed my eyes and steeled my resolve. "You know what to do?"

"Yeah," Solberg said. His voice had deepened some and sounded oddly like the Terminator's. "Bring Laney home."

"Be careful," I said, but he had already hung up. I dropped the phone back into my pocket, kicked off my flip-flops, and played out the coming drama in my head: Aalia meandering down the debris-strewn hallway, shouting for drugs. Jackson worrying, telling Laney to keep quiet, locking her in the bedroom, opening the door into the hall, glancing . . . But wait, what if he locked her in a different room? The bathroom maybe. Somewhere without a window to—

"What the hell you doing?"

I stifled a squawk but jumped as someone glared at me through the windshield of the broken Geo.

"I didn't mean to bother you. I'm just—"

"Get away!" shrieked the guy in the car. His face was wizened, his hair stretched out of his head like gray antennae.

"Don't—"

"Get out of my yard!"

"I'll—" I began, but just then the sound of breaking glass crackled through the neighborhood. I swore as I watched shards spray down from a third-floor window. After one more frantic glance at the aggravated car-sitter, I dropped my robe to the cracked asphalt and kicked off my flip-flops. The homeless guy emerged from the Geo to stare at me like I was the second coming, but I was already running, hotfooting it down the shattered sidewalk toward the apartment building, counting in my head, trying to guess how long it would take for Jackson to realize Laney had broken the window. How long before he could believe she had jumped through the shattered glass and landed safely on the weedy dirt below. How long before he would careen into the hall to chase her. I had no way of knowing. Adrenaline was pumping through me like hot tequila by the time I reached the building.

It wasn't until then that I realized I'd been followed by the old guy from the Geo.

"Whatcha doin'?" he rasped, but at that second I heard someone hiss an expletive from above. I glanced up, saw a dark form leaning from the window, and knew my plan was working. Elaine had broken the window and subsequently hidden.

I bolted toward Thirty-seventh.

"Hey! Come back!" screamed Geo.

I stumbled on the curb, almost fell, and glanced back. Half-dressed and lean as a greyhound, Geo was catching up. I shrieked as his fingers brushed my back, hacked up a burst of speed, and cut an angle between two houses. Marigold lay dead ahead. I hit the asphalt just as a car turned from my left and screeched to a halt ten feet from me. I froze in the headlights.

The driver's door opened. "LAPD! Put your hands where I can see them."

"Not me!" I was panting like a field hound. My pursuer seemed to be long gone. I made a frantic motion toward Thirty-seventh Street. "The apartments."

"Just relax now."

Another cop stepped from the passenger side. "What's going on, ma'am?"

"Kidnapped! Apartments! Third floor! Elaine!"

"Take a deep breath."

"Patricia Ruocco is up there!" I shrieked. "Naked."

They looked at each other, then launched themselves in their squad car and squealed off down the street. Alone and abandoned, I ran after them. By the time I had panted up to the third floor, Laney was standing in the hallway, wearing Solberg's T-shirt.

Jackson was lying on the floor, cradling his ribs and gritting his teeth. The two officers I'd met moments before stood over him, guns drawn. A cracked bat lay in the corner. Aalia was nowhere to be seen.

Elaine's gaze met mine. Her eyes were wide, her face pale, but she was well. Safe. Whole. "Emma wasn't naked," she said.

I bent double, trying to breathe as I slanted a look at her.

"In that episode of *Starsky and Hutch*. Everyone was fully clothed," she said.

"Yeah, well, I didn't think Jackson would believe you'd somehow obtained a pair of jeans on your jump to freedom."

"Or you just really like running around East L.A. naked."

"Yeah." I dug the heel of my hand into my side to relieve the pain. "That's probably it."

"You okay?" Laney asked. Her voice had gone soft.

"A little out of shape," I said, still trying to breathe. "But other than that I'm fantastic."

"You really are," she said, and smiled through her silent tears.

34

Any couple that begins a marriage by inviting both of their families to the same ceremony clearly deserves whatever they get.

—Dr. Henri Farthing,
marriage counselor

The wedding took place at the top of Yosemite Falls. The bride wore hiking boots and a fine sheen of perspiration. I was sweating like a paratrooper from the climb. Beside me, Rivera barely looked winded.

Mist had enveloped the lower regions, wreathing the valley in silvery spray, leaving just glimpses of paradise below.

A handful of guests had been airlifted in. I have no idea how Solberg had managed it, but as the newlyweds kissed, a golden eagle swooped down from a craggy outcropping of red rock. For a moment it was perfectly backdropped against the bubbling perfection of a blue-velvet cloud and a fit violinist's poignant rendition of classical music.

I felt my throat tighten with tears.

"How you holding up?" Rivera asked. We hadn't had much time to discuss things.

I turned to find him watching me and shrugged. "This is the first time my bridesmaid's dress didn't have an ass bow the size of the Mojave and I don't get to wear it."

His gaze never left mine. "She looks happy."

I glanced at her. "She had a near-death experience. She's not thinking clearly."

"How'd you know she'd break the window, then hide in the closet?"

I took a seat on a nearby rock and watched the ridiculously happy couple. Maybe if I was lucky Solberg would die of ecstasy. Although, I had to admit, he had really come through in the clinch. Jackson's medical report said he had sustained three broken ribs and a cracked humerus. It couldn't have happened to a nicer abusive millionaire junky.

"Actually, I thought she'd hide under the bed," I said.

"I'm told there wasn't a bed. Just a mattress."

"On *Starsky and Hutch,* Emma hid under the bed."

Rivera gazed out over the silvery, mist-shrouded valley. "Who pretended to be Emma? Starsky or Hutch?"

"It was Emma's sister. Hutch's love interest. Almost broke my heart. I had a huge crush on him. Had his poster on my wall for most of a decade."

Rivera shook his head.

"What? You didn't think he was good-looking?"

"I think you're a nut job," he said. "But I'm kind of glad you're alive."

I stared at him a moment, then glanced away. "I'm sorry I didn't call you right away. Jackson said there would be retribution if the cops got involved." I could feel the tears welling up again. But at least it was just a remnant of fear now and not some stupid-ass emotion brought on by the flight of an oversized raptor soaring on the haunting strains of "Für Elise."

"Is that the term he used? 'Retribution'?"

I nodded. "In Glendale the night he was shot, and on the phone."

"So that's how you knew it was him."

"That and my twenty-one-second conversation with Laney."

"I never thought that *Texas Ranger* show would be worth all the daylight it took to film it."

"Are you kidding? Do you know why Chuck Norris doesn't wear condoms?"

"Please. Not Chuck Norris jokes."

"Because there is no protection from Chuck Norris."

"Oh God."

"The chief export of Chuck Norris is pain."

He groaned.

I smiled and watched the flight of a distant bird. "So it wasn't Nadine who broke into my house at all."

"She did send the letters. But Lavonn was responsible for the B and E. Nadine just saw the opportunity for some airtime when the cops showed up at her door."

I scowled. "Any publicity is good publicity?"

"I guess that was her line of reasoning, but you'd think that would exclude incarceration," he said.

"She's trying to start her own business."

"Just like Jackson."

I gave that a moment's thought. "So he was the original producer of Intensity?"

"Looks like it. Nothing's sure yet, but he seems to have the necessary knowledge. He owns a fair amount of real estate, some of it under other names. We're searching for labs."

"With all that money you wouldn't think the packet Lavonn shoved in my pocket would be particularly significant."

"I suppose he didn't want you finding it and putting two and two together. Besides, it was a hefty amount. I'm surprised you didn't notice it in your jacket pocket."

"I had a few other things on my mind. I wish I had made the connection earlier, though. Before Lavonn vandalized my poor house."

"She said she was scared what Jackson would do if he got out of the hospital and found out she'd lost a quarter kilo of his shit. I guess it seemed more logical to rip your house apart than to leave the bastard."

"She may not have been thinking really clearly. I mean . . . she took the rosewood recipe box instead of Laney's jewelry."

He shrugged. "Girl's got a thing for rosewood. And drugs haven't been known to make people any smarter."

"So in the end she panicked and grabbed Laney's jacket hoping it was mine."

"Then Jackson comes home, learns he's out a small fortune in drugs, and decides to recoup his losses."

"Lavonn's conviction should help Micky's cause," I said, then shuddered despite the sunlight. "Do you think Jaskson was watching my house when Laney left that morning?"

"Better that than hiding in your backseat."

"Are you still on a backseat kick?"

He watched me. "I can't believe Aalia got you back there before I did."

"You snooze, you lose."

The corner of his mouth kicked up a quarter of an inch. "Have you heard from her?"

"No. Ramla's worried sick, but I think Aalia just needs . . ." I shrugged, scanning the silvery beauty below me. "Freedom."

"That what *you* need?"

I brought my attention back to his dark-coffee eyes. "What are you asking, Rivera?"

Our gazes melded for several moments before he shifted his to Laney and Solberg. They looked happy enough to fly, laughing and holding hands as they conversed with their well-wishers.

"You drive me crazy," Rivera said.

He shifted his gaze back to me. A muscle bunched and loosened in his jaw.

"Stop," I said, voice dry against the happy couple's gaiety. "You're making me giddy."

"You take too many chances, my old man has the hots for you, and sometimes you act like you don't have a brain in your head." His scowl had darkened toward midnight. He drew in a long-suffering breath. "But I think I love you, too," he said, and pulling me into his arms, he kissed me.